CHRISTMAS COCOA
HEARTWARMING HOLIDAYS SWEET ROMANCE BOOK 2

ID JOHNSON

Copyright © 2017 by ID Johnson

All rights reserved.

No part of this book may be reproduced in any form or by any electronic or mechanical means, including information storage and retrieval systems, without written permission from the author, except for the use of brief quotations in a book review.

Cover by Sparrow Book Cover Designs

Photo image by Jill Wellington via Pixabay

❦ Created with Vellum

For my nephew Payton who is a remarkable young man.

NEWSLETTER

Get several of my books for free when you sign up for my newsletter here:
  https://books.bookfunnel.com/idjohnsonnewslettersignup
  or sign up here:
  https://www.subscribepage.com/f3d2p5

CONTENTS

Chapter 1	1
Chapter 2	11
Chapter 3	19
Chapter 4	27
Chapter 5	37
Chapter 6	49
Chapter 7	63
Chapter 8	75
Chapter 9	87
Chapter 10	105
Chapter 11	115
Chapter 12	129
Chapter 13	143
Chapter 14	151
Chapter 15	165
Chapter 16	173
Chapter 17	185
Chapter 18	197
Chapter 19	211
A Note from the Author	219
Also by ID Johnson	221

CHAPTER 1

The crisp November breeze billowed around her, stirring up the leaves and sending them shooting up into the cobalt morning sky. Delaney Young could sense the sun still sound asleep on the other side of the mountains, not yet ready to climb from beneath the solace of her blanket of fluffy cirrus clouds, content to put the day off a bit longer in order to catch a few more moments of undisturbed slumber. For Delaney, however, being a baker often meant rising long before most of the residents of Charles Town, West Virginia, ever left their last refreshing cycle of REM sleep, and as she hurried to her red Dodge Charger, she was thankful that she had a career she loved and enough energy to unwrap herself from her comforter and the land of dreams.

The dashboard clock said it wasn't quite 4:30. It was cold outside, but not frigid enough to take more than one crank to start her car, despite the fact that she had left it in the carport the night before instead of driving the few hundred yards more to the unattached garage her grandfather had built decades ago. Once the threat of snow became more certain, she'd go the extra mile, but for now, at least there was a bit of cover and easy access to the kitchen entry of the farmhouse she shared with her grandmother.

Delaney turned to look behind her as she backed down the winding driveway that led to the country road she'd lived on most of her life. There was very little traffic this time of day, or any time of day, for that matter, and she made her way onto the lane with no problems. The heater hadn't quite had a chance to thaw her fingers yet, so she rubbed her hands together and blew into them for a moment before pointing the car in the direction of town and easing her foot onto the gas pedal.

Even though the three-bedroom farmhouse, complete with picket fence and chicken coop, was a few miles outside of town, it never took her more than ten minutes to get to the downtown area where her bakery, Delaney's Delights, fit in nicely amidst the other quaint little stores one might expect to see in any antiquated shopping area in one of thousands of similar communities around the country. Yet, there was no doubt in Delaney's mind as she pulled onto the main highway leading to Charles Town that this community was special. While other graduates of her class from Washington High School had complained about boredom and busybodies, claiming they would do whatever they could to get away as soon as possible, Delaney had always known she would never leave Charles Town, and as soon as she had graduated from culinary school in Frederick, Maryland, which really wasn't even that far away, she had returned to start her own bakery, a dream she'd had ever since she was a little girl burning her fingers on the Easy-Bake Oven her grandmother had purchased for her for Christmas when she was four.

Delaney's grandmother, Nora Jean, or Nana, as everyone lovingly called her, had needed someone to move in with her about the same time, and things had just worked out that, as soon as Delaney returned from school, she could live in the farmhouse and keep an eye on her aging grandparent. Even though Papa Fred had passed away when Delaney was a little girl, she had wonderful memories of walking the dirt path between her own home and her grandparents' modest dwelling. Summers filled with fishing on the pond, chasing lightning bugs with her older brother and cousins, and listening to Papa play the harmonica had been reason enough to compel her to take the upstairs bedroom that had been her father's when he was a little boy and help Nana take care of household chores and remember to take her medicine. At seventy-two, she was beginning to show her age, even though she could still get around quite well and would have never admitted to anyone that she needed help. She would say that she missed her only granddaughter, however, and when Delaney asked her if she'd like some company, Nana had gladly accepted Delaney's request to become her roommate.

The living arrangement had certainly helped with the bills. She'd received a good scholarship to attend culinary school but had some student loans to consider. On top of that, she had rent on the bakery due the first of every month, and while the space itself wasn't large, it was in the prime shopping area of the little town. Many of the buildings on that side of the street, including the bakery, belonged to Mr. Henry Gaston, and while he was a fair landlord, like everyone else, he wanted his money when it was due. It had been a bit intimidating taking on such a responsibility fresh out of school, but now, four years later, Delaney's business was doing quite well, and she was able to employ a full-time worker, as well as several part-timers who often took the shifts Delaney would rather not have herself—like weekends, afternoons, and occasionally early mornings, though most of the time Delaney still preferred to come in early and get the baking done herself. She didn't trust a whole lot of people with her recipes, particularly her award winning cocoa recipe which was extremely popular this time of year.

Delaney pulled her car into her usual spot behind the building in the "employee only" parking lot for the area and rested her head back against the black leather seat for a moment. She had always been a morning person, and sometimes she liked to take a moment to enjoy one last minute of solitude before she jumped into her day. The sky was still completely dark, and though she knew there were a few other shop owners nearby embarking on their Thursday, she could neither hear nor see anyone else in the world, which made her feel both important and insignificant at the same time. In this wide world full of billions of people, she was the only one occupying this particular spot at this particular moment. What might this day have in store for her? As she pulled her keys from the ignition and grabbed her purse, she was full of optimism, even though chances were this day would be a blur of baking and customers, of exhaustion and aching feet, and then of moments around the kitchen table listening to her grandmother chat about days gone by. Nevertheless, some days did tend to be more significant than others, so Delaney chose to start off each one with the hope that this one would be special.

By the time her co-worker, Edie Strawn, made her way in the back door at a quarter to seven, Delaney had given up on the idea that this Thursday would be anything special. She'd already made dozens of doughnuts, muffins, croissants, and more pots of coffee and cocoa than she could count. She was just starting to make a batch of what she referred to as "afternoon goodies," usually cookies or cakes, items people tended to request later in the day, and was happy to have someone man the front counter while she tended to the oven.

"Mornin'," Edie called, closing the door and sneaking her purse into their secret hiding spot. "Been busy?"

"Yes," Delaney called, wiping flour off of her hands onto her apron. "I'm not sure what's going on, but I swear business has picked up this month. If it keeps up, I'm going to have to find someone to cover this first hour. I can't get everything done that I used to in that hour between opening and when you come in."

"More business is good," Edie said, tying a matching red apron around her waist. She was about ten years older than Delaney, in her mid-thirties, with red, curly hair that tended to have a mind of its own. She was also taller and wider, with a no-nonsense attitude and two children at home she was practically raising on her own since her husband was a truck driver who worked long hours and didn't come home nearly as often as Edie would've liked. She was a hard worker, though, and Delaney had hired her the week she'd opened her bakery. Edie had never called in sick or missed a shift for any reason, and Delaney tended to think of her more as a partner than an employee.

"That's true. More business is good," Delaney agreed, opening the oven and sliding two cookie sheets full of super-sized chocolate chip cookies inside. "But I don't know who I can get to come in that early. The high school kids won't want to get up and work an hour or so before making it to school, and it's really hard to find anyone else willing to get up at the crack of dawn."

"I wish I could help you out," Edie said, checking a tray of muffins on the cooling rack to see if they were ready to put out, "but I can't drop off Billy and Samantha any earlier."

"Oh, I know," Delaney replied as the bell over the door out front let them know that they had another customer. "I'll figure something out. Maybe I should put a notice up or something."

"That's a good idea," Edie called over her shoulder as she made her way to the counter. "We could use someone for an hour or two. Especially if it stays this busy until Christmas. And maybe someone will be looking for some extra money this time of year."

Delaney heard her greeting Mr. Williams, one of their regulars, so she didn't bother responding, but she did think putting a "Help Wanted" sign on the door was a good idea. She wasn't sure what kind of help she might get for a few hours each morning, but it wouldn't hurt to start looking. It seemed more and more people were trickling into town bright and early and deciding to stop off for a morning treat on their way to work. While she usually recognized almost every customer who came by, this morning there had been several she didn't know, and a few had mentioned they usually drove right on by Charles Town on their way to surrounding cities for work, but they'd recently heard of the quaint downtown area and had decided to give it a try. Whatever was bringing people in, Delaney wouldn't complain, but she'd either find some help or fall over trying to get everything done at once. Otherwise, she'd have to get up even earlier to get everything prepped before the customers started rolling in, and while she loved getting up early, setting her alarm for anything before 3:45 seemed almost impossible. Somewhere in the misty hours of the morning, there was a line that divided night owls and early birds, and Delaney wasn't too keen on discovering what that magical time might be.

One good thing about being busy was that the day tended to fly by.

Delaney tended to stay at the bakery longer than necessary most days, but when they were particularly busy like they were today, her day went even longer. The afternoons were covered by a couple of high school girls who usually made their way in around 3:30 depending upon whether or not they had meetings after school. By the time Joanna Kinney and Courtney Tobak arrived, Delaney had already put in at least eight hours, often closer to nine, and while Edie tended to stay until 4:00 most days, she was supposed to be off at 3:00. The day was spent chatting with customers, refilling the display case, wiping off the half-dozen tables where more and more people were tending to enjoy their treats, and trying to bake more of whatever was selling best, which today seemed to be chocolate croissants and banana nut muffins. At 3:20, Delaney looked up at the clock and realized she hadn't even taken a lunch break.

Hustling back into the kitchen to throw a tray of brownies in the oven, Delaney heard the back door open and looked up to see Joanna's smiling face. Delaney chose to use the word "dainty" to describe the slight blonde. She wore glasses and had frizzy hair which she usually wore in a ponytail, though the tendrils that framed her face refused to be tamed. A junior at Washington High, her mother dropped her off and picked her up most days as she still hadn't gotten her driver's license, and Delaney knew she was a bit socially awkward due to her overwhelming shyness. "Hey, there, Joanna!" Delaney said with a warm smile, sliding the brownies into the oven and double-checking the temperature. "How was school?"

"Good," Joanna replied as she tied her apron around her waist.

Delaney knew the chances of her saying more without a prompt were slim to none, so she asked about a project she knew she was working on. "Did you get to work on your proton model today?"

"Uh, yeah," Joanna nodded, pushing her glasses up with her index finger. "We got a little bit of time to work on it in class."

"That's good." Delaney smiled at her, hoping to somehow pass off some of her own enthusiasm to the girl, though none of her other attempts had ever been successful. Joanna stood in front of her for a moment, as if she couldn't decide whether or not the conversation was over. She took a step toward the front, like she wanted to pass Delaney by and go tend to whatever needed doing in the shop, and Delaney sighed, stepping backward out of the way. While she was hopeful that, eventually, with some effort, she could bring the girl out of her shell, she was too tired to give it much attention right now, and a few minutes later, the back door opened again, this time the whirlwind that always accompanied Courtney hitting Delaney in the face along with the chilly November wind.

"Oh, my gosh, Delaney," Courtney was saying, perhaps even before she was fully inside. "You will not believe what happened at lunch today!" Before Delaney even had a chance to attempt a guess, the brunette with long, free-flowing hair, complete with red lowlights, launched into a story about how one of her friends had asked some boy to the Winter Formal in front of the entire lunchroom, and he said no, embarrassing her friend, but also embarrassing Courtney who had to eat lunch next to her as if nothing had happened. At the end of the long-winded story, which contained more "likes" than Delaney could even, like, count, Courtney said, "Ooh, so needless to say, I won't be able to make my shift Saturday, if that's okay."

Confused, Delaney leaned back against the prep counter behind her. "I'm sorry—I guess I didn't quite follow that, Courtney. Why do you need to miss your shift on Saturday?"

Courtney sighed in a way only a teenage girl can do. "Because I have to go get my dress for the dance. Like I said, Holly is hoping that Rich will change his mind, so she's going to go ahead and get her dress. Well, I have to go with her. I mean, it isn't like I can let her go by herself. And if she gets hers before I do, I could totes end up with the same dress, and that would not be cool. Anyway, I haven't asked off in, like, three weeks. So—you don't mind, right?"

Delaney wasn't sure she understood the logic at all, but part of the risk in hiring teenagers was recognizing that they might need off from time to time, so even though she knew that meant she would have to cover the Saturday shift—something she wasn't particularly excited about—she nodded. "Okay. What is it ten to two?"

"Yup. Oh, thanks, D—you're the best!" Courtney said flinging her arms around Delaney's neck. Before she could respond, Courtney was off to the front, joining her exact opposite, Joanna, behind the counter as Edie greeted her and then came to the back. Delaney realized she was still leaning on the counter, the same puzzled expression likely still on her face.

"You okay there?" Edie asked, nudging her as she took her apron off and tossed it over her arm.

"Oh, yeah," Delaney replied, pulling herself out of her thoughts. "I was just thinking about Saturday. Courtney's not coming in. So I guess I'll cover that. Francine and Bonnie will be in that morning as usual, right?"

"Far as I know. They hardly ever miss, and I'm sure they'd let us know by now if they weren't coming."

Francine Pratt and Bonnie Gann were older women who only worked Saturday mornings and occasionally came in if Delaney found herself in a jam. They were retired from their regular jobs, loved baking, and liked to make a little "pocketbook money" as they called it. Delaney realized the timer was about to go off on her brownies and bent to check to see if they were done. "And Joanna will be in from, what, noon to close?"

"Yes, but if you get someone new to come help you in the morning, you might see if she can also work that afternoon shift with Joanna. She might be able to handle it by herself most of the year, but during this Christmas rush we seem to be having, I think things might be a bit too busy for her on her own," Edie replied, throwing her purse over her shoulder.

Delaney nodded, knowing Edie was right. Part of the problem of living in a small town was not always having the help one needed to run a small business readily available. "I'm glad for the extra traffic, but I wish I knew what was causing it. Do you think it'll let up after the holidays?"

"Why don't you ask your friend Melody?" Edie replied, pausing for a moment in front of the back door. "I think she's the one bringing them all in."

Once again, Delaney found herself confused. "What do you mean?"

"She's been wrestlin' up business for her mom's antique store, right? People are saying they heard about downtown Charles Town online. Whatever she's doing to bring folks in must be trickling over to us, too."

As Edie wished Delaney a good evening and made her way out the back door, Delaney carefully considered what the older woman had said. Melody Murphy had been her best friend since before high school. She knew Melody had returned from Chicago recently to help her mother run their antique shop, just a few doors down from Delaney's Delights, but she wasn't aware that her friend had brought her marketing skills along with her. That made sense, though. She knew Murphy's Antiques and Collectibles had hit a bit of a slump since Melody's father, Tim Murphy, had passed away a couple of years ago. If anyone knew how to bring people in, it was Melody, and if she was doing some sort of social media marketing campaign to draw attention to the antique dealership, it could very well benefit the rest of the small business owners on the square.

"Is that a 'Help Wanted' sign in the door?" Courtney asked as she brought in some dirty dishes and set them in the sink.

"Yeah," Delaney replied, silently debating whether or not she should do one last load of dishes before she headed home. "I thought we could use an extra pair of hands around here, particularly in the morning before school and on Saturday. Do you happen to know anyone?"

Courtney seemed to consider the question, resting a finger against her perfectly proportioned chin. "No, but I'll keep my ears open. Not everyone's mom makes them pay their own car payments like mine," she muttered and then walked past Delaney back out front.

Deciding to help the girls out, Delaney crossed to the sink and began to work on the dishes that had begun to stack up again already, even though she could swear she had just washed them. Courtney's mom was a bit of a rarity these days. They were what most would consider an upper-middle-class family, yet Courtney was still responsible for making her own payments on the Taurus she drove. It was just that sort of ambition her own parents had inspired in her, and even though at times she thought her father might have been disappointed that she became a baker instead of a doctor or business major, she knew he was proud of her for working so hard to build her own business.

Finishing up the last of the dishes, Delaney dried her hands on a nearby towel and went back up front to let the girls know a few details before she took one more glance around and headed home. Even though there were still several patrons in the bakery, she knew that between Courtney and Joanna, they could handle it. They might have been polar opposites personality-wise, but they were both responsible teenagers. Delaney's exhaustion finally overcame her and she grabbed her coat and purse and slipped out the back without even taking off her apron.

CHAPTER 2

The scent of deliciousness filled Delaney's nose when she opened the back door, and she instantly felt her mouth begin to water. Aromas of roasted chicken, carrots, and a medley of other vegetables wafted through the air, and she paused for a minute before hanging up her coat, the wayward apron, and purse, inhaling deeply. While most of the time she tended to think about how much she was helping her grandmother by moving in with her, in moments like this, she remembered that she was also a beneficiary here. No one made chicken soup like Nana Nora Jean.

"That you, Delaney?" her familiar voice called from the adjoining living room.

"Yes, Nana," she replied, approaching the crockpot, her stomach beginning to rumble.

The shuffling of slippers behind her alerted Delaney that Nana was making her way into the kitchen. She wasn't as spry as she used to be, but so far, she didn't require any type of assistive device, so long as she took her time. "That chicken soup is done, honey, if you want to go ahead and fix a bowl. I know it's not quite supper time, but something tells me by the looks of you that you skipped lunch again. You're getting too thin, darling."

Delaney didn't wait to be told twice. Grabbing a bowl out of the cupboard above her, she reached for a ladle and carefully set the glass lid on the counter next to the slow cooker. "Do you want some?" she asked as she poured two heaping ladles full of steaming deliciousness into her bowl, ignoring her grandmother's comment that she was too thin. She knew she was not the stereotypical plump baker, but she was also on her feet almost non-stop and still tried to get some exercise in every evening when possible.

"No, dear. I just ate lunch a little while ago. I'll eat my share later." Nana placed the lid back on the crockpot and bent down to look at the settings before turning the heat down, peering over her glasses as if she couldn't quite decide whether she needed them or not.

Delaney took a seat the table and was surprised when Nana came over and sat down next to her. "Aren't you going to miss *Judge Judy?*" she asked. There were only two programs her grandmother cared to watch most days. One was the courtroom reality show starring Judith Sheindlin, who her grandmother said she envied for her no-nonsense personality, and the other was *The Young and the Restless*, which Nana had been watching since Delaney's father was a little boy.

"No, it's okay. I watched the earlier episodes," Nana replied, adjusting her glasses. Nana's hair was short and almost a steel gray color. Her eyes were a pretty blue, and Delaney had always wished hers were that color instead of the deep brown of her father and grandfather. Nana was petite and had always been lithe. Her grandfather said she was built like a ballerina, which had often made Nana blush, and Delaney hoped when she was her grandmother's age she would still be as trim as the woman sitting next to her. Besides her eyes and warm smile, the most endearing part of Nana was her hands. Soft and gentle, they knew just how to clean a boo boo, soothe a broken heart, mend a tattered toy, and as Delaney was reminded, make a loving meal for her family. It had been Nana's cocoa recipe that had inspired Delaney to love creating in the kitchen so long ago, and though Delaney had modified the recipes she had learned from Nana over the years, the one thing she would never change is pouring her own heart into everything she made, just like Nana did.

CHRISTMAS COCOA

"This is delicious, Nana," Delaney said between bites of the hearty soup. "Thank you for making it."

"You're welcome, dear. It's the least I could do. I know how hard you're working these days. Not to mention coming back home and doing all the things this old grandma just can't do anymore."

Delaney chuckled. "Nana, you do plenty. I do have a few things to check on outside, and I'll throw in a load of laundry, but that's nothing."

"Delaney, you always were such a sweet girl," Nana said, patting her granddaughter's hand. "How was the bakery today? Did you sell a lot of cookies?"

Nana always asked about cookies, as if that was all Delaney baked, though she knew the bakery had a lot of different offerings. Nodding, Delaney said, "We've been swamped the last few weeks. I think I'm actually going to have to hire another part-time worker, Nana. I don't know if it's the holidays or if people are just giving into their craving for sweets more these days, but business has definitely picked up."

The warm smile Delaney loved spread across her Nana's face. "That's good to hear, dear. Is there anything I can do to help you? You know, I could bake a batch of my famous snicker doodles tomorrow and you could take them with you to the bakery."

"Oh, Nana, you're so sweet," Delaney said, finishing up her soup. "That's okay. We can manage. Thank you for offering. I'm just going to have to get someone to cover the front for an hour or two before Edie comes in in the morning. Oh, and before I forget to tell you, I'll be working Saturday this week."

"You will?" Nana asked, her forehead crinkling. "Why is that?"

Shrugging, Delaney stood and walked her bowl over to the sink. "One of the high school girls had something come up. It's not a big deal."

Behind her, she heard Nana let out a sigh. "Well, darling, just don't work yourself too hard. It seems like you never have time to spend with your friends anymore."

Delaney thought about her grandmother's words as she put her bowl in the dishwasher. It had been a while since she'd done anything fun. Thoughts of going out made her briefly think of Bradley—and then promptly push that memory aside. "If anything interesting pops up, Nana, I'll be sure to take advantage, but as for now, there's not a whole lot going on."

Nana sighed again, and this time Delaney turned to look at her. She wondered if she'd bring up her ex-boyfriend—something Nana did from time to time—but she didn't. Instead, she asked, "What about Melody? She's back in town. Maybe you could go see a movie or go out for dinner together, like you used to, when you were in high school."

Folding her arms across her chest, Delaney considered her grandmother's advice. She hadn't seen much of Melody since she moved back to town. It seemed they were both extremely busy. It might be nice to get together with her friend and see how she was doing. Melody wasn't quite herself anymore since her father had passed away so suddenly, and Delaney had been worried about her, but every time she stopped by the bakery, she seemed like she had a million things to do. "Maybe…" Delaney replied, thinking she might call Melody later and see what she was up to.

"Or…" Nana began, and Delaney could tell by the lilt of her voice what was to come next, "you know my friend Viola from church has a grandson about your age who lives over in Harper's Ferry. Maybe the two of you could get to know each other a little better?"

There it was. Delaney bit back a sigh of disgust, knowing her grandmother's intentions were good, even if she didn't quite understand that Delaney did not want to be fixed up with her friend's grandson—or anyone else. "Nana, no thanks." She busied herself straightening up a few items on the counter that didn't need straightening and then considered exactly what she needed to throw in the wash.

"I'm just saying," Nana continued, turning to face her, "it's been—what? Six months since, uhm…"

"Bradley," Delaney supplied, the disgust even more prevalent now with thoughts of the lawyer from Baltimore whose decision to end their relationship abruptly because he suddenly couldn't handle the long distance anymore had shocked her and left her despising all men, a sentiment she was only just now beginning to get over.

"That's right. Bradley. Six months is a long time to go without a date when you're young and beautiful."

"Nana," Delaney said, sighing and stopping in front of her grandmother who was now turned sideways in her chair, "thank you for thinking of me, but I don't think now is a very good time for me to be dating—Viola's grandson or anyone else. I'm so busy at the bakery, and with the holidays coming up, things tend to get a little overwhelming. Maybe after the New Year, if Viola still wants to fix me up with..."

"Mervin," Nana said with a smile.

Delaney wrinkled her nose, then realizing she was being rude and judgmental, changed her expression back to a more neutral affect, "Mervin? Maybe... maybe in January I'll have more time to think about dating again. Okay?"

"All right, dear," Nana replied with a sigh. "But don't wait too long. A young woman like you should be out there enjoying life, not spending her evenings and weekends with an old lady like me."

Stooping to slide her arms around her Nana's shoulders, Delaney said, "Oh, Nana, there's no one else I'd rather be with." She felt her grandmother's arms wrap around her waist and give a gentle squeeze before she kissed the soft, wrinkled cheek she loved so well and then straightened up. "Okay. I'm going to toss in a load of clothes. Why don't you go see who Judge Judy is reprimanding today?"

"All right," Nana said, using the table to pull herself up and waiting a second to get her balance before she headed into the living room. "You know, I plum forgot to watch my story this morning," she called as Delaney headed off down the hall toward her nana's bedroom to get the clothes she was intending to wash.

A few feet away from the bedroom door, Delaney stopped and turned to hear what her grandmother was saying. "You forgot?" she repeated. "Again?"

"I know," Nana called. "That's twice this week. Not sure what's getting into me."

She heard the creak of her grandmother's favorite recliner as she spun on her heel to get the clothes out of the hamper. "Hmmm," she mumbled allowed, lifting the only half-full container and heading back down the hall toward the kitchen. The laundry room was just off the small dining area where they usually took their meals, next to a large walk-in pantry her grandfather had added on many years ago when he first realized what a chef his new bride was.

Raising the lid to the washing machine, Delaney put in the contents of her grandmother's hamper, threw in a gel tablet of detergent, closed the lid, and set the washer for a load that consisted of both lights and darks. Her grandmother despised Delaney's "new fangled" washer and dryer, preferring her old ones where items still had to be separated by color and fabric, but Delaney had insisted that if she was going to be doing the laundry, she needed something that didn't take up so much time. The new appliances had been some of her first purchases once Delaney started making an income from her bakery.

Taking the hamper back toward her grandmother's room, she puzzled over this new wave of forgetfulness. There had been times in the past when Nana might occasionally forget something, but forgetting to watch her favorite show was unlike her, and now that it had happened twice in the same week, Delaney wondered if there was anything else she'd forgotten.

After the hamper was back in its usual position, she made her way into the living room and took a seat on the plaid couch next to the recliner, waiting for a commercial break to inquire about the rest of her grandmother's day. This sofa had been here as long as Delaney could remember, as had most of the other furnishings in the room, including all of the knickknacks and collectibles that lined the shelves on the walls and the pictures of children and grandchildren that hung above the couch and elsewhere in the room, which included portraits of her father and aunts dating back to the 1960s. Delaney loved that this was the one place in the world she could be assured of sameness and consistency. Her mother, on the other hand, loved to redecorate, and even though her parents had lived in the same house just a mile or so up the road since before Delany was born, sometimes walking into their house seemed foreign, and Delaney spent too much time looking around in an attempt to pinpoint what had changed from the week before.

Once an advertisement came on, Delaney asked, "Nana, did you remember to take your medication this morning?"

With a stifled chuckle, Nana replied, "Of course, darling. Just because I forgot my story doesn't mean I forgot everything."

"No, I know, Nana. Of course not. I just… it's not like you to forget your show. You love that show."

"Well, darling, that's what happens when we get old."

Delaney nodded, hoping that's all it was. She had friends whose grandparents had begun to show signs of dementia at ages far younger than her grandmother's current seventy-two, and she couldn't imagine what it might be like to lose her Nana in any capacity. "Maybe I could set a timer to remind you—or set the DVR to record it."

Nana made a dismissive wave with her hand. "Oh, Delaney, don't be silly. If an alarm went off in the middle of the day, I'd think the house was on fire. And you know I can't figure out that blasted DVR remote. It's fine, honey. I'll figure out what those folks are up to tomorrow. You know, I think that Graham is up to no good. And that Ashley, she better get her act together."

Delaney giggled and nodded her head, though she really had no idea what Nana was talking about. It'd been so long since she watched a daytime television show regularly, she couldn't have even named one character on any of the soaps. "Well, if you change your mind, let me know. I'm going to go out and make sure the wind didn't blow down any more branches on top of the garage last night."

"Okay, dear. You be careful out there. Bundle up. It's getting cold out."

Stopping to pat her grandmother lovingly on the shoulder, Delaney made her way to the back door, hoping that this memory lapse was nothing to worry about. She made a mental note to mention it to her father the next time they spoke and set about putting her coat and gloves back on. Even though she was fairly certain the old tree next to the garage was nothing to worry about, she felt responsible for Nana now, and she wanted to make sure there wasn't anything inside or outside that could harm her in any way. It was the least she could do for the woman who had always done so much for everyone else.

CHAPTER 3

The sharp scent of pine and spruce, mingled with the earthy smell of freshly plowed soil filled his lungs as Josh Taylor stood near the top of one of many rolling hills looking out over the vast expanse of the Taylor Christmas Tree Farm. It was early, and like most days this time of year, it would be long, but at least it was Saturday, so he would have no out-of-town deliveries. While the crowds hadn't quite started making their way to the little village his parents had created over twenty years ago, he knew they'd be there soon enough. Thanksgiving had passed, and the joy of the holiday season was now upon them. While he had long associated Christmas with physical exhaustion, he also loved the spirit of the holidays, and getting to spend this time of year with his parents and extended family once again made getting through the long days a bit more tolerable.

Josh removed his stocking cap and ran his hand through his unruly brown hair. He knew it was time for a haircut, but he liked letting his wavy hair grow a bit long this time of year. As the November breeze picked up a bit, he remembered why; there was just something freeing about feeling the wind in his hair. Unfortunately, that was about the only part of him that felt free these days. He placed the black stocking cap back on his head and shoved his hands deep into the pockets of his matching coat, letting out a sigh before returning to the four-wheeler that had brought him this far, and with one more glance around at the saplings dotting the outskirts of his parents' land, he headed back to the house.

His mother had insisted that the little village his father built for the Christmas crowds be set far away from their actual home. Josh passed by the little shops and the reindeer pen on his way to the log cabin his father had constructed practically on his own before Josh or his brother and sister were even born. While the rough-hewn timbers on the outside gave the appearance of a larger version of what one might have seen sprinkling the West Virginia hillsides a hundred years ago or more, on the inside the home was much more accommodating. Though it was cozy, it was big enough to welcome visiting family, complete with an ample kitchen where his mother would spend the majority of her day if she were allowed.

Pulling the ATV to a stop near the two-car garage, Josh stepped off and stretched. He'd gotten up before dawn to go check on his father's newest planting, trees that wouldn't be ready for a few more Christmases, and planned to spend most of the day out in the western acreage harvesting trees that would make for a merry Christmas this year. But first, he would enjoy the spread he was certain his mother was preparing for breakfast. His mouth watered thinking of the eggs, bacon, sausage, and homemade biscuits he imagined she was cooking right now in anticipation of the arrival of his brother, sister, their spouses and children, as well as anyone else his father may have commandeered to work on the farm that weekend.

Before Josh even made it inside, he heard his father's voice and realized he was sitting on the porch swing, phone in hand, having a bit of a heated discussion with someone, and Josh paused to see if everything was okay.

"No, I understand. If he's lost his driving privileges, Faye, then I guess we'll have to figure something else out. I get it. It's just I wish you would've called me last night so I could have found someone else to go. Yes, I know. I agree, it is important to teach them responsibility when they are young. Okay—yes, send him over and I'll put him to work." Kent Taylor said his goodbyes and hung the phone up, letting go a sigh of frustration as he did so.

As if he'd just noticed Josh standing nearby, Kent grimaced and attempted to force a smile, but it didn't quite come out the way he intended, and Josh could see that he was clearly put-out about something. "What's going on, Dad?" he asked. Faye was Josh's cousin, and as far as he knew, her son Will was set to make a delivery run to a few of the lots this morning. From what he could tell by listening to his father's end of the conversation, though, it sounded like that wasn't happening.

"Will stayed out too late last night and missed his curfew," Kent explained, running a hand through his thinning hair, which he kept much shorter than Josh's, keeping its tendency to break into waves in check. "Faye has suspended his driving privileges, which I don't blame her for, but had I known she was considering that as a punishment, I wouldn't have arranged for him to take those trees to Winchester today."

Josh nodded, everything he suspected becoming clear. "Well, it sounds like she's still going to bring him over to help, so that's good."

"Yes," Kent nodded, "but you know he's better at driving than he is anything that has to do with actual physical labor."

Josh chuckled. Will was one of the lankier, scrawnier family members that worked on the tree farm. Most of the time, he tired out, or quit from a lack of motivation, long before the rest of the team was ready to take a break. "Is Mackenzie still bringing over Payton and his friend Robert?" Josh asked, referring to his older sister and her son, who was not old enough to drive yet, but he was strong and a hard worker. He was also usually good for bringing a friend or two who wanted to earn a little gas money.

"Yes, and your brother is coming, as well as a few of the other cousins. But we have a lot of trees to bring in today. Your mom will definitely be busy at the village now that Thanksgiving is over, and next weekend will likely be one of our busiest. We need to get at least a few hundred more trees down to the village, and then you've got deliveries to make almost every day this week."

Josh nodded. He was very familiar with the business of his schedule. He had already started making the trips to different lots this past week, delivering hundreds of trees to towns in three states, and his mom had been on the phone with dozens more retailers the last few days scheduling drop offs for the coming weeks leading up to Christmas. While Josh didn't mind the monotony of driving around the countryside taking the trees to various towns where he knew they would make for many a happy holiday, he also enjoyed working the land with his father, brother, and other members of the Taylor clan. That's what weekends were for this time of year. However, seeing the desperation on his father's face and knowing there were very few people he trusted to actually deliver the trees and speak to the clients, Josh said, "I can take this load."

Kent's eyebrows raised, and Josh knew it was because his father understood how much Josh looked forward to having his weekends off from deliveries. "Are you sure, Son?" he asked. "I could ask Travis to do it."

Chuckling at the thought of his older brother attempting to tactfully interact with the various retailers he'd have to speak with when dropping off the trees, Josh said, "Sure, Dad. It's fine. It shouldn't take more than a few hours, right? I'm sure I'll be back in time to get some work done out there in the mountains with you."

A look of relief washed over Kent's face. "I hate to even ask you. I know you get tired of all the driving during the week."

"You didn't ask me," Josh reminded his father. "I volunteered. It's not a big deal, Dad."

"Still," Kent said, standing and crossing the few steps so that he was standing next to his son, who was a good half-foot taller, "I know how you feel about the farm, and the fact that you're willing to take all of your vacation time to come out here and help us means a lot to your mom and me. It makes me proud to hear you say you're willing to do whatever it takes to make this a profitable year for us."

Josh shrugged and carefully studied the wood grain in the porch between his work boots. "Dad, I love the farm. It's not that I don't. I just don't know that it's my dream, you know? At least, not the way that it's always been yours. But I want to help. You know I wouldn't be here if I didn't want to."

"I know," Kent interjected quickly, patting his son on the shoulder. "I understand. Maybe, while you're out there today, you can think about what we talked about."

Holding back a sigh, Josh nodded. "I will," he confirmed, then forcing a smile, he added, "I am definitely not leaving before breakfast, though." The aroma of freshly cooked bacon made his mouth water, and he paused for a second to take a deep breath before pulling open the screen door, holding it for his dad.

"I can't fault you there," Kent replied, pushing open the large oak door where his wife had already hung a beautiful, handmade wreath she'd created from pine trimmings. "As long as you're on the road by 9:00 you shouldn't have any trouble making it to Winchester on time. Although, I will need you to go through Berryville and stop off at Gallows. They've ordered twenty trees."

Following his father across the living room and into the kitchen, Josh repeated, "Gallows in Berryville and then on to Winchester. Got it."

"I always thought Gallows was a funny name for a Christmas tree lot," Lydia Taylor said as she slid plates across the counter to her husband and son, both heaped to the brim with the country breakfast she'd just prepared. "It always made me wonder if they used to specialize in a different sort of product also made from lumber."

Josh chuckled as he sat down at a barstool across from his mother and next to his father. While there was a perfectly good dining room table in the adjoining room, eating breakfast in here on the weekends was always a bit more intimate, and he knew his mother would continue to prepare more food as he and his father ate in anticipation of the rest of the family members and crew who should be there in an hour or so.

"I believe that is a family name," Kent explained, digging into his eggs. "Mmm, mmm," he proclaimed, and after swallowing, added, "even better than your last." It was a comment he made each time his wife prepared a meal for him, and even though she had heard it thousands of times through the years, it always brought a blush to her cheeks and a smile to her lips.

Lydia Taylor was fairly tall and insisted that her sons got their height from her, while her daughter was stuck with Kent's average height. She wore her dark hair cut to shoulder length, and while she had put on a few pounds over the years, mostly from sampling her own creations, she was definitely able to keep up with her grandkids. Josh watched as she pulled a cookie sheet filled with steaming biscuits out with one hand and popped another in with the other, thinking his mother could make her way around this kitchen blindfolded. "Are you going to be making the deliveries then today, honey?" she asked, glancing back over her shoulder at her youngest child.

"I am," Josh said between bites of bacon. "I guess Will got himself into a little trouble."

Lydia shook her head and leaned against the counter in front of them. "That doesn't surprise me. Still, he's almost eighteen years old. It's too bad he can't get his act together."

"He's a good kid," Kent chimed in, defending his fallen delivery boy. "He just needs a better father figure."

"Or a good swift kick in the pants," Lydia muttered as she wiped at the counter with a tea towel, though Josh was fairly certain there wasn't a speck of crumbs or splatter of liquid anywhere in the kitchen to be found, despite his mother's continued food preparation. "Thank goodness none of our kids ended up being slackers like your cousins' children."

Clearly trying to avoid a conversation highlighting the downfalls of his distant family members, Kent said, "Are you excited to have the granddaughters help you in the shop today?"

Lydia's face brightened at the mention of the two little girls. "Oh, yes. I think we'll be busy, too. Bridgette is excited to make another wreath, and Chloe wants to be in charge of the reindeer."

Kent chuckled. "That Chloe. She'll make sure everyone pets them properly, I'm sure."

Josh loved his two little nieces, his brother Travis's girls. One of the things he loved most about visiting his parents during this time of year was watching their faces light up at the mention of Santa Claus or anything Christmas related. This was such a magical season, particularly for children, and he was happy to get to share the holidays with the girls while they were still small enough to believe in the splendor of it all. Bridgette would be six soon, and Chloe was only three. Looking at his parents' faces when they spoke of their youngest grandchildren made Josh wonder what it would be like when he had his own kids someday and he could bring them by to visit their grandparents.

"Well, if you're going to Berryville, you should stop by Charles Town on your way," Lydia said, pulling an advertisement out of the newspaper sitting next to them on the counter. "I guess I didn't realize what a quaint little downtown area they have over there."

Having grown up in Shepherdstown, Josh was no stranger to the surrounding area, and he had visited Charles Town many times when he was younger, mostly just to have something else to do on the weekends or during high school sports competitions. He didn't quite share his mother's enthusiasm, however, though he listened as she continued to discuss the flyer.

"The antique store looks interesting," she continued, "and they are having a festival in a few weeks. There's a diner and a cute little bakery. I wonder if they have any treats we could sell in the shoppe."

"You already make enough cookies and cakes to fill up the shoppe twice over," Kent pointed out, taking a sip of his orange juice.

"Oh, I know," Lydia replied, scarcely looking up from the sheet of paper. "I just love new ideas, that's all. If you're in a hurry, I suppose I could run over there sometime this week and check it out. I just thought, you may as well stop by for a cup of coffee, see if there's anything inspiring. I just love this time of year. Everything is so festive and magical. Why not see a new place?"

"Charles Town is definitely not a new place," Kent reminded her. "Wasn't it founded by George Washington's brother."

"Yes, smarty," Lydia said, finally setting the ad down. "That's not what I meant. A place you haven't visited in a while—some place with fresh ideas." The timer on the oven made a chirp, and she went to check on her biscuits.

As Kent rattled on about how there was enough adventure awaiting him on the western acreage, Josh picked up his mother's flyer and gave it a look. It was a well put together photo spread of a few older buildings decorated for Christmas, with lots of smiling faces and an invitation to check Charles Town out for the holidays. With a shrug, he thought, "Why not?" He hadn't been there in years. Maybe he would stop by the bakery for a cup of coffee if he had time. May as well see what Charles Town had to offer if he had to head that direction anyway. It wasn't how he had planned on spending his Saturday morning, but then, some of the best things in life happen with absolutely no preparation whatsoever.

CHAPTER 4

Saturday mornings had a tendency to be busy, and even though the shift Delaney was covering for Courtney wasn't supposed to start until 10:00, she found herself standing in the back popping muffins into the oven well before 9:00. Wiping a trickle of sweat off of her brow onto the back of her hand, she surveyed the trays of treats stacked along the far wall, mentally calculating whether or not she needed to start on another batch of... something.

It had been a good decision to come in early. Despite Francine and Bonnie being very capable of running the shop without her on a typical Saturday morning, today, they were swamped. It was as if everyone and their brother had decided today was the perfect day for a doughnut, a croissant, or some other of Delaney's creations, and both women were busy up front with customers most of the morning while Delaney kept them in fresh supply with items to sell. She'd already made more batches of hot cocoa than she could count, and the tin of her secret recipe was going to need refilling soon. That was one thing only she made, and she only did so under cover of darkness, either before the other ladies came in or after they'd all gone home. There was no way she was going to risk letting that recipe get into anyone else's hands.

As Delaney took a pile of empty muffin tins over to the sink, she heard Francine say something to a customer about, "having to ask the boss lady." She set the pile down with a clatter and wiped her hands off on her apron, wondering what the question might be that only she could answer.

She made her way toward the front, seeing Francine walking her direction and met her a few feet outside of the kitchen. "There's a young man here who'd like to speak to you about the 'Help Wanted' sign," the older woman explained. Francine was short and plump, just the sort of grandmotherly-type figure one might expect to see baking cookies, and oftentimes new customers assumed she was the owner. It wouldn't have surprised Delaney to hear that this was the case with the teenage boy standing on the other side of the counter now, his hands shoved deeply into the pockets of his khaki pants.

"Hi," Delaney called as she neared the front counter. Offering her hand, she said, "I'm Delaney. Were you asking about the opening?"

Shaking her hand with a nervous smile, he replied, "Yes. Hi, I'm Cameron Baker, and I just thought… with a name like mine, this might be just the place for me."

Delaney giggled. She had to give him credit for trying. He was tall and thin with spiky black hair cut at a jarring angle, and from that perspective he reminded her of some of the skateboarders she'd seen around town and on television. He wore a plaid button-down shirt beneath his heavy jacket, and while it looked like it could've used pressing, she was impressed that he had worn something other than the jeans and T-shirt or sweatshirt most younger applicants tended to throw on when they stopped by to inquire about a job.

"It's nice to meet you, Cameron," Delaney replied. "I'm looking for someone to help out for a couple of hours every morning at opening. I'd also need some help on the weekends. Before you fill out an application, do you think those hours might work for you?"

Without hesitation, he replied, "Sure. I go to high school, but I could come in before that. I don't have to be there until 8:00."

Delaney thought about the hours she would need him. It was really from about 6:00 when the bakery opened until she was done with the morning baking that she needed someone to watch the front counter. If he could work until 7:30 or so, that should work. "Why don't you take an application, and go have a seat over there and fill it out? I'll come over when you're done and we can chat some more."

"Okay, great," Cameron said, the nervous smile back. He ran his hand through his hair, and Delaney marveled as the spikes bent but did not break, bouncing right back into place once his fingers had passed through.

Bending down below the counter, Delaney grabbed an application off the stack she'd pulled out earlier that morning. So far, despite the hundreds of people who had already been in the shop, no one had inquired about the sign. Apparently, people wanted to spend money this Christmas, not make any. Handing the simple form over to Cameron, and digging a pen out of her apron and giving that to him as well, she said, "Here you go. Just let Francine or Bonnie know when you're done, and they'll come back and get me."

"Thank you," Cameron said, his smile a bit more relaxed now, and he took the paper over to one of the empty tables, sat down, and began to fill it out.

Delaney looked around the room. There was only one other empty table, and a few people stood in various locations in front of the window and bulletin board, clearly waiting on Bonnie to finish putting together their orders. She recognized a few of the faces and waved, wishing the townsfolk a good morning, but she didn't know everyone, and before she could return to the muffins she'd put in the oven, the bell above the door chimed two more times, signaling even more hungry patrons. Whatever was going on to bring so many people in, she was glad for it, even if this might be the most exhausting Christmas yet.

She had just finished removing the muffins from the oven and decided she could turn it off for a while since they had a good supply of their best sellers waiting on the racks now when Bonnie hollered for her to come back up front. Cameron waited on the other side of the counter, his completed application in hand, and Delaney offered him a reassuring smile, remembering what it was like to be a teenager interviewing for her first job, though hers had been at the newspaper down the street, not at a bakery.

"You ready?" she asked, gesturing back toward the table he'd just vacated.

"Yes, miss," Cameron replied with a nod.

Delaney tried not to giggle at his formality, thinking at least he hadn't called her "ma'am" and led him back over where they sat across from each other. He slid the application across to her and Delaney checked it over. "Oh, so you just moved here from California?" she asked after reading a few lines of his history.

"Yes, miss. We've lived here for about a month."

"What brought you to Charles Town?" she asked, folding her arms on top of the table and looking up to meet his brown eyes.

"Well," Cameron began, briefly biting his bottom lip before continuing, "my dad lost his job. So he came back here, thinking he might be able to get a trucking gig where my uncle works. He's hoping to start next month. In the meantime, he's taken a job at a gas station, and my mom's working at a convenience store in Martinsburg. I just thought I should be helping out some, especially since I have younger sisters and brothers, and it's almost Christmas and all."

Delaney's eyebrows arched. "That seems like a noble cause," she said with a smile. "How old are your brothers and sisters?"

"My sisters are fourteen and eight," Cameron replied, "and my brothers are ten and six. I can't really work too much after school because I go home to help my sister look after the younger kids, but in the morning my mom drops everybody off at school before she goes to work."

Swallowing a lump in her throat at the thought of such a young man having that kind of responsibility already, Delaney nodded and returned her attention to the application. "You've mowed lawns and done some work for the park crew? Tell me about that."

"Oh, yeah," Cameron began. "I started mowing lawns in my neighborhood in California when I was about twelve. I was hoping to save up for a new bike, but... that's not what I ended up doing with the money." He had a distant look in his eyes, and Delaney wondered if some family emergency had come up and prevented him from using the money he'd worked so hard for on the object he intended. "And then during baseball season, I would work around the park near our house, mostly picking up trash and pulling weeds. It wasn't an official job, I guess, but I got paid a little bit, and I learned a lot from working with Mr. Joe, the head groundskeeper."

Delaney smiled as she saw Cameron's countenance change. "What did Mr. Joe teach you?"

"He taught me that it's important to work hard, to follow through, and not to let people down when they're counting on you. And that's why I want to help my family. I want my brothers and sisters to have a nice Christmas, even if it's not what they had before, when my dad had a better job."

Nodding, Delaney appreciated his candor. So far, his answers indicated he was just the type of young person she was looking for. "Do you know anything about baking?"

"Honestly... no," Cameron admitted. "I mean, sometimes my mom gets those break-apart chocolate chip cookies and I help Gail—my sister—bake them for the little kids. But that's about all I know. I'm willing to learn, though," he added, "and I'm usually pretty quick at catching on."

Delaney giggled at the comparison between her creations and the cookies he was referring to. "There probably won't be too much baking involved, but you might have to watch the oven from time to time or take something out and put it on the cooling racks."

"I can do that," he chimed in with an assuring nod.

"How are your customer service skills?"

"Good," Cameron replied confidently. "I know how to count change, I'm usually pretty good at talking to people, and I like for customers to have a good experience."

"All of those things are very important in our industry," Delaney said. "When people come into Delaney's Delights, they are looking to treat themselves or a family member. We want them to know they're not only getting a superior product that they can't just pick up at a grocery store, but they're also getting an experience—hometown charm, that's what we're all about."

"I think that shows," Cameron spoke up, glancing around. "Everyone is smiling and having a good time."

"Yes, and while there have been a lot of new customers lately, we want to keep them coming back. Believe it or not, some of these people drove quite a ways to experience downtown Charles Town, and we want to find out who they are and why they're here without being invasive so we can make sure we remember them if they ever come back."

"I saw something on Facebook about that," Cameron nodded, "and on Instagram. That's a pretty good slogan they've got going."

"What's that?" Delaney asked, not quite sure what he was referring to.

"Oh, you know. The ads. 'Downtown Charles Town, the Heart of Home.' It's kind of catchy. I can see people liking that, especially at Christmas time."

"Right," Delaney nodded, though she wasn't quite sure what he was talking about. She absently wondered if it had something to do with her friend Melody's work to drive sales to her mother's antique shop. Either way, she had a good feeling about Cameron, despite his lack of direct bakery or retail experience. "Well, Cameron, I think you'll fit right in here. How would you feel about coming in Monday morning at 5:45 and we'll get you started?"

"Really?" Cameron asked, a broad smile breaking across his face. "That would be great! Thank you so much!"

"Certainly," Delaney replied, offering him her hand, which he shook with gusto. She went over the sort of identification she would need in order to officially hire him and asked him to bring it with him. "Wear something similar to what you have on now, and you can park around back. I'll be here, so just knock on that back door, and I'll let you in."

"Okay," the teen replied as Delaney walked him over to the door. "Thank you so much," he repeated, offering her his hand one more time, and Delaney shook it before watching him make his way back out the door, waving at him as he went and giggling at the little skip in his step she witnessed as he made his way down the sidewalk.

Once he was gone, Delaney made her way back around the counter intending to go file his application in a filing cabinet in the back when an unfamiliar voice caught her attention. The deep tenor was not one she remembered hearing before, but he must have been talking to her when he said, "I think you just made that young man's day."

Delaney turned to see a tall man with wavy brown hair sitting on one of the barstools at the end of the counter sipping what appeared to be a mug of her cocoa. She knew instantly she'd never seen him before as she was certain she would remember him. He had a warm smile and hazel eyes. The unassuming air about him was intriguing, and she stopped mid-step, turning to reply. "I guess so," she said with a shrug, approaching the stranger. "He seems like a good kid."

"I would agree," he replied, taking another drink before setting the cup aside. "Attitude is everything, and he seems to have a great one."

Delaney smiled, and leaning on the counter with her free hand, she asked, "And are you an expert on hiring teenage help?"

He chuckled softly, and Delaney liked the way the sound rolled around her ears. "Something like that. I work with a lot of kids at my parents' Christmas tree farm this time of year, and some of them are a little more worth their weight than others."

She gave a nod of agreement. "Well, Cameron will be the first young man I've employed, but he seems like a good kid. Anyone who wants to help out their family at Christmas seems like they deserve a shot to me."

"I totally agree," he replied. He looked at her for a moment, as if he was trying to memorize her face, and Delaney felt a bit of red creeping up her neck from the weight of his eyes. "By the way, I'm Josh." He offered his hand, and Delaney shook it, noticing his hands were not as rough as she would have expected from a self-proclaimed tree farmer. "I take it you're Delaney?"

She realized that she hadn't given her name and felt the blush intensify. "Oh, yeah. One and the same. You're not from around here, are you?"

"No," he replied, rather quickly. "I mean, I guess that's all relative. I grew up in Shepherdstown. I live in DC now. But I come back for the holidays every year to help out my parents."

"Just like Cameron," Delaney said, realizing why he must have been so empathetic to the teenager's story.

"Something like that," Josh nodded. "You know, I must have driven past Charles Town dozens of times the last few weeks delivering trees, but I never stopped to check it out. This is a nice little place you've got here."

"Thank you," Delaney said as Bonnie slipped between her and the counter to pull out a particular croissant for a customer. "Yeah, we've been really busy lately. I'm not sure what's going on."

"It might have something to do with this," Josh explained, reaching into his pocket and pulling out a mostly red piece of paper.

Delaney took it and looked it over. There it was. "Downtown Charles Town, the Heart of Home," she read silently. While she had no way of knowing for sure, the prominent display of Murphy's Antiques and Collectibles at the top of the grouping of pictures displaying lots of festive shops in the vicinity let her know this had to be Melody's work. Not far below the picture of the quaint shop was a photo of Delaney's Delights, a happy little girl resting her hand on the door as she smiled for the camera. "I hadn't actually seen this, but I keep hearing about it."

Josh ran his hand through his wavy hair. "It's a nice piece of marketing. Whoever did that is a professional." Then, with a chuckle, he added, "Maybe Taylor Tree Farm should hire this marketer."

Setting the paper back on the counter, Delaney asked, "Oh, are you in a slump?"

"No," Josh replied quickly. "We do just fine. I was just thinking... advertising can never hurt."

"Right," Delaney nodded, wondering if he was being completely honest or if there was something he wasn't saying, not that it was her business. "So are you working now?" she asked, realizing she was being a bit nosy but wanting to continue the conversation with the handsome stranger, despite the fact that she could see out of the corner of her eye that Bonnie and Francine could probably use her help.

He let out a sigh and then offered what appeared to be a forced smile. "I am. I don't usually deliver on Saturdays, but our irresponsible teenager needed to take the day off."

"That stinks," Delaney replied with a nod. "I guess you do know about kids who lack responsibility. I'm kind of in the same boat, actually. I mean, my teenager is out shopping for a dress for the formal at the high school, but she did kind of leave me hanging at the last minute. I don't usually work on Saturdays either."

"I do," Josh clarified. "That is, while I'm helping out at the farm I work just about every day, but I usually try to work with the trees on Saturdays, help my dad and my brother bring them into the lot, that sort of thing. Once we get busy, I'll spend most of the weekend hauling trees in for customers who've gone out and cut down their own perfect tree."

"Oh, that sounds so nice," Delaney said, smiling. "It must be great to know you've contributed to someone's merry Christmas."

His smile seemed genuine as he said, "It is pretty rewarding, actually. A lot more than my day job." He took another sip of his cocoa. "Well, Miss Delaney, I can see that you are pretty busy, and I've got trees to deliver. It was really nice meeting you. I hope your new employee works out."

"It was really nice meeting you, too," Delaney replied, meaning it. "Good luck with the trees," she added as he stood, and not only did she feel a little silly about her last comment, she noticed just how tall he was as she had to tip her head slightly to meet his hazel eyes.

He seemed to be stifling a chuckle as he said, "Good luck with the cocoa. Best I've ever tasted, actually. Glad Bonnie recommended it."

"Bye, Josh. Thanks for stopping bye," Bonnie said in response to her name, waving over the shoulder of the customer she was helping.

"Thank you," Delaney said, wishing she had the opportunity to explain about the cocoa, but he was already walking toward the door, and she knew any sort of commentary now would seem out of place and desperate, though she really didn't want him to leave. There was just something about him—and it wasn't even the fact that he was tall and handsome. For some reason, he seemed familiar to her, like she'd already known him for a long while, and at the same time she felt drawn to him, as if she needed to get to know him better.

With one hand on the door, Josh looked back over his shoulder and smiled at her before he pulled it open and walked out into the cold November air. Delaney felt her knees buckle just a tad, and she was thankful that the breeze from the door reached her enough to cool her burning cheeks.

"Now, that's a good lookin' feller," Bonnie whispered in her ear as she went around her to get something from the counter.

"Uh huh," Delaney agreed, still staring after the door. It wasn't until she heard Francine calling her name—and she must have called it more than once judging by her tone—that Delaney finally pulled her eyes away from the door and tried to focus on her work. While she wasn't sure at this point whether or not fate had just interjected itself into her life or this was just one of those chance encounters that might leave one wondering for a few weeks, she was hopeful that someday soon she would see Josh Taylor again.

CHAPTER 5

The trip to Berryville, and then on to Winchester, wasn't that long, but it had given Josh a chance to think. All the driving he'd been doing recently left him alone with his thoughts much more so than his usual 9:00 to 5:00 job as an IT specialist for a big firm in Washington, DC, and as he headed back home from his last delivery, it wasn't thoughts of programming or circuit boards that filled his mind —it was the image of deep brown eyes and a warm smile the likes of which he'd never witnessed before.

Stopping by Delaney's Delights had been a whim. He'd intended to swing past the antique store on the top of the flyer to see if they had anything his mother might like for Christmas, and he'd found a lovely bracelet there. The shopkeeper, an older woman by the name of Sarah he'd learned, recommend he stop by the bakery, so he'd done so, intending to grab a coffee to go. Once Bonnie suggested he try the cocoa and accidentally put it in a ceramic mug instead of a to-go cup, he decided to sit for a moment and enjoy the ambiance. That's when the owner, possibly the most beautiful woman he'd ever seen, caught his eye. Now, Delaney was about all he could think about.

Pulling the truck off of the main highway onto a back road that led toward home, he realized it was foolish to spend a lot of time picturing her pretty smile. After all, Washington, DC, was over an hour away, even without traffic. And there was always traffic. He'd only be staying with his parents for another month or so, then he'd be returning to the hustle and bustle of big city life. Not only would he be far away from Delaney, he'd be very busy, and he knew those long distance relationships never worked.

Besides, what were the chances she was even interested in him anyway? A beautiful girl like that probably already had a boyfriend or a husband (even though he hadn't noticed a ring.) Still, she'd been great to talk to, and he couldn't help but notice the twinkle in her eyes. It was too bad he couldn't meet a woman like that who lived closer to home. He would've asked her on a date in a heartbeat.

Nearing the farm, he finally pushed thoughts of Delaney out of his mind, which allowed another perplexing issue to creep into his awareness. He hadn't been too surprised the week before when his father had told him he'd like to retire soon—and that the only person he trusted to take over the farm was Josh. While he'd been honored to hear his father talk about how his responsibility and understanding of how to cultivate the land and care for the trees made him proud, Josh had always assumed his older brother would take over the farm when his dad was ready to hang up his saw and shovel the final time. Kent had explained that his oldest son, Travis, just didn't have the work ethic Josh had, and he was fairly certain Travis wouldn't want to leave his position at the car dealership anyway. He was good to work on the weekends a few times a year, but that was it. Josh was the one who understood how Taylor Tree Farm needed to be run, how making Christmas magic was an honor and a privilege. Kent said he knew that Josh liked his life in Washington but that Josh's home was here, with his family, working the land.

Josh had told his father he'd think about it—and that's exactly what he was doing now as he pulled the truck and trailer into the drive that led to the house. He'd spent many years and lots of money on student loans to get his degree in computer science, and while he wasn't fond of passing long days cooped up in an office, he did enjoy his work. He didn't get a lot of recognition or appreciation, but the company he worked for was a good one, despite it being a headhunting firm, and he had made several friends over the past four years in the big city as well. The question had caught him off-guard, and he definitely needed to consider his options. While he enjoyed working alongside his father and the rest of his family for these few weeks each year between Thanksgiving and Christmas Eve, taking on the farm full-time was an option he'd never really given much thought to. Not only was it potentially a lot less income, there was also a chance he could lose the whole thing with a failed crop or two.

He pulled the truck into its usual spot, the best for loading the trees once they were brought in, and climbed down from the cab. Glancing at the time, he knew that his father, brother, and the rest of the crew would still be out in the western acreage gathering trees for next weekend. He intended to head out there, but first he wanted to stop by the shops and see how his mother and nieces were doing. He'd spotted several cars in the lot on his way in, and they hadn't asked for a lot of help actually selling the trees, so she may have needed a hand. Josh climbed aboard one of several ATVs and headed off in the direction of the Christmas village he and his father had built a few years ago, hoping his mother hadn't been overly busy all day.

It took just a few minutes for him to cover the half-mile or so that brought him to the parking lot next to the village. He pulled to a stop near the fence and noticed at least a half dozen cars in the lot, which was pretty good for this late in the afternoon still in the month of November. He stepped inside and saw a few families milling about, some looking at pre-cut trees, another standing outside the reindeer pen. There was a gift shop where his mother generally hung out, ringing up trees and other assorted Christmas collectibles. She also sold her baked goods in a candy shoppe next door, as well as hot drinks—though in retrospect Josh wasn't sure he could ever call the concoction they mixed up here hot cocoa after having tasted Delaney's. Though the stores appeared to be separate entities from the outside, there was a large walkway between them on the interior, which allowed Lydia to monitor both sides and help guests with collectibles and candy at the same time.

Josh was relieved to see his nephew, Payton, helping a customer at the tree shaker. Most of the time, they shook excessive needles off of trees as they brought them into the village, but whenever a customer cut their own tree down, it would need to be shaken before it could be tied up and strapped to their vehicle. This was not a job his mother was particularly good at, and Payton was one of the more reliable teenagers in the crew even though he was also one of the youngest. Josh gave him a quick wave before he headed toward the shop to see if his mother was managing the customers okay while keeping an eye on his nieces, Bridgette and Chloe.

Lydia was working at the crafting table she had set up near the cash register when Josh walked in. Bridgette and Chloe were giggling, ribbons and glitter everywhere, and Lydia had a smile on her face. Josh knew Lydia loved all of her children and grandchildren, but these two gifts from his brother Travis were her pride and joy.

"Girls, I think you got more glitter in your hair than on the ornaments!" Lydia laughed, brushing a strand of sparkly blonde hair out of Bridgette's face.

"What are you girls up to?" Josh asked with a smile.

"Uncle Josh!" both little ladies proclaimed as they skipped over to him and wrapped their arms around him.

"We're making ornaments," Chloe said in her sweet baby voice.

"And mine is gold and silver!" Bridgette added. Her smile was missing one front tooth on top, and with her freckles and pigtails, Josh couldn't help but think she'd look perfect on a Norman Rockwell Christmas card.

"That looks like so much fun." He squeezed both girls and then waited for them to let him go so that he could check in with his mom. A scurry of footsteps and flying dress hems later, the girls were back behind the table carefully selecting their next glitter colors.

"How was your drive?" Lydia asked, patting her youngest son on the cheek. "Everything go okay?"

"Yeah, just fine," Josh replied, stopping in front of the counter. There were no customers in the shop right now, but he could tell

CHRISTMAS COCOA

from bare spots on a few shelves that his mother had been busy. "You able to manage down here?"

"It's been a challenge," Lydia admitted with a chuckle. "We haven't been this busy in November for as long as I can remember. But Payton came down to help, and the girls have been assisting with the candy selections, so we've been making it."

"Assisting with the selections or sampling the candy?" Josh asked, resting his hands on his hips and giving the girls a mischievous look. He could tell by their giggles they'd had a few pieces themselves.

Lydia lovingly ran her hand across each girl's hair. "Both, I do believe," she admitted. "It's been fun though." Leaning in, she added, "I can't say I'll be able to manage them every weekend, but today has been memorable."

Josh nodded, giving a chuckle. He knew what she meant. The closer they got to Christmas, the busier it would be, and they would need to bring in even more help to make sure no customer had to wait too long to get what they needed. "Well, I just wanted to swing by and check on you before I head up to help dad. I assume he's still over in the western acreage?"

"He is," she confirmed. "They've brought in three loads already, and he said they had at least one more to get in today. And then they'll all need shook, tied, and some of them loaded... all that fun stuff."

"Right," Josh nodded, knowing full well how the routine went since he'd been helping his father with the process since he was about Bridgette's age, though things had gotten a lot busier the last few years. "Do you need anything before I head out?"

"No, I think we've got it handled," Lydia said, still smiling.

"Good," Josh replied. "Holler if you need one of us."

"Will do!" Lydia assured him.

"Bye, princesses," Josh said, lovingly patting each girls' head.

"You're not going to stay and make ornaments wiff us?" Bridgette asked, struggling with the T-H sound because of her missing tooth.

"Not today," he replied. "I've got to go help Grandpa with the trees."

Though both of their little faces looked crestfallen at first, a quick redirection from Grandma got them interested in a new shade of glitter, and Josh was able to make his way out the door, glancing briefly over his shoulder at the two little angels as he made his way to the ATV. He was hopeful that someday he'd find the right woman and settle down which would allow him to contribute his own little cherubs to the grandchildren pool. For now, he would try to focus on Christmas trees, though, as he started up the four-wheeler, his thoughts of starting a family led him back to the beautiful smile of a certain baker, and he spent the few minutes it took riding out to join his father wondering what sort of a mother Delaney might one day be.

DELANEY HAD JUST FINISHED ADDING her secret ingredient to the cocoa mixture and putting its container back into the hiding place where she kept it so that the other employees wouldn't suspect that's what made her cocoa so much better than everyone else's when she heard a knock on the back door. She glanced at the clock on the wall and saw that it was twenty till 6:00, which meant Cameron was five minutes early, a good sign on his first day. She brushed her hands off on her apron and went to let him in.

"Good morning, Miss Delaney," he said, a bright smile on his face indicating that he must be a morning person.

"Hi there, Cameron," Delaney, said stepping back so that he could enter the bakery. "You can just call me Delaney."

"Oh, okay," he replied, a sheepish grin on his face. He was dressed in khakis again with a nice button down shirt, and this one appeared to have been freshly ironed, judging by the creases. He had a backpack slung over one shoulder, which Delaney assumed was for school later. "I brought the paperwork you needed." He handed her the requested documents.

"Awesome," Delaney said. "If you want to grab a damp cloth and go wash down the front counter and the tables, I'll get this taken care of.

You can put your backpack over here," she said, gesturing to the place where the ladies stored their purses.

"Yes, miss," Cameron answered as he slid his backpack off and placed it in the specified location.

"You really don't have to be so polite." Delaney stepped over to the little area where she kept the "business" part of the bakery. She had a small desk next to a filing cabinet. Without even sitting down, she began to fill out the paperwork she'd need in order to formally hire him. "You make me feel old."

"Sorry," Cameron muttered, and Delaney glanced up to see some color in his cheeks. "My mom always tells me it's important to be polite."

"Your mom is right," Delaney agreed writing Cameron's date of birth into the appropriate box and shuddering to see that he was so much younger than her. *Almost a decade....* "But we are all friends around here."

"I'll try to remember that," he said as he grabbed the cloth she'd asked him to get and dampened it. "What's this?" he asked, peering into the large metal container where Delaney kept her finished cocoa mix.

She glanced over her shoulder. "Oh, that's my cocoa. It's a secret recipe. I'll finish it in just a second. Just be careful not to get it wet—or spill it." Images of the dark powder tumbling to the ground filled her mind, and she secretly prayed that Cameron wasn't a klutz like one of the other kids she'd hired last year who couldn't seem to keep anything in its container.

"That's cool," Cameron replied, and Delaney wondered if he really thought it was cool or if he was still being mannerly. Cameron went off to the front of the store, and she could hear him wiping everything down, the screech of chair legs on tile letting her know he was being thorough. Technically, nothing really needed wiping as she had just disinfected everything when she came in about an hour ago, but it was something easy for him to do that didn't take a demonstration or careful directions.

Once she was done, she called, "I have your paperwork back for you, Cameron."

He appeared in the doorway. "That was fast."

"It's not so hard when you're a small business. If you'll come over here, I have a few things for you to sign and then you can put these away."

Cameron put the dirty rag on the sink, washed his hands, and wiped them on a paper towel before tossing it and coming over to the desk. A few minutes later, he was an official employee, and Delaney gave him a high five before stepping past him to go turn the lights on up front and flip the sign. It was time for Delaney's Delights to open.

Luckily, they weren't too busy for a Monday morning, and she was able to show Cameron how to use the cash register. She also showed him how to make the coffee and where they kept everything he would need for making all of the various drinks they offered, including the cocoa. Once she was sure he had the hang of it, she returned to the kitchen to finish making her secret concoction, though she did come up front for the first two customers. By then, Cameron had proven he was able to handle the work, and Delaney returned to the kitchen, a smile on her face.

Delaney went about making sure they had plenty of fresh treats on hand just in case they got busy and between batches, she went up front to check on Cameron and show him how to refill cups, lids, straws, and other items when he wasn't with a customer. She also showed him where they kept the list of other work that could be done if he wasn't busy. Once she returned to the kitchen, she heard him talking with one of their regulars, Mrs. Sampson, and smiled. The kid really seemed to know what he was doing.

As Delaney finished mixing a batch of muffins, her mind began to wander. She'd spent most of the weekend thinking about the conversations she'd had with Josh—the tree farmer from Shepherdstown. She couldn't quite put her finger on what it was, but she couldn't get him off of her mind. Maybe it was that heartwarming smile, or the way his hazel eyes sparkled when he talked about Christmas. While she knew chances were she wouldn't see him again, she was hopeful that maybe he would stop by, and every time the door chimed, she secretly hoped it was him.

She knew she was acting silly. The goofy grin she'd been wearing most of the day before wasn't lost on her grandmother, and she'd had to make up a story about one of the customers telling a joke in order to get out of it, ending with, "I think you had to be there." But still, after Bradley had broken her heart, Delaney wasn't sure she'd ever be interested in dating again. If nothing else, it was nice to know that spark of interest could still be lit when the right guy came along. Whether or not Josh Taylor was that guy remained to be seen, particularly if he never returned to Delaney's Delights. How would one go about hunting him down if he didn't come back for another cup of cocoa?

"Miss... I mean, Delaney?" Cameron called from the doorway, startling her back into reality.

"Oh, hey, Cameron," Delaney said, hoping her face wasn't red as she brushed her hair off of her forehead with the back of her hand, glad she hadn't dumped the muffin mix when she jumped. "What's up?"

"Are you okay?" he asked, clearly holding back a grin.

"Yeah. Just... thinking. I guess I forgot you were here."

He smiled and nodded. "It's almost time for me to go to school, and I was just wondering if there was anything else you'd like for me to do before I go."

Delaney looked up at the clock hanging on the wall above her head and saw that he only had five more minutes before he needed to take off if he was going to get to school on time. "Are there any customers right now?" she asked, unable to see the front from where she stood.

"No," Cameron replied. "And I refilled everything and wiped the tables and counter down. I also washed the front window and the glass in the door."

Her face lit up. "You're so good!" she said, putting the muffins aside and stepping over to him. "I guess there's nothing else for now then. You can put your dirty apron in that bin over there, and I'll get you a clean one tomorrow. Eventually, I'll get one with your name embroidered on it." She knew Nana would be excited to get to make an apron for a new employee, especially since this one was a male—something new and interesting to chat about with the ladies at church, no doubt.

"All right," Cameron said as he untied his apron and approached the dirty laundry bin. After he tossed it in, he looked around for a moment awkwardly, and Delaney wondered what he might be thinking. "So… tomorrow then?"

"Oh, right!" she replied, realizing she hadn't even talked to him about a schedule. "Yes, if you could come every morning at this same time, that would be great."

"Cool," he replied, with a smile.

"You're sure you'll make it to school on time?" she asked, glancing at the clock again.

"Oh, yeah," he answered, slinging his backpack on. "I'm a fast peddler, and it's not that far."

Delaney hadn't realized he didn't have a car until that very moment. It made sense though. Why would a kid who needed a job to help out his family have a car? She thought it was too bad he wouldn't be able to save his paychecks to get one either. "Okay—well be careful on your way to school. You did a great job today, Cameron. Thanks again."

"Thank you," he said, with a smile. He waved at her and made his way out the back door. As he went, Delaney absently thought she needed to make sure he could pick up some hours on the weekend, if he wanted them, to help with his situation at home and maybe let him earn enough for some wheels. Business was booming right now; it just made sense that she'd let him work if he wanted to. Otherwise, he wouldn't be making much more than a hundred bucks a week before taxes and that wasn't enough to help his family and still have some money for himself. He was a good kid, and if today's performance was any indicator of what she could expect, she hoped he'd be working for her until he graduated from high school and went on to college.

Just to be safe, Delaney went to the front and checked the till. She added up what she'd started the day with and looked at receipts to see what had been sold. Everything added up correctly, and with a sigh of relief, she muttered, "And he's not a thief. Good kid, that Cameron." The bell over the door rang, making her jump, and Delaney forced a smile at one of her regulars, even though she was disappointed it wasn't Josh Taylor. As she went about fixing Mr. Eberson's cocoa, she wondered if Josh Taylor would ever enter her establishment again. She certainly hoped so.

CHAPTER 6

Delaney was attempting to concentrate on Nana's directions as she gingerly placed one of several glass snowmen on the fireplace mantel, though there was either a disconnect between the speaker and the task-performer or Nana wasn't quite sure exactly where she wanted each one and was changing her mind as she went. Delaney thought it was likely the latter, but since she had nothing better to do on her Sunday afternoon (other than sit around and wonder what Josh Taylor was doing!) she decided to humor her grandmother by making the minuscule changes as she was told.

"Move that one just a bit to the left," Nana instructed from her recliner. "No, not that far. Back a little. That's good. Now, let's go back to the one on the end, the one with the silk hat. No not that one. The other one. Yes, him. Can you turn him just a bit to the right? Not that much…."

Delaney knew how important these keepsakes were to her grandmother. Most of them had been gifts from her grandfather, and every single one of them had a story. "How about this?" she asked, giving it a teeny tiny nudge. "Is that enough or maybe a bit more."

"That looks nice," Nana assured her. "Are your arms getting tired, dear? Do you want to rest a spell?"

Glad to hear that she had finally perfected the display, at least for now, Delaney came back down from her tippy toes and returned her arms to her sides. "Maybe a short break," she conceded. "I think we only have about five more to go."

"I do love this time of year," Nana said with a smile as Delaney cozied up next to the fireplace in an old rocker. "All the lights are so beautiful. The smells bring back such memories. I just wish your grandpa were here." Her voice trailed off in sadness, and Delaney felt her heart melt just a bit.

"I know you miss him," Delaney said, a sympathetic look on her face. "He loved Christmas, too. Didn't he?"

"Oh, yes," Nana said, the smile returning to her face. "He would go out and chop down a tree, bring it in, and we'd decorate it. He loved picking out presents for the kids. He got you a doll once, when you were just a little thing. Do you remember that?"

"I do," Delaney nodded, the thought brightening her mood. "I loved that doll. I think it's still up in the attic at home."

"You know, when I was little, we didn't have much, but my papa—that's what I called my father, Papa—he would always make sure us kids had something to unwrap Christmas morning. There were twelve of us, you know?"

While she did know that, hearing it always made her shake her head. "I know," Delaney said, not able to imagine having so many brothers and sisters.

"Sometimes it was just a corn husk doll, or a used book. Once, he gave me and each of my sisters a new ribbon for our hair. Oh, but we treasured those items, we really did. Because we knew how hard he worked for them. Nowadays, kids just expect their folks to give 'em whatever they ask for, no questions asked. And I suppose most parents do just that. But those kids miss out on learning the value of a gift. It's real sad, now ain't it?"

"Yes, it is," Delaney agreed, thinking of Cameron and his family and how he was doing everything he could to make sure his younger siblings had some nice gifts for Christmas.

"At Sunday school this morning, Brother Mitchell talked about how important it is that we concentrate on the gift of Jesus this time of year. I think we're beginning to lose that, as a country. Don't you?"

Her class had discussed a similar topic, and Delaney couldn't help but nod along. "I do think it would be nice if things were simpler. People are so busy now. Sometimes I wonder if they even slow down enough to notice what's going on around them. That's one of the nice things about having those tables in the bakery though," she mused. "Seeing families come in and spend a quiet moment together over a special treat warms my heart. I hope that the children will remember those times for many years to come."

Nana beamed at her proudly. "You're such a good girl, Delaney," she said. "I know someday you are going to make someone a loving wife, and you'll be one of those mothers who takes time for the important things in life."

Though she wasn't quite sure how her grandmother had made the leap from her comment to such an accolade, Delaney said, "Thank you, Nana. I hope so."

"I know so," Nana confirmed. "I know you're still a bit down about that boy—what's his name?"

"Bradley," Delaney supplied, the smile gone from her face. She was fairly certain Nana could remember his name and just chose not to speak it when she could get away with it.

"But you just wait and see. There's someone so much better out there for you."

"Thanks, Nana," Delaney said again. "But I don't think it's Viola's grandson Mervin." Pulling herself out of the chair, hoping to alter the conversation, Delaney approached the mantel. "Now, where shall we place the next Frosty?"

"How about you put that one with the green scarf over there next to the one holding the candy cane?" she directed.

Delaney pulled the requested snowman out of the box on the coffee table and put him where she supposed Nana wanted him to go. Once adjustments were called out, she made them, trying to hide her smile. Someday, she'd see a snowman and miss these moments.

After the last of the snowmen was placed—at least tentatively, barring any changes in Nana's perception—Delaney went back to the rocking chair. "Do you want me to get the tree down from the attic next?" she asked. Sunday was about the only day Delaney had to work on projects such as this one. Even though the day before she hadn't had to cover any shifts, and she'd let Cameron pick up some hours as well, most Saturdays she was working on other bakery related tasks—such as advertising, accounting, and ordering, just to name a few—and though she tried to save Sunday for church and family, it was also her big home project day.

"You know, sitting here reminiscing about the trees your grandfather used to bring in, I think I might want to have a real tree this year," Nana said, her face puckered up in deep thought.

Delaney was surprised. She could never remember Nana having a real tree. She'd always said she didn't like the sap or the needles, and as soon as the fake trees started looking remotely like real ones, she'd been the first to pick hers up from the Montgomery Ward catalog. "Really?" she asked. "I'd love to have a real tree if you're sure you're not worried about it making a mess."

Nana chuckled. "Sometimes life gets messy. I guess I've learned that by now."

"Well, all right then," Delaney smiled. "A real Christmas tree it is!"

"Do you know some place where we can get one? It doesn't have to be today, I suppose."

Suddenly, Delaney realized exactly where she needed to get her Christmas tree. "Yes, Nana, I do know where we can get a real tree," she replied, trying to keep the grin off of her face.

Nana was not fooled. "Delaney? What's that expression, dear? Your eyes are gleaming like an old alley cat in the full moon."

Bursting out into a fit of laughter over her grandmother's comparison, Delaney took a moment to regain her composure. "It's nothing, Nana. We just had a Christmas tree farmer come into the bakery last weekend. I think it would be nice to get our tree from a small business if we can."

Not being one to miss a thing, Nana said, "I see. And who was this tree farmer?"

Trying to keep her face composed and the color from her cheeks, Delaney cleared her throat and said, "I think his name was... Josh or something. I'm not sure. He was from Shepherdstown. I'll have to look into it."

With a broad smile, Nana asked, "And was this Josh a good-looking feller?"

Giggling at the phrasing of the question but trying to feign disinterest, Delaney replied, "You know, I didn't really notice. He was nice, though. We just chatted for a few minutes. It's been over a week. It just stuck in my mind because I don't get to talk to too many small business owners from surrounding areas."

"Yes, I'm sure that's the only reason why," Nana nodded, but Delaney could tell she was onto her. Still, Nana let it go. "All right, sweetie. I guess that's enough decorations for today then. Why don't you see about going to get a tree next weekend, and that'll give us some time to get the ornaments and lights down from the attic. I sure hope those lights aren't in a tangle like they used to get sometimes when I'd let your grandfather put them away unsupervised. That man sure could get his strands in a jumble."

Delaney laughed, picturing her grandfather holding a giant wad of tangled up Christmas lights. "I put them away very carefully last year, so I'm sure they're just fine," she assured her nana.

"Good. Now, where's that remote? I want to see if there's any good Christmas pictures on yet. I sure hope they play *White Christmas* soon. I love that movie."

"Nana, the remote is on your lap," Delaney replied, her forehead crinkling in concern.

"Yes, of course it is," Nana said with a dismissive shrug.

Delaney eyed her carefully but didn't say anything more as she went about taking the snowman box back to the attic. Nana had forgotten her show again one day this week. She'd also forgotten to feed the barn cats, a job she still insisted on doing, even though Delaney didn't like her stooping down to fill the bowls on the back porch, and one day she'd come home from the bakery to find Nana's pocketbook in the refrigerator. She said she'd gotten it out to check her wallet for a business card for a local flower shop that made deliveries she'd gotten from a friend at church and was carrying it with her when she went about making dinner. She must've set it down in the fridge by mistake. Delaney understood that everyone had mental slip ups from time to time, but the more frequently they began to happen, the more concerned she became, and she wondered if it was about time to go visit a doctor about Nana's memory and focus.

She made her way up the narrow steps to the small attic space and slipped the box over the lip onto the floor, thankful that she wouldn't have to haul the Christmas tree down from its corner this year. The smell of mildew and dust was overwhelming, and she rushed back down the ladder and shut the door attempting to hold her breath the whole time. She knew people who loved old things, and while Delaney appreciated memories of days gone by, she would rather avoid that smell when given the choice.

Making her way to her room to get out her laptop and look over the month's budget, Delaney thought about her grandma's suggestion. Surely, she would be able to find Taylor Tree Farm online and go there to pick out a tree. While it was tempting to stray from her work and look it up right then, she decided not to. What if the website was full of pictures of Josh, a wife, and smiling children? She wasn't ready for something like that—not now anyway. Besides, she'd need to enlist someone to go to the tree farm with her; approaching a man she'd just met on her own seemed a bit scary. This mission called for a best friend, and since it was time for her and Melody to do a little reconnecting anyway, Delaney resolved to question her oldest pal first to see if she might be up for a bit of recon—and Christmas tree shopping. She decided to talk to Melody later and started looking over the budget, impressed with the bottom line she was seeing. Assuming that Melody had something to do with that as well, she made a mental note to ask her about her advertising campaign. If Melody's ads had brought Josh into her bakery, then her friend definitely deserved a lifetime supply of cocoa and all the muffins she could eat. And with these figures, Delaney could afford it!

CHRISTMAS COCOA

❄

THE WEEK after his excursion to Charles Town passed quickly for Josh as he made his deliveries during the day and helped his father tend to the trees in the evenings. The village was only open on weekends, so they had all week to make sure that there were enough trees available for the next weekend, but since they'd sold most of the supply they had on hand the day before, his Sunday afternoon was full of trips to the village from the various locations around the farm bringing in fresh trees. He also used his tractor to bring in load after load of trees that families had cut down themselves from the selection of trees closer to the village. At least he could listen to the Redskins on the radio.

The farm opened for business after church on Sundays, and just as they had been busy the day before, the parking lot was practically full by the time Josh returned with his second load of trees. He wasn't sure where all of these people were coming from, but he loved to see the smiles on their faces when he dropped off the trees they'd picked out themselves. One little girl was so excited, she couldn't stop jumping up and down, shouting, "This is the best Christmas ever!"

Josh truly hoped it would be, though he felt like his Christmas was getting lost a bit in the hustle and bustle of helping out at the farm. He'd yet to watch a Christmas movie or hang an ornament, though his mother had done a spectacular job of decorating the cabin, as she always did.

As busy as he was, Josh had spent a great deal of time during the week in solace, and in those quiet times, making deliveries or moving trees across the property, his mind wandered to that pretty girl he'd met the week before. Unfortunately, none of his transports that week had brought him anywhere near Charles Town, with most of the lots he visited being in the opposite direction, into Maryland and Pennsylvania, but he decided if he didn't see Delaney soon, he'd have to stop by for another mug of cocoa. After all, there was simply no replicating that taste.

"You wanna go help Mom out in the shop for a minute?" Josh's dad called as he pulled the tractor to a stop near the shaking station. "I think she sold that giant Santa—the one that dances and sings—and the little old lady who's purchased him is going to need some help getting him loaded into her vehicle."

Josh knew his father's back wasn't in the best shape, so most of these types of activities fell to the younger man, which was no problem. Recalling when her mother had put that Santa on display a few years ago, Josh gave a chuckle. His father said she'd never sell that thing, and though it took her a while, clearly he was wrong. "Sure, Dad," he said. "I guess there really is a customer for everything."

Lydia was chatting with an older woman Josh didn't recognize as he made his way into the shop. "Here's my son," she said, walking over to rest her hand on his shoulder. "He'll be happy to help you get Santa in your car."

"Oh, goody," the older woman replied. "This is such a lovely place. I'm so glad I happened upon it. Everything is just so festive. It really reminds me of a time gone by."

"We're so glad you stopped in," Lydia said with a smile.

"There's just one thing," the woman continued, gesturing with one hand at the Styrofoam cup she held in the other, "this cocoa is not nearly as tasty as the rest of your baked goods." She held out the cup for Lydia, who took it from her promptly.

"I'm sorry," Lydia said, clearly a bit embarrassed. "It's just the ready mix kind."

"I understand, dear," the woman said with a smile. "And it only cost a quarter. Still, your cookies were divine and I loved the cinnamon almonds. Just needed something tastier to wash them down with."

Before she could say anything more, Josh asked, "Shall we get Santa loaded into your sleigh?"

The woman giggled. "If my old station wagon is a sleigh, then I guess so, son."

Catching his mother's eye, Josh winked and approached the unboxed Santa, trying to determine the best way to go about picking him up. He decided to wrap his arms around Santa's midsection, and

Lydia rushed to get the door so that he could squeeze through, the older lady following.

All the way to the car, the customer chatted about her grandchildren and how much they would enjoy seeing this dancing Santa when they came to visit for Christmas in a few weeks. By the time Josh had Santa snuggled into the backseat, he felt he knew all there was to know about the Chambers family and their traveling plans. He didn't mind though; getting to meet new and interesting people was a part of this job he truly enjoyed. It certainly beat sitting at a desk in an office building surrounded by the same few dozen people all day long.

"Have a Merry Christmas, Mrs. Chambers," Josh said, waving as the woman climbed into the driver's seat.

"You, too, son," she replied, smiling broadly. "I hope you have some Christmas magic in your life this year. You've certainly help spread some!"

Josh thanked her and watched as she pulled out of her parking spot before making his way back toward the shop to speak to his mom. He hoped he had half the energy Mrs. Chambers displayed when he was her age.

Lydia was rearranging some items to fill in the space left by the Santa. "Now, what in the world can we put here that will be as eye catching and interesting as that Santa?"

"I'm not sure we have anything that meets that description," Josh admitted stopping beside her to survey what she'd done so far. He definitely didn't have an eye for displays and would have to leave that to his mom. "She sure was nice," he added as his mother puzzled over the placement.

"Yes, although the comment about the cocoa seemed a little unnecessary," Lydia agreed. "It's more of an ambiance setter than an actual refreshment. That's why it's only a quarter."

Josh chuckled. He'd wondered if the remark hurt his mother's feelings. Certainly it had. "Well, maybe some people are used to drinking higher end hot chocolate—like from Starbucks or whatever."

Lydia waved at him dismissively. "I wish we could charge the three dollars they do for a drink then."

While he was wondering what size drink his mother was ordering from Starbucks that only cost three dollars, Josh didn't ask. "I had the best cup of cocoa in Charles Town last Saturday when I stopped by on the way to Winchester."

She turned to face him now. "You did? I didn't know you'd stopped in Charles Town."

Remembering that he hadn't mentioned it to her for fear he'd accidentally slip up and reference stopping by the antique store and eventually spoil her present, Josh shrugged. "You suggested it. I just wanted to see if your flyer was accurate."

"And was it?" she asked, turning back to begin moving some items around on what was left of the display where the Santa had been.

"It was nice," Josh replied, trying to keep his tone nonchalant. "Anyway, I decided to grab a cup of coffee from that bakery, the one in the picture, and the lady at the counter suggested I try the cocoa instead. She said it was an award winning recipe."

"I didn't know they had cocoa contests," Lydia muttered, still shifting merchandise. "Maybe the large snowman over there…."

"I didn't either," Josh admitted. He was about to sneak back out the door, realizing his mother was more interested in the shop than the cocoa discussion and knowing full well the only reason he'd mentioned it at all was because he wanted to speak of his experience to someone. While he was not about to reveal anything about Delaney to his mom or anyone else, he felt like he'd been keeping a secret bottled up for several days now, and talking to his mother about the cocoa relieved a bit of the pressure anyway.

Lydia was listening after all. "Well, if our cocoa is so awful, maybe we should see about trying another brand. I wonder if that bakery would let me use their recipe, or if they have a mix we can purchase. I'd hate to turn away people from the lot because of our horrific cocoa."

Chuckling, Josh said, "Maybe if I head toward Charles Town this week, I'll stop by and ask."

"I think you're headed back north all week," Lydia replied, turning to look at him. "You might have a trip that direction next week, but those big lots in Maryland really want our trees, and we've gotta give them what they want." She returned her attention to the display and repositioned a few smaller collectibles before she mumbled, "Unless they want cocoa."

"Mom, don't take it personally," Josh recommended, squeezing her shoulder. "It's a packet from the store—not something you made."

"I know, honey," she said, wrapping her arm around him. "I just want everyone to have a perfect Christmas. I don't know how much longer your father and I are going to be able to do this, and I've yet to have the perfect holiday I've always imagined in my mind. I guess I was hoping this might be it. And while cocoa is not the end of the world, if it's something we can fix to make our customers' experience better, I suppose we should." She let out a sigh and then continued. "Surely I have a cocoa recipe in the kitchen somewhere."

"I'm sure you do," Josh encouraged her, though he would still like to use his cocoa reasoning as an excuse to stop by Delaney's Delights.

Lydia rested her head against her son's shoulder. "I'm so glad we have you here to help us out, Josh. This place means so much to your father. It's a shame he won't be able to continue for too much longer, but he's just getting to where it's… too much."

She didn't need to rehash everything for him; Josh was aware of his father's failing health. Working long hours out in the field would do that to a person, no matter how well they took care of themselves. "I know, Mom," he said quietly.

"I don't want you to feel pressured into making a decision, but I have to think about what we will do if you decide not to take this place on. There are some extended family members who might want to purchase it, I suppose. But ultimately, it will probably be sold to someone who wants the land for other purposes, and while we'd intend to keep the house and a few acres, I'm not sure what it would do to your father to see all of this gone."

A lump formed in Josh's throat, and he did his best to swallow it. He couldn't imagine all of this not existing. The village, the trees, the barns, the feeling visitors got when they pulled into the lot knowing they were practically stepping into Santa's village.

Before Josh could comment, Lydia continued. "There's something else, Josh. I'm starting to worry about his memory more and more. The other day, I walked into the kitchen to see him just standing there. I watched for about a minute before I said anything, and when I finally did, he said he'd forgotten what he came for. But he was just… staring into space. I'm afraid he's becoming more forgetful. I'm afraid he might… forget something important. Like to put the truck in park or put the guard on one of the saws. At least when he's in the house, I can keep a better eye on him."

While Josh was well aware that his father's memory and focus had been slipping over the years, he had definitely noticed a pronounced difference this year as well. It was quite alarming since Kent wasn't really that old, relatively speaking. He'd always been sharp and detail oriented. Now, he seemed to fumble for words, to lose his train of thought, and to forget to do things that had always come second nature. Josh didn't want to tell his mother that Dad had misplaced the keys to one of the tractors the other day and it had taken them hours to find them. When they finally turned up, they had been in his pocket all along.

"I know you're worried, Mom," he began, "I am, too. What does Dr. Nelson say?"

"He says that's just part of being old. He recommended some supplements, and your father has been taking them. I don't know if they're helping."

"Maybe it's time to see a specialist," Josh suggested.

Lydia nodded. She opened her mouth to say more, but the bell above the door chimed and a family walked in. The children, a boy and a girl about Bridgette's and Chloe's ages, let out exclamations of wonder as they darted around taking in all the Christmas magic.

"I'll see you later, Mom," Josh said as he stepped away, leaving his mom to dote over the children and help the customers. He said hello to them and made his way back outside.

The December air had a small bite to it, but he welcomed the refreshing sensation on his face as he watched his father across the lot, standing near the shaker station, talking to Payton. Ever since he realized a few years ago that his father's memory was beginning to fade a bit, Josh started considering what he could do to help. He had discovered some apps that were supposed to help provide information to family members, help keep track of appointments, and possibly sharpen cognitive skills, but the more he thought about how apps were changing lives in so many other ways, the more Josh thought there might be a way to use smartphones to help with memory loss. As a computer information systems manager, he was well aware of how technology could improve lives. Over the last few years, he'd spent some of his spare time designing an app that would help people in the early stages of dementia not only improve their memory skills but also serve as a reminder of what they needed to do next in their daily routine. While he was still working on it, the basic premise was that the phone could operate as a memory stimulator, giving prompts and interacting with the user in a way that would help them remember what they were doing and what they needed to do next, as well as interact with them in a way that improved brain function. There was still a lot of research that needed to be done before his idea was even ready for early stage programming and design, but hearing his mother voice her concerns about his father made Josh realize he needed to do something that could help. And if his app had the potential of helping just a little bit, he needed to give it the time and attention it deserved.

For now, however, he had another trip to make out to gather more trees. With his gloves on and his stocking cap pulled tight, Josh made his way through what was turning out to be quite a crowd of people toward the tractor. There just didn't seem to be enough time in the day to get everything done, but he would have to find a way to make time. His father was much too important to him for there to be any alternative.

CHAPTER 7

It was easily the busiest Monday Delaney could ever remember at the bakery. She'd come in bright and early to get as much prepared as she could, and Cameron had been on time as well, but he'd been so swamped up front with the breakfast crowd that she'd ended up having to stop baking to come and help. By the time Edie got there, they were desperately in need of more cocoa and completely out of their most popular chocolate-chocolate chip muffins. Cameron had been reluctant to leave to go to school, but Delaney sent him out the door anyway. Now, it was well past noon and she hadn't gotten a chance to sit down for even one minute. She would be happy to see Courtney and Joanna arrive after school, though she was fairly certain she wouldn't be able to leave them if business continued to boom in the afternoon as it had all morning. They wouldn't be able to handle it.

She had completely forgotten that she was going to call Melody and ask her about going to the Christmas tree lot until her friend came by for a treat after lunch. While Melody had mentioned that she would stop by frequently since she visited her mother's antique store almost everyday to deliver new products, Delaney didn't see nearly as much of her as she'd expected to, and she wasn't sure if they were both busy or if it was the distance being so far apart for several years had brought to their relationship. Melody had gone to school in Chicago and lived there for a few years only recently having moved back to help her mother out at the shop.

Perhaps it was the fact that she didn't actually get much time to speak to her friend when she did stop by that was acting as a deterrent. That was certainly the case today. Every time Delaney started to come over and ask how Melody was doing, another customer would enter through the front door or someone would ask for a refill. Finally, after more attempts than she could count, Delaney got a second of spare time and slid over to where her friend was sitting, looking at her phone as she sipped her cocoa.

"Hey," Delaney said, waiting for Melody to look up. They both had long brown hair and similar complexions. Often times in high school, they were mistaken for sisters. "Sorry. We're just so busy. I feel like there's twice as many people here as on a regular Monday afternoon." She glanced at Melody's mug to see if she needed any more cocoa and decided she was okay for now.

"I've noticed there's been a lot more traffic lately, too." She looked around the bakery and then returned her attention to Delaney. Every table was full, and it was a little noisy with the chatter and the festive Christmas music Delaney had playing to add to the ambiance.

She'd been meaning to ask if Melody was the one who made the flyer, and now seemed like the perfect opportunity. "I think maybe some of your advertising has had something to do with it," Delaney replied, probing for a response. "Lots of people say they didn't even realize Charles Town had such a quaint little shopping district."

Melody's eyebrows arched momentarily before she said, "Not people from around here." She repositioned her mug on the counter. "Everyone who lives in Charles Town knows that."

Delaney surveyed the room and noticed a lot of unfamiliar faces. A lot of the people she'd spoken to that morning were not from Charles Town. "No, a lot of them are from out of town. It's really kind of cool."

Melody glanced around again, her green eyes crinkling at the corners. "What makes you think that they learned about Charles Town from me?"

Several people had either mentioned seeing an online advertisement or a flyer, and while Delaney had the sheet of paper Josh had left on the counter at home, she'd managed to procure another one from an elderly gentleman who lived near Berryville. "This?" she said, pulling it out from beneath the counter and sliding it across the table so that Melody could see it.

A look of recognition washed over Melody's face as she glanced at the sheet of paper. It was evident to Delaney that her suspicions were correct and that Melody had designed this particular advertisement. "I'm glad that it's helping," she said, offering a small smile, and Delaney was surprised she wasn't more vocal about her contributions, though she had always known Melody to be very humble; she never seemed to understand the positive impact she had on others.

Now seemed like a perfect time to segue into the topic Delaney had been dying to discuss with Melody for over a week now. There just hadn't been time, and she'd felt a little silly bringing it up at all since her hopes that Josh might show up on his own had begun to fade, but since Nana had planted the idea in her mind the day before, she could hardly contain her enthusiasm. Trying to act as casual as possible, Delaney mentioned, "And… it brought in a really cute Christmas tree farmer from Shepherdstown."

She could tell by Melody's reaction that she knew immediately what Delaney was getting at. A twinkle in Melody's green eyes, she leaned forward and quietly asked, "Delaney, did you meet a boy?"

Delaney felt the heat rising in her cheeks as she sheepishly said, "Maybe." She dropped down on the counter so that she could lean in more closely to talk to Melody, hopeful that Edie was too busy with the other customers to eavesdrop, though she was fairly sure that her coworker and friend already suspected something was up. She continued, "He stopped by last Saturday. Said he usually drives right on through or around Charles Town when he's out making his deliveries, but he wanted to check out the downtown area for himself."

Even though it had been over a week since she met him, and she'd only spoken to him for a few minutes, she couldn't get the memory of those sparkling hazel eyes out of her mind. "Melody—he's so cute. And nice. And... I really want to see him again." She looked up at her friend, hopeful that she understood exactly what she meant and that she wouldn't think she was being silly for having a crush on a man she'd only just met.

A small giggle escaped Melody's lips before she said, "Well, why don't you just drive over to Shepherdstown and pick out a nice Christmas tree? Did he tell you the name of his farm?"

Trying to give Melody the impression that she hadn't become obsessed with Josh—after all, she hadn't even Googled the tree farm yet—Delaney replied, "He did. I was thinking about that." She leaned up and brushed her hair behind her shoulder. "I think they do most of their sales at lots—but maybe they sell trees there, too." Josh hadn't really given her a whole lot of details about exactly what he did on the weekends, but she remembered he'd mentioned staying there and helping his parents, rather than driving the truck, on Saturdays.

Melody gave her a nonchalant shrug. "Doesn't hurt to drive over and find out."

Delaney nodded and then bit her bottom lip. She knew that Melody's late father had been quite passionate about Christmas and that he had some well-established rules about exactly how certain Christmas related tasks had to be done. She glanced at her friend and then looked away, not exactly sure how to broach the subject. Finally, she simply asked, "Have you picked out your tree yet?"

She could see Melody's shoulders tighten up. "No, we were going to go Saturday, but mom decided to stay home and make some soup for Mrs. Tresco. She fell and broke her hip." Melody met her eyes only for a second before looking away.

Delaney wasn't quite sure how to proceed. They'd known each other a long time, and while she normally wouldn't hesitate to ask her for help, things were different now. Nevertheless, the most direct way seemed the most logical. "Maybe... you could go with me?" She watched as Melody's eyes widened and her face seemed to pale even more than usual.

Melody began to shake her head before words even came out of her mouth. "Delaney, you know my dad's rule: Only Murphy's pick out the Murphy Christmas tree."

Despite her sympathy for her friend who had lost her father only two years ago on Christmas Eve, Delaney began to grow frustrated. She wasn't asking Melody to buy her own Christmas tree—she was simply asking her to go along as Delaney picked out hers. Beyond that, the fact that Melody seemed to pick and choose which of her father's rules she wished to follow suddenly bothered Delaney more than she had realized. Melody's father had insisted on naming her after one of his other passions—music—and she had been aptly named. Every year, the residents of Charles Town had looked forward to hearing Melody sing at the local Christmas Festival. However, once her father passed away, Melody stopped singing altogether, and Delaney, like most people, had difficulty accepting her reasoning. Why would she stop doing something that brought herself and so many others such joy? Perhaps that's why she found Melody's response to her inquiry particularly annoying. Without thinking about how it might be perceived, Delaney asked, "So you're strictly following your father's guidelines this year?"

Melody's eyes narrowed a bit, but she didn't seem to get what Delaney was hinting at, not yet anyway. "Trying to," she replied with a nod.

"Then I guess you'll be singing at the festival...." Delaney began, watching the heat rise in her friend's face.

"Delaney—don't." Melody's expression seemed to be a warning that she was growing quite agitated, but it was ignored.

"Well, I just thought, if you're following all of his rules...." Delaney continued, realizing she was treading on thin ice about two seconds too late. Unlike the times they'd teased each other about countless unimportant issues in high school, clearly Melody was not taking this inquest quite the same way.

"Do not go there." Melody's face was turning a bright red now and her breathing seemed shallow and quickened.

Instantly, Delaney felt remorseful about pushing the issue. "I'm sorry," she began. She realized this had more to do with the change in her friend than she realized, and once Delaney began to explain, more emotion came out than she originally expected. "I didn't mean to upset you. I know this time of year is a delicate balance for you, trying to keep your father's memory alive while dealing with the anniversary of … the accident." With a sigh, Delaney placed her hand on top of Melody's. "I just miss you, Melody. I miss the old you, the happy you. I just thought, maybe, it might be a way to bring some of that joy back into your life, if you were to sing again."

Pulling her hand away, Melody said "Delaney, I'm not having this conversation right now." She took her mug and slid it across the counter as she rose from her barstool.

Delaney felt awful for being so pushy. "No, don't go. I'm sorry." She reached for Melody's hand again, and this time hers wasn't shoved aside. "I promise I won't mention it again. Here, let me get you a refill."

Melody held her gaze for a moment, then with a deep sigh, returned to her barstool. Delaney picked up the bright red ceramic mug and crossed to the hot cocoa machine, trying to place her emotions back in check. While concern for Melody's disposition were certainly part of her reason for asking the series of questions that subsequently agitated her friend, she knew she was also being selfish. Not only did she want to spend more time with Melody, to have the girl back she'd known and loved for so many years, she also expected Melody to go out of her way to help her with a mission she really had no obligation to assist in fulfilling. Delaney felt ridiculous for letting her scheme come between them.

She returned to the counter to see that Melody was taking deep breaths and seemed to have calmed down. Sliding the mug across to her, Delaney offered a sympathetic smile, afraid to say more lest she upset Melody to an even greater degree.

"I'm sorry, Delaney. I shouldn't have gotten mad at you." Melody smiled in return and took a sip of the freshly topped-off cocoa.

Shaking her head, Delaney replied, "I shouldn't have pushed so hard. I've hardly had a chance to speak to you at all since you've gotten back, and I made you uncomfortable. I'm sorry."

Melody looked her in the eyes and said, "It's okay." She seemed to consider the situation for a moment before she continued. "You know, just because I can't get my Christmas tree with you doesn't mean that we can't go together to pick out your tree. If you still want me to go with you on Saturday, give me a call. We need to spend some quality time together anyway."

Delaney's eyes widened. She was shocked to hear her friend come to such a contradictory conclusion so quickly, but she was pleasantly surprised. Deciding to lock her into the agreement before she had second thoughts, Delaney smiled and said, "Thanks, Melody. Oh, I hope you get to meet Josh. He's really nice." Thoughts of his beautiful eyes filled her mind, and before she realized it, she was no longer as concerned about offending Melody as she had been a few moments ago, thoughts of Josh consuming her.

"I can't wait to meet him." Melody was giggling at her, and Delaney felt the heat in her cheeks again. While she wanted to think of something witty to say in response, a middle-aged woman with a small child next to her was calling for Delaney's attention and she pushed thoughts of Josh out of her mind for a moment as she turned to attend to her other customer.

A few minutes later, Melody stood and began to gather up her things. Delaney excused herself from a man who was still trying to decide which kind of cookie to try and stepped over. "I'll give you a call in a day or two and we can work out the details."

"Okay," Melody said, still smiling. "It'll be fun to hang out again."

"Yes," Delaney agreed. "I'm really looking forward to it." It had been so long since she'd had a chance to spend quality time with Melody. Even if she didn't see Josh, at least she'd get to visit with her friend.

"Have a great afternoon," Melody called over her shoulder as she headed for the door, and Delaney glanced at the time, wondering where the day had gone. By then, the gentleman was ready to order his treat, and she slid back down to help him, wishing her afternoon help would arrive already so she could go take a short break.

JOSH LOVED the view from the back porch of his parents' log cabin, particularly when the sky was as clear as it was this evening, and he could see what appeared to be thousands of stars overhead. In the distance, he saw rows of trees covering the hillside, and beyond that, a thin shadow of smoke wound its way into the twilight sky, evidence that someone in the distance was enjoying a cozy fire.

Still stuffed from the delicious dinner of homemade lasagna his mother had made, he found his way out to the solace of the porch, hoping to spend a few moments pondering his predicament. It had been a long week, though he'd gotten little accomplished other than delivering hundreds of trees to different lots in the tri-state area, and while he had a sense of fulfillment at having assisted his parents with that aspect of the farm, he still wasn't sure what to do about the other lingering questions.

One of the family's many outside pets, an old bloodhound who was almost as round as he was tall thanks to the scraps he got after dinner each night, waddled his way up the steps and rammed his head into Josh's hand, insisting he be petted. Chuckling, Josh said, "Hey there, Critter. Have you had a rough day, too?" He scratched the dog between the ears, and when he dropped to his back to have his belly rubbed, Josh complied. "Must be rough living on the land out here, huh?" Of course the dog didn't respond, and after he'd had his fill of stomach scratching, he flipped over and came to rest on top of Josh's well-worn work boots.

The door opened and Kent came out, two mugs in his hands. "Mind if I join you?" he asked.

"No, please," Josh replied, gesturing toward an Adirondack chair that matched the one he was sitting in.

His father handed him a steaming cup of coffee then sat down, letting out a sigh as he did so. Josh thanked him and took a sip. Like most things in the kitchen, his mother certainly knew how to make a good cup of joe. "What's Mom up to?" he asked, eyes still focused off in the distance.

"She's decided that the banister needs some garland," Kent began, "which means she's got to make it first."

Josh chuckled. No store bought garland for the tree lady. "That ought to take her a while," he replied, resting his mug carefully on the arm of the chair.

"It would take a normal human a while, but your mother will likely have both sides of the railings fully decorated with garland she's whipped out of the air before you and I can even finish our beverages."

Though it was a slight exaggeration, picturing his mother waving a wand made of a blue spruce limb and creating perfectly even garlands adorned with pinecones and berries made Josh smile. There was no doubt his mother was amazing, both of his parents were, and he felt very blessed to have each of them.

They settled into a comfortable silence, both content to sit in each other's company and peer out into the distance without having to say anything at all. Eventually, Critter got stir crazy and lumbered his way off of the porch, which broke the silence enough for Kent to hesitantly ask, "So, how were your deliveries this week?"

"Good," Josh replied, realizing that was likely just an opening question. "I'm glad we got enough cleared to keep the village fairly stocked. Something tells me we are going to be busy this weekend."

"It's nice to have so many customers," Kent agreed. "This will definitely be our most profitable season yet."

It was difficult to manage a business that really only made money one time a year, and though his parents worked hard all year long, November and December saw the vast majority of their income. Hearing that this season would set them up nicely for the new year was reassuring. "People seem to be full of Christmas spirit right now, that's for sure."

Kent cleared his throat, and without responding to Josh's remark, he asked, "Have you given what we talked about much thought?" Josh didn't answer right away, not sure how to continue, so Kent added an unnecessary clarification. "Do you think you might want to take over in a year or two?"

There was so much to consider. He had a life in Washington, one he hadn't planned on discontinuing for the foreseeable future. While he'd managed to save quite a bit of money since he'd started working at Stokes and Stokes, he wanted to make sure he had enough to provide for a potential family before he took over such a volatile business. Whether it was one year or two really would make a big difference, but Josh wasn't sure he would even be ready five or ten years from now. With a sigh he hoped didn't sound too frustrated, Josh replied, "I've been thinking about it, Dad. I'm just not certain yet. I think... I think I need some more time to make sure I do what's best for all of us."

Saying nothing, Kent took a sip of his coffee and nodded his head. He stared out into the trees, and Josh's shoulders slumped. His father loved those trees, loved this place. How could he possibly put him in a situation where he might lose all of it? "I'm sorry, Dad...."

"No, don't apologize," Kent cut him off. "I understand you need more time. Take all the time you need. It's not an easy decision. And your mother and I want you to do what's best for you. If you decide the tree farming business isn't for you, we'll find a way to make it work."

"I can't imagine all of this being gone," Josh exclaimed, running his hand through his hair. "I want to do what I can to make it work. But... I love my career—not necessarily my job, I guess, but working with computers, building programs and helping people find solutions to problems they don't have the information to understand. I have friends in DC, not a lot of them, but some good ones. It's just hard for me to imagine what I might do with myself the other ten months out of the year."

"There is always work to be done on the farm," Kent reminded him, "but maybe you could do both. I know Shepherdstown isn't as fancy as Washington, DC, and folks around here can't pay like they can there, but believe it or not, some people here actually do own computers."

Josh couldn't help but laugh at his father's joke. Shepherdstown was small, and people held on to the culture of their hometown life, but of course there were business that needed IT support, people who had home computers that needed fixing. There was a possibility he could find extra work in that capacity to make ends meet and fulfill his need to work with technology. Not to mention, he'd have lots of extra time to work on his app. It might be nice to be his own boss and not have to answer to anyone, particularly people who didn't understand his work well enough to truly appreciate him.

"Take your time, Son," Kent assured him, patting his arm. "I've got a year or two left in me, I reckon. If I can hold out a while, maybe Payton will want to take over the farm."

Josh's eyebrows raised; Payton wasn't old enough to drive yet. There was no way his father could continue to work as hard as he did now until Payton could take over, if he even wanted to. "Dad, we'll figure something out, I promise," Josh said. "I hadn't really thought about trying to find time to work with computers locally, but let me see what that might entail. If I could make that work, maybe I could find a way to balance the two. And if I have a year or two more to continue with the firm, maybe I can feel more confident financially."

"All right, Son." Kent offered him a warm smile and then refocused on the hillside, adjusting his glasses as if he was straining to see a particular tree, and after a long gaze in his father's direction, Josh turned to look off into the distance as well.

The solace of the country evening may have been interrupted by weightier considerations, but hopefully he could find a way to return his thoughts to more relaxing subjects—such as the app he was mentally designing and a way to solve his mother's cocoa problems while simultaneously relieving a certain compulsion he was having himself. Josh remembered that Delaney mentioned the fact that she rarely worked on Saturdays, so he knew traveling into Charles Town tomorrow wouldn't do him any good, but he had checked his schedule and he was set to make a few trips in that general direction early in the week. It might be a few miles out of his way, but surely he could justify the extra time and gas money so that he could inquire about securing some of that award winning cocoa for the village. It seemed like a valid reason to him. As he settled back into his seat, taking a sip of his cooling coffee, he replaced thoughts of the farm and his father's failing health with visions of deep brown eyes and a warm smile that made his heart skip a beat.

CHAPTER 8

Delaney pulled her Dodge Charger down the winding lane that led to the top of the hill and her parents' farmhouse. Though it wasn't too much bigger than Nana's, it was made of brick with a large wraparound porch. Driving this road made her remember the long trudge from the school bus every afternoon, usually in the snow it seemed—though she supposed there were plenty of snowless days—and the relief of finally making it to the door where her mother always greeted her, often with a plate of chocolate chip cookies and a tall glass of milk.

Today, as she pulled in beside her father's old work truck, her parents were in the yard, a tangle of Christmas lights around their feet wending their way up the porch railing next to a ladder she assumed her father had scaled at some point since the porch seemed to be about half-done. Even though they lived out in the middle of the countryside, the house was situated atop a hill, which not only meant the long walk home ended in an incline, but cars could see the house from several of the country roads in the distance, so her parents always put up a fair share of lights. Besides, her mother loved the twinkling, multi-colored lights, so even if she would've been the only person in the world to see them, Delaney was certain the house would be fully decorated each season.

She stepped out into a crunch of snow. While the flakes were no longer coming down, the sky warned more was to come. Delaney was just fine with that, but she pulled her red winter coat closer around her and grabbed her hat and gloves from the car before she joined her parents. "Why didn't you call? I would have come to help."

David Young was a big man, but a gentle giant, and as Delaney approached, he dropped the lights he'd had in hand and wrapped his daughter in a hug. "Good morning, honey. We didn't want to make you get up early on a Saturday and stand in the snow while we worked out all the knots in the lights. Besides, you just hung Nana's lights all on your own."

Hanging Nana's lights was not a big deal since she only asked for them to be placed on the roofline of her front porch, which wasn't nearly as large as her parents' nor as high or steep. It had only taken her about an hour. This looked like it might take her parents all day. "I still would've helped."

"Good morning, darling." Delaney's mother, Maggie, had the same color of brown hair as her daughter, but Maggie's was wavy, unruly, she said, so she kept it short and often pulled back with clips on either side of her pretty face, as it was today. When her cheek brushed Delaney's it was freezing cold, an indicator they'd been standing out here longer than she'd first expected. "Are you excited to go pick out your Christmas tree? How is Melody?"

Ignoring her questions at first, Delaney exclaimed, "Mom, you're freezing."

"I'm fine," her mom assured her. "I'll go in and warm up in a few minutes."

"You need a warmer hat," Delaney suggested, looking at the thin one her mom had on that barely even covered the tips of her ears.

"That's what I've been saying," her father agreed. He was dressed as if he were about to summit Mt. Everest.

"Maybe Santa will bring me one for Christmas," Maggie chided. "Now, tell me again where you're going."

Delaney felt the color rush to her face but tried to play it off. The last thing she needed was for her parents to know there was a young man involved. "Melody and I are driving over to Shepherdstown. It's called Taylor Tree Farm. It's quite the quaint little Christmas village." Delaney had finally gotten around to searching for the farm online after she'd spoken to Melody earlier in the week, and she was pleasantly surprised at all the farm had to offer. She was honestly shocked she'd never heard of it before.

"And is Melody doing all right?" Maggie continued.

Glancing back at her father, who seemed to be listening though he was now wrestling with a ball of tangled Christmas lights, Delaney replied, "I think she's doing okay. We haven't had a chance to spend a lot of time together, so I'm hoping that we'll get to chat some more today."

"You work too hard," Maggie noted, shaking her head, her forehead creased.

Stifling a sigh, Delaney replied, "Melody has been working a lot, too. It's just a busy time of year, Mom. Besides, both of you taught me that hard work is important, you know?"

"Yep—nothing like a full day's work to make you feel proud," David chimed in, the lights now threatening to consume him.

Chuckling, Delaney asked, "Do you want some help, Dad?"

"I've got it," he asserted rather quickly. "Now, about the truck. Remember, don't go over sixty, and if any lights come on, you pull over and call me immediately. Got it, kiddo?"

Delaney's true purpose for stopping by was to borrow her father's pride and joy—a '64 Chevy pickup he lovingly referred to as Bertha the Beast, Bertie for short. She sat in the driveway next to where Delany had parked her Charger. Though she was fairly certain she wouldn't be selecting a tree so big it couldn't fit on the roof of her car, she worried about the sap, and she thought they may as well take the truck, just in case. "You got it, Dad," she replied, knowing how much the truck meant to him. She was surprised he'd even said she could take it.

"And when you bring it back, maybe you could stay for supper?"

Maggie requested, her eyebrows indicating Delaney had better say yes. "It's been a while since we had the chance to sit around and talk."

Some time had passed since she'd really visited with her parents. She saw them often enough, but she didn't really get the opportunity to chat. Thinking she should mention her concerns about Nana to them, Delaney nodded. "That sounds like a great idea, Mom."

"Good. I'm making your favorite chili tonight, so come hungry."

With a giggle, Delaney replied, "Sounds delicious. Thanks, Mom."

Her mother wrapped her in an embrace one more time before wishing her a good trip and turning to assess the lights again.

"Keys are in it," her father said as Delaney squeezed him and gave him a peck on the cheek. His hands were so full of Christmas lights, he could do little in return. "Be careful."

"Always am," she replied, and with a wave, she headed off toward the monstrosity, double-checking her pockets that she had her wallet, gloves, hat, and phone. She'd leave the keys in the Charger in case her parents needed to move it. The likelihood of anything getting stolen in these parts was slim to none.

Delaney had to turn the starter twice; the second time, she caught her father's concerned eye, but the engine finally fired up, and she let it run for a second as she hooked her seatbelt. With another wave, she backed down the drive to the spot where she usually turned around and cranked the wheel so that she was headed back to town.

The roads were fairly clear since the snow wasn't that thick and no more had fallen in the last few hours. By the time she reached town, the streets were damp but all of the snow had either melted or been carried away by other passing cars. She checked the time and saw that she still had a few minutes before she needed to swing by Melody's house, so she decided to stop by the bakery and check on how things were going. If last Saturday was any indication, they would be busy.

She pulled the truck into her usual spot and pulled the keys out of the ignition, hoping it would start again. It was a bit of a drop down to the ground and there was no running board, so she took her time getting out. Pushing the heavy door shut, she made her way to the back door.

It was locked. And her key was at her parents' house with her car keys. With a sigh, she banged on the door, hoping it wasn't so busy that no one would hear.

A few minutes later, Cameron pulled the door open, cautiously, as if he wasn't certain whether or not he'd actually heard a knock or if it had been his imagination. "Oh, hi, Delaney," he said, his face morphing into a smile. "Didn't expect to see you today." He stepped out of the way so she could enter the warm kitchen.

The smell of baking muffins filled Delaney's lungs, a scent that she'd never grow tired of. "Thanks. I didn't have my key. I just stopped by to see how things were going. Been busy?"

He didn't need to say anything for her to find her answer. Looking through the narrow opening between the kitchen and the storefront, she could see a crowd of people even larger than the record crowds they'd had earlier in the week. "It hasn't been slow for a minute," Cameron replied. Even with all five of us here, we've been pretty busy."

"Hey, what are you doing here?" Bonnie called, hurrying to the oven just as the timer went off. She slipped a large red oven mitt on her hand and began to pull out trays of steaming muffins.

"Just came by to see how it was going," Delaney replied. Instinctively, she began to help move the muffins to the cooling rack after slipping on another oven mitt which was laying on the counter. "I've never had five employees working at the same time."

"You have now," Bonnie said. "Six counting you. We've been working the whole morning without a break."

"Crazy," Delaney muttered.

"I'll head back out front," Cameron called.

"Oh, fiddle," Bonnie exclaimed as he passed by her. "I forgot to refill Mrs. Pentecost's cocoa."

"I'll get it," Cameron assured her with a smile.

"Thank you, Cam," Bonnie said with a sigh of relief. Then, turning to Delaney, who had just set the last tray of muffins on the rack and returned to place her oven mitt in the correct drawer, she said, "That boy is a very hard worker."

"I know," Delaney agreed. "He's really smart, too. And good with the customers."

Bonnie nodded, and leaning back against the counter, clearly happy for a short break, she added, "He's always got the little old ladies smiling."

"I'm so glad we found him," Delaney said, glancing around to see if there was anything else she needed to do before she left. "Everything okay?"

"Yes, just busy. You should go though. Aren't you headed off to Josh's tree farm?"

Delaney felt the color rising in her cheeks. It had been Bonnie who convinced Josh to try the cocoa in the first place, and if she hadn't given him a mug instead of a to-go cup as he'd requested, she never would have met him. Bonnie had claimed it was an accident, but Delaney knew better. Bonnie had a reputation for being a bit of a matchmaker, and while she'd never attempted to fix her boss up with anyone before, Delaney was happy for the tactic Bonnie had used to make Josh linger in the store a bit longer that day. "Yes, I'm going."

"Well, good luck, honey," she said, patting Delaney's arm. "He's a cutie. And he seemed pretty bright, which means he'll know what he's getting with a girl like you."

While Delaney knew she meant what she said, she couldn't help but feel as if she were being flattered. "Oh, stop. It's not even a date, Bonnie. I don't even know if he'll be there."

"He will be." She winked, as if she knew something, though Delaney was certain she was just being optimistic.

"Do you need anything before I go? Is the cocoa holding up?"

"We've gone through a lot, but we'll be okay for the rest of the day, I think. I haven't had to open the emergency tin yet."

Delaney was the only one who made the cocoa, so on days when she wasn't there, she always made sure there was enough to go around and even had an emergency supply available. If the workers had to open it, they were to call her immediately. Even though many people thought of cocoa as a seasonal drink, people ordered it year round due to Delaney's secret recipe, so each time she stopped by, she always checked on the cocoa, even in the summertime. On a day like today, she wouldn't be surprised if they didn't sell twice as much as they were used to.

"Okay. Let me go up front really quickly and make sure everyone's doing all right."

"They're fine," Bonnie called, but Delaney stepped around her and went to check, just in case.

What she saw was a bit surprising to her. Despite the hustle and bustle of customers, Cameron was whispering something into Joanna's ear, which made her giggle from her station behind the cash register. He quickly stepped away to attend to another patron without even noticing Delaney behind them, but she was shocked to see Joanna even acknowledging Cameron. The girl had worked there for almost a year now, and never had she seen her voluntarily speak to any young man. She'd say the bare minimum to customers, often with a nervous expression on her face, always with a timid air about her. Joanna seemed so relaxed and free when Cameron spoke to her, it made Delaney smile. Perhaps Bonnie had been up to something with the teens as well.

Though Cameron and Joanna seemed to be in high spirits, the second Delaney saw Courtney's face, she knew something was wrong. The girl had a dishtowel in one hand, as if she'd just returned from wiping down the tables, and she came to a sudden stop with a huff as Delaney surveyed the supply of treats under the counter. "Is everything okay, Courtney?" she asked, once she was sure nothing needed to be refilled.

"Yes, I guess," she said, though her voice did not sound convincing. "It would help if some people didn't think everything was so hilarious." She tossed the cloth onto a counter and crossed her arms.

Delaney could tell immediately that Courtney was jealous of the attention Joanna was getting from the new male employee, and while she felt a bit of sympathy for the more popular girl, she couldn't say she wasn't glad. It was about time Courtney shared some of the spotlight. "It's that time of year," Delaney said, playing it off. "Everyone's in good spirits." She turned to check the cocoa and saw that it was full.

Deciding to bring Melody a treat, she grabbed a couple of to-go cups and began to fill them, hoping Courtney would let it go and get back to work.

"I guess," she exhaled, the end of the world clearly on her mind.

Delaney held back a chuckle. "How's your boyfriend. What's his name? Kyle?"

"Kyler is fine," Courtney lamented, leaning against the counter next to Delaney. She had her head tipped up as if she were studying the ceiling. After a long pause, she returned her focus to her boss. "Say, would it be all right if I left just a few minutes early on the twentieth? Like, an hour?"

Momentarily confused, Delaney thought about what the current date was. "You mean next Saturday?" she asked.

"Yes," Courtney replied. "It's the Winter Formal, and I want to make sure I have plenty of time to get dressed and do my hair."

Despite the fact that Delaney knew for sure they'd be very busy that day—there was a lot happening in the downtown area for Christmas, such as meeting Santa at the library—she nodded. "Sure, that sounds fine." She figured she'd have to come in and help out anyway, so an hour probably wouldn't make that big of a difference.

"Great," Courtney sighed. "I'm sure Joanna won't need to leave early," she added. "I don't think she's going."

The comment sounded innocent enough, but it made Delaney look from Courtney to Joanna, who was just a few steps away and might have even overheard if she wasn't talking to a customer. "Why isn't she going?" Delaney asked, returning her attention to Courtney.

She shrugged dismissively, as if it wasn't a big deal. "I don't know. She never goes to dances. We don't really... hang out at school, so I don't really know her business."

Once again, it wasn't the message but the tone that made Delaney's stomach tighten up. Even though she'd been fairly popular in high school, she'd tried to be a friend to everyone, and the way Courtney made the statement, it led Delaney to believe that Joanna might be having trouble making friends at school. It made sense—she was overly shy and a bit awkward. But it had never occurred to Delaney that Courtney might not treat the other girl the same way at school as she did here, where they seemed to get along fairly well.

Delaney glanced up at the clock and saw that it was almost time for her to meet her friend, but since Melody only lived a few blocks away, she set the drinks aside, and waiting for Courtney to get back to work and for the customers to dissipate, she sidled up next to Joanna.

"Hey, how's it going?" Delaney asked, offering her a smile.

Joanna peered over her shoulder at her boss without turning around. She adjusted her glasses and said, "Fine, I guess. Busy."

"Right," Delaney nodded. "You and Cameron seem to be getting along pretty well."

It was a risky endeavor, but Delaney took the chance. Instantly, Joanna's face turned as red as a beet. "Yeah," she mumbled. Her lips twitched as if she knew she was expected to say more, but nothing else came out.

Thinking she needed to proceed with caution, Delaney changed the subject. "We are really busy today. Thanks so much for being here, Joanna. I know I can count on you to serve our customers with respect and a great attitude."

"Sure thing," Joanna nodded. That seemed to put her at ease a bit more, since Delaney's compliments were not a rarity. The young girl glanced around as if she were looking for something to do to make herself useful before she had another customer to ring up.

Delaney took a chocolate muffin from under the counter and dropped it in a bag, knowing those were Melody's favorite. "Can you ring this and two cocoas ups?" she asked, and Joanna began to punch the correct buttons on the keyboard. Even though Delaney could do whatever she wanted to in her own bakery, she often went ahead and rang up any items she consumed to set a good example for the other workers and to make sure her numbers came out correctly each evening.

Already knowing how much it would be, she slipped the cash out of her wallet and handed it over, taking her change and dropping it loudly into the tip jar hoping the patrons would remember it was there. "Thanks, Joanna," she said as she gathered up the cocoas. Acting as if it were an afterthought, she paused on her way back to the kitchen. "Oh, and if you need to leave early to go to the Winter Formal, just let me know. I'm planning on being here next Saturday."

Joanna's face was red again, and her eyes widened behind her thick lenses. "I don't think... I'm going to go," she mumbled.

Delaney realized Cameron was now standing just a foot or two away, and she thought perhaps she should let the conversation drop, but before she could stop herself, she asked, "Why not? It might be fun. I used to go to a lot of dances with my friends."

Her blush somehow managing to grow even deeper, Joanna turned her attention to the cash register buttons. "Yeah," she muttered again. "Maybe."

Though she wanted to ask why Joanna wasn't interested in going, Delaney didn't press it. With a sigh she patted her on the back and said, "Have a good afternoon." Her attention returned to Cameron, who was frozen in place, one eyebrow raised, his eyes trained on the back of Joanna's head. "Thanks for your hard work, Cameron."

That jolted him back from wherever he'd disappeared, and with a sheepish smile, he replied, "Thanks for the opportunity, Delaney. I hope you have fun picking out your Christmas tree."

While Delaney had mentioned her plans to him the morning before when they were the only two in the store, she had not mentioned Josh, and she could tell by his nonchalant tone that Bonnie hadn't either. "Thanks. I'm sure I will."

Delaney waved at Courtney and Francine, who she hadn't even had the chance to speak to, then headed back through the kitchen. Bonnie was busy with the baked goods, so she didn't stop to say more, just shouted a, "See you later," and headed off toward the truck, still puzzling over the teenagers and wondering if things had been so complicated when she was in high school. She guessed they must have been, but she'd been so focused on academics and culinary arts, she hadn't really had too much time to concern herself with what other people were doing. She'd dated some, but never had a serious boyfriend, and while she had friends who were gaga over one guy or another, she tried to keep the drama to a minimum. She hoped that whatever was going on with Joanna, she would be all right. She was a sweet girl, pretty, too, in her own way. Surely, she had friends at school and boys who were interested in spending time with her, didn't she? It certainly seemed like Cameron might be, and he was about as good a guy as they got in Delaney's book.

Climbing back into the truck with two cocoas and a muffin was a feat, but she managed to do it, and once she'd dug the keys out of her coat pocket and said a silent prayer that the engine turned over, she put the key in the ignition and breathed a sigh of relief when she heard the motor catch. She backed out of the lot, hopeful that there would be no more drama in her day and that she could make it to Taylor Tree Farm without the butterflies in her stomach causing her heart to explode. She had no idea what she would say when she got there, but she was hopeful that Bonnie was right and Josh would be available—and remember her—and not be completely shocked that she'd shown up unexpectedly.

CHAPTER 9

Despite the fact that the alleged point of this trip was to spend time conversing with Melody, both girls were extremely quiet most of the way from Charles Town to Shepherdstown, which would take about thirty minutes. A light dusting of snow covered the road, and from time to time, Delaney flicked the wipers on to clear the softly falling flakes. For the most part, they rode in silence, Delaney trying to come up with something interesting to say to Josh should he remember who she was and want to know why she was there, and Melody likely thinking about the man she'd arranged to meet at the tree farm. When Melody had shown up the day after they'd made their initial plans and asked if she could invite some friends, Delaney's curiosity had been piqued. When she'd learned it was the new handyman all the women in town were raving about, she'd been more than pleasantly surprised. Melody deserved to meet a good guy, and she was hopeful that Reid and his son Michael would make her friend forget all of the unpleasant memories she'd recently come to associate with this time of year.

The closer they got to Taylor Tree Farm, the more knots Delany got in her stomach until she was certain that an ultrasound would reveal something resembling her father's Christmas light catastrophe.

She had the radio off because she knew Melody didn't like Christmas music anymore, but she tried to concentrate on the tune she was playing in her head, and her hand began to tap against the steering wheel either to the beat or because of her nerves.

The GPS prompted her to turn onto a narrow country lane as Melody assured her that Josh certainly couldn't have forgotten her so quickly—as if she was quite memorable—and Delaney tried to take deep slow breaths. She still had no idea what she should say.

Delaney had the opening to the parking lot in her sights when Melody offered, "Well, if he is here, and you get a chance to spend some time with him, let me know if you need me to come rescue you. I hope he really is as nice as you've described."

A large sign in red and green proclaimed this to be Taylor Tree Farm, and as she swung the truck into the parking lot, she said, "Thanks." That's about all she could manage at the time as her stomach seemed to be sliding up her throat. She turned the truck off, and turning to face Melody, who was peering around the parking lot expectantly, she said, "Wish me luck."

Melody turned to face her, a reassuring smile on her pretty face. "Luck! It'll be great. Who wouldn't want to get to know you better? And if he doesn't—then he's an idiot, and you don't need him anyway."

Realizing she'd been overly focused on herself and not even considering that Melody must also be nervous, Delaney placed her hand on her friend's arm. "Thanks. And good luck with... Michael. I know that's who you're here to see." Melody's face reddened, and Delaney tried not to laugh. Clearly, it was more than just the little boy who had led Melody to invite the pair to meet them today.

Grabbing her hat and gloves, she opened the door and carefully hopped down from the truck. She could hear a child's voice on the other side of the truck shouting Melody's name and couldn't help but giggle at the sweet sound. She slipped her gloves on and used the mirror on the truck's door to make sure her hair looked okay as she carefully placed the hat on her head before going around the front of the truck to meet Reid and his son Michael.

As she rounded the corner, she heard Reid asking Melody if the truck was a '63, and before her friend could respond, Delaney said, "It's a '64, actually. I'm Delaney." She reached around Melody, and he took her hand. Delaney could see why Melody was attracted to the handyman. With piercing blue eyes and sandy blonde hair, he had an air about him that seemed lighthearted and fun. The little boy standing between them was absolutely adorable with his mop of blond hair and beaming smile.

"Reid, nice to meet you," he said, releasing her hand. Then, gesturing back to the truck, he added, "It's a classic."

Smiling, Delaney replied, "Thanks. It's my dad's pride and joy. I'm surprised he even let me borrow it, but I wasn't sure I could get a Christmas tree on the roof of my Charger."

With a shrug, Reid said, "Oh, with the right bungee cord hacks, you could, but why chance it?"

"Exactly," Delaney agreed, thinking of what tree sap might do to her paint job. Turning her attention to the little boy, she said, "And you must be Michael? I'm Delaney. It's nice to meet you. I've heard so much about you." She offered her hand to him as well.

He reached out and took her hand with his mittened one, and Delaney was impressed with his manners. "Nice to meet you, too. Are you and Miss Melody sisters?'

"No, but people ask us that a lot," Melody explained as both she and Delaney giggled.

Winking at the sweet little cherub, Delaney said, "We are like sisters." She put her arm around her friend's shoulders. "Are you ready to go find a Christmas tree, Michael?"

Hopping up and down in the freshly fallen snow, he exclaimed, "I can't wait!"

"Well, then let's go," Reid suggested, and Delaney turned to lead them in the direction of the tree lot, swallowing the lump that had formed in her throat.

Meeting Melody's friends had been a nice distraction, but as they neared the large snowman holding a sign that said, "Taylor Tree Farm," in festive red, Delaney's nerves threatened to overwhelm her. So many catastrophic scenarios played through her mind, and if she wasn't aware of the people following her, she thought her feet might stop moving. She generally had no problems talking to anyone, but she'd been thinking about seeing Josh again for so many days, the idea that she might be standing in front of him again in a matter of moments was unsettling. *What if he wasn't even there?*

She heard Reid and Michael talking behind her, but she wasn't paying attention to what they were saying. While she was certain the little village laid out in front of her was just as quaint and charming as it had been when she'd looked at it online earlier in the week, she wasn't really able to focus on that either. She glanced around nervously, wondering where Josh might be. She saw some workers; they were easy to distinguish thanks to their green aprons, but she didn't see Josh anywhere, and she wasn't sure if she should feel relieved or disheartened.

A hand on her shoulder brought her back around, and Melody's voice in her ear caught her attention. "Do you see him?"

Sighing, Delaney turned to face her. "No."

"That doesn't mean he isn't here," Melody assured her. One of the tree farm employees was headed their direction, though from the expression on his face he was on a mission, not on his way to greet them. He looked young, and the comment Josh had made about working with teenagers came to mind. She absently wondered if this was the boy who hadn't been able to make the delivery the day that Josh came to Charles Town. "Maybe you should ask one of the other workers."

Delaney's eyes widened. "What am I going to say? 'Hi, my name is Delaney and I just drove all the way from Charles Town to see if Josh was working today'?" She'd been over this scenario a dozen times, but none of the inquiries she'd rehearsed seemed to be quite right, and now faced with this dilemma, she wasn't sure what to do.

Melody bit her bottom lip, and Delaney could see the beginnings of a smile playing at the corners of her mouth. "Maybe you should've worked that out before you drove all the way from Charles Town."

Before she could even attempt to explain that she had been trying to work that out—for days—she realized that Reid was stepping forward to intercept the young man headed in their general direction. Delaney held her breath, not quite sure what he might say.

"Excuse me," Reid said smiling at the young man, his tone light and nonchalant. "Is Josh around?"

From here, Delaney could see that the boy's name was Payton, and while he didn't look exactly like Josh, she could see a resemblance. She wondered if they were related. Payton replied, "Um, yeah. He's out on the tractor right now bringing in a few trees for customers, but he should be back in a few minutes. He'll be over by the shaking station." He turned and gestured in the direction he'd just come from.

"Thank you," Reid said, and as he turned back to face them, Payton hurried on his way. Echoing Payton's tone, as if they hadn't just overheard exactly what the boy had said, Reid repeated, "He's out on the tractor right now bringing in a few trees for customers, but he should be back in a few minutes."

A wave of relief at getting past the first obstacle washed over Delaney, and even though she felt a bit nauseous realizing this meant she'd actually have to explain to Josh why she was here, an overwhelming sense of gratitude made her feel ten times lighter. "You're a lifesaver!" she proclaimed, hurling herself at Reid. "I could kiss you." Realizing what she'd said and seeing a shade of red start to creep up his neck, Delaney released him and assured him that she was not being literal. "I won't—but I could." She looked at Melody to make sure she knew there was absolutely no intention of imposing on her mind, and she could see in her friend's smile and the twinkle in her eyes she was amused, not threatened.

As she stepped away, Reid shrugged. "Asking questions is one of my specialties. I learned it from Michael. He can ask forty-five questions in a minute. Easily. Without taking a breath."

Melody began to giggle, and Delaney assumed there was an inside joke there she was not privy to. "Well, he's an awesome teacher," Delaney replied, shoving her hands into her coat pockets and smiling at Melody, happy to see her friend in such a good mood.

Turning his full attention to Melody, Reid said, "All right. We have some reindeer to greet." Delaney didn't miss the intensity behind his smile. Whether or not Melody realized it yet or not, she couldn't be sure, but this guy was definitely into her.

Delaney realized that Michael wasn't with them, and glancing over her shoulder, she noticed him standing over by the reindeer pen. "Okay. I'll just have a look around at the trees and come find you in a bit."

Melody reached out and squeezed her shoulder. "Good luck," she said as she and Reid headed off in the direction where Michael was playing.

While she wanted to say, "You, too," she couldn't risk Reid overhearing, so instead she just waved at both of them, and taking a deep breath, she slowly headed over in the direction of the shaking station, intending to stand around and admire the trees for a little while before, hopefully, Josh showed up on the tractor, and she said something witty and charming to make him remember just what a great conversationalist she had been during the five minute long discussion they'd shared over a week ago. Sighing, she attempted to focus on the lovely scenery before her, not the dragons buzzing around in her stomach.

Delaney wandered among the trees for a few moments, looking at tags and comparing different varieties. She knew from her exploration of the website that she would be able to borrow a saw and forage into the woods to cut down her own tree if she wanted to, but thought picking out one of these pre-cut trees was probably more her style. When she heard the sound of an approaching tractor in the distance, she felt a lump forming in her throat again, and tried to stay focused on the trees. "The last thing he needs is to see me standing up here like a big dork, as if I was stalking him," she muttered, hoping no one was close enough to hear her talking to herself. She looked around, and while the lot was full of many smiling, happy people, no one seemed to be paying her any mind. She glanced over her shoulder to see precisely how close the tractor was and felt relieved when she saw he was still about two football fields away. That might give her one last chance to get her act together.

Stepping around behind the tree, Delaney decided to try to make herself as invisible as possible so she could determine when best to approach him. She glanced down at her outfit and realized now that red may not have been the best option. She knew she looked great in this color, but there would definitely be no way to hide with a backdrop of green trees and white snow.

Even from here, she could see that he likely wouldn't notice her anyway. He had a far off expression on his handsome face, as if he were attempting to solve all the world's problems as he drove a tractor pulling a flatbed full of various coniferous trees. She'd worried that he wasn't quite as attractive as she'd made him out to be in her head, though with his personality it wouldn't really matter to her. As he drew closer, however, she could see that, if anything, she'd forgotten just how good looking he really was. Her heart fluttered as her eyes traced the outline of his strong jawline and his perfectly formed nose. She couldn't quite make out his hazel eyes, but that's one feature that had definitely stuck with her. Tufts of his dark hair stuck out around the sides of the black stocking cap he wore, his tall frame evident behind the wheel of the late-model tractor.

Eventually, he came near enough that she could've stepped out and waved to get his attention, but she decided that would be a bit much, so she kept her position behind the tree, trying to focus on the springy needles before her, while she listened to what was going on near the shaking station.

The tractor engine turned off, and she heard a voice, presumably the young man from earlier say, "You need some help unloading them, Uncle Josh?"

"No, I've got it," Josh replied. "Go ahead and start shaking them as I bring them off."

"Okay," was the response, and Delaney peeked around the tree to see Josh hauling the trees off of the trailer one at a time. He was preoccupied with his back to her most of the time, and she watched him set each one against the small building next to the machine that shook off the loose needles. The sound of the machine as it whirred to life was overwhelming, and Delaney swore her teeth were shaking. She wondered how she would even have the chance to speak to Josh at all if the machine was still on by the time she decided she should approach him.

She saw that it was Payton running the machine, and he flipped it off between trees, which would give her a chance to say hello, should she find the courage to do so. As Josh brought the last tree around, he said something to a woman standing nearby that Delaney couldn't make out over the shaker, then turned as if he was headed back to the tractor. Deciding it was now or never, Delaney forced her feet to begin to trudge through the snow, hopeful that Payton would kill the machine in time for her to call his name.

He was next to the tractor just about to climb back into the driver's seat when Delaney found herself less than a foot away. The machine was still whirring behind her, and short of hurling herself at him, she wasn't sure how she might get his attention. If he were to leave again, there was no way she'd have the courage to continue to stand here pretending to look at trees for who knew how much longer.

With a deep breath, Delaney cupped her hands around her mouth and shouted, "Josh!" She had only gotten the first sound out when the machine abruptly stopped leaving her standing right beside him screaming the "osh" part of his name at the top of her lungs. Before he could even turn to face her, Delaney felt crimson filling her face and knew she must be about the same color as her coat and hat.

Josh turned around rather quickly, possibly startled at the sound of most of his name being shouted at such close proximity in an unfamiliar female voice. Delaney braced herself, afraid he might think she was a lunatic or have absolutely no recollection of her at all. She wasn't certain which would be worse. And though his eyebrows were wrinkled in confusion when he first turned, immediately his countenance changed and a smile of recognition splintered across his handsome face. "Hey!" he said, taking his foot down off of the step-up to the tractor he'd been about to mount. "You're the girl from the bakery. Delaney, is it?"

Instantly, Delaney felt her stomach muscles relax and the color in her face begin to return to normal. "That's me," she said laughing. "I wasn't sure if you'd remember me or not."

"Oh, no, of course I remember you," Josh said, and Delaney noticed that with the comment he began to look a little flushed himself. "What are you doing here? Did you bring your family to find a Christmas tree?"

He had completely turned to face her now, his hands shoved deep into the pockets of his gray coat and his hazel eyes smiling at her inquisitively. "I came with my friends," Delaney began to explain. Gesturing in their general direction she said, "That's my friend Melody over there with Reid and Michael." She didn't think there was any point in trying to fill him in on how she'd technically just met Reid and Michael a few minutes ago.

Josh glanced over in the area she was pointing. "They look like they're having fun," he said.

Delaney noticed Michael running around with some other kids, only knowing it was him because she recognized his coat from earlier. Melody and Reid were sitting on a bench nearby. They did look rather cozy together, and Delaney absently hoped things were going well.

Drawing her attention back to Josh, she said, "Yeah, so anyway, I just wanted to say hi. I know it's been a few days since you came in, but when my Nana suggested we get a live tree this year, I immediately thought of Taylor Tree Farm." She chuckled nervously and silently hoped she didn't sound like a dork.

If he thought so, he didn't let it show. "Well, that's quite a compliment," he replied. "It's a bit of a drive from Charles Town."

"True," she admitted, shoving the snow around with the tip of her boot. "But I looked it up online, and we really don't have anything like this in Charles Town. Your family has really gone all out to make this a memorable experience."

Josh was clearly proud of the place. He looked around, nodding, as if he needed a reminder of exactly what his family had built here. "It definitely has a hint of Christmas magic you won't find anywhere else."

"I totally agree," Delaney nodded. "You should've seen Michael's face when he first noticed the reindeer." Again, no need to mention she hadn't seen Michael's face when he first noticed the reindeer because she'd been too busy freaking out over trying to find Josh, but she could imagine what he must've looked like, and she was certain it had to be magical.

"Yeah, my nieces love them, too," Josh agreed.

"What do you do with them the rest of the year?" Delaney asked, the question just popping into her head. Could reindeer acclimate to West Virginia summer weather?

"My dad borrows them from a farm up north every holiday season," Josh explained. "They aren't actually ours. Although, we do try to get the same ones every year if we can so they sort of feel like our adopted pets."

"I see," Delaney replied. The snow was beginning to fall again, and she glanced up at the sky, thinking about what a wonderful winter day it was turning out to be. When she returned her eyes to Josh, she realized he was staring at his tractor, as if had somewhere he needed to be, and Delaney remembered that he was working. "I'm sorry," she offered. "I didn't mean to interrupt your schedule."

"Oh, no, not at all," Josh stammered. "I mean, I do need to head back out and gather up the rest of the trees these customers are waiting on, but it looks like they are all enjoying the reindeer or the shops."

Delaney glanced around and could only see a couple of people waiting by the shaker with several more trees leaning against the building. As if looking in its direction some how brought it back to life, the shaker began to roar again, and Delaney wanted to throw her hands over her ears to force the noise out of her mind.

She didn't realize Josh had stepped closer to her until she turned back around, her head almost colliding with his as he leaned in to speak directly into her ear. There was a rush of warmth as her cheek brushed his, and Delaney felt her knees grow weak. He smelled like fresh balsam and pine needles with a faint minty undertone, and she had to concentrate to make out what he was saying. "Do you want to go for a ride on the tractor? I'll take you out to gather some more trees and give you a little tour," he shouted into her ear.

While she hadn't been expecting that at all, she couldn't help but smile. Since her grandfather had been a farmer, she was used to tractors, and her dad still used one to mow his land. Still, it had been a while since she'd been on one, and she'd never been anywhere with a man as attractive as Josh. Using the shaker as an excuse, she leaned in close to his ear and shouted, "Sure! That sounds fun. Just let me tell Melody where I'm going."

She stepped back and Josh nodded, with a smile, and Delaney fumbled to get her phone out of her pocket, unable to pull her eyes off of his for a moment. Eventually, she got the device out of her coat pocket and sent Melody a text.

"I'm going out for a tour of the farm on Josh's tractor. Hope you don't mind!" Once she hit send, she returned her attention to Josh but kept her phone in her hand in case Melody had an objection. From the looks of things, she seemed to be doing just fine with Reid, but then there was most of a Christmas tree village between them, so it was a little difficult to tell.

"You'll have to ride on the trailer," Josh was explaining, still shouting over the machine. "I hope that's okay."

"Yeah, that's fine," Delaney replied. "I grew up on a farm, so it's no big deal."

"Really?" Josh asked, his eyes widening. He glanced over her shoulder as if he were trying to see if Payton was about finished so they could stop shouting, but the machine continued to whir.

"Really," Delaney replied, feigning offense. "What—did you think I was a big city girl or something?"

Josh chuckled. "No, but you always look so... put together. I was just a little surprised."

Delaney wasn't exactly sure what that meant or why it was funny, but she thought it must have been a compliment of some sort, so she decided to ask what he was implying later if she had the chance, when there wasn't so much noise. She felt her phone buzz in her hand and glanced down to see that Melody had replied. *"No problem. Just be careful."*

Whether her friend meant be careful of farm equipment or strange men she just met, Delaney had no way of knowing, but rather than clarify, she sent a text back that said, *"Will do. If you and Michael and Michael's dad decide to head back to town, just let me know."* While she felt bad that she wasn't getting to speak to Melody as much as she had anticipated, clearly her friend was having a good time, and she didn't want her to feel obligated to hang around all day if she had a chance to ride back with Reid, particularly if things continued to go well with Josh.

After she hit send, she looked up to see Josh smiling at her. "My friend said to have fun," she explained. "So I think we're good to go."

"Perfect," Josh shouted, and as he led Delaney around to the back to help her aboard the trailer, the shaker machine finally switched off. "We could probably squeeze into the cab, but you might be more comfortable back here," he explained. Even though the trailer was very low to the ground and there was a step-up, he offered his hand, and Delaney took it. She felt a warm, tingly sensation shoot up her arm, despite the fact that they were both wearing gloves, and once she was standing on the back of the trailer, she was hesitant to let go. Eventually, she did and settled herself down on the splintery, needle covered wood, ready for an adventure.

"Ready to go?" Josh asked, still standing next to the trailer, a crooked smile on his face.

"Let's do it," Delaney nodded, and she watched him saunter off to the front of the tractor. A moment later, the engine turned over, and he began to slowly turn the tractor around. Several children stopped what they were doing to wave at her, as if she were in some sort of Christmas parade or aboard a magical Christmas tractor, and Delaney couldn't help but giggle as she waved back, doing her best to imitate the beauty queens she saw on TV.

Josh was driving rather slowly, which Delaney appreciated. Though she was used to farm equipment, it had been a while since she'd found herself on a tractor trailer, and this one looked as if it got quite a bit of use. The countryside around her was lovely, and she took a moment to breathe in the fresh air, trying to push her excitement at getting to spend some time with Josh aside so that she could appreciate the beauty of the snow as it danced through the air, blanketing outstretched branches of green and covering the hillsides in white lace.

A few minutes later, Josh brought the trailer to a stop not too far from the village. He turned the engine off and dismounted. Delaney decided to wait for him to see if he might offer his hand again. He was already talking as he came around the back of the tractor. "Most people don't venture too far away from the village, even when it isn't snowing," he explained as he paused beside her.

"It's so beautiful out here," she said, still breathing in the fresh mountain air. "And peaceful."

"It is easy to forget about the rest of the world when you're out here, that's true," Josh agreed. He offered her his hand, and she acted as if she hadn't been waiting for it, making a faux surprised face as she placed her hand in his and jumped down from the trailer. "Was your ride okay?" he asked.

"Yes," Delaney assured him, reluctantly letting go of his hand and brushing the back of her jeans off. "I hope we don't have too many trees to gather, though, or else it might not be too comfortable going back in." She laughed, hoping he knew she was joking, although the thought of riding back buried in trees wasn't exactly appealing after all.

"Nah, I think there's just these three," Josh replied, gesturing at a few trees lying on the ground scattered amongst their standing counterparts. One of them was quite large, but Delaney didn't think they could fill up the whole tractor. "I was thinking, though, if you really want a tour of the whole farm, it would probably be best to take the four wheelers. I mean, if you're not in a hurry. Or if you weren't just being polite."

Delaney could tell from the way he asked the question that he was a bit nervous to hear her answer, and she couldn't help but smile, trying to hold back an anxious giggle of her own. "That sounds like a lot of fun," she replied. "Melody said she can always catch a ride back with Reid if they get ready to go."

"Oh? You didn't all come together?" he asked, clearly confused. The snow was coming down just a bit harder now and some had accumulated atop his hat. Delaney was tempted to brush it off.

"No, Melody and I rode together and met Reid here. She just met him and… well, I guess it's a little complicated. But he's a very nice guy, and she won't have any trouble hitching a ride."

The confusion lingered for a moment before Josh shrugged, as if to say he didn't quite understand but that it didn't matter. "Okay, well, if you want to help me haul the trees over to the trailer, you're more than welcome to. Otherwise, feel free to look around, and I'll be done in a few minutes."

"I don't mind at all," Delaney replied, happy to have the chance to do some farm work again. Josh led her over to the tree furthest from the tractor, and she watched as a cardinal took flight from a nearby spruce, the red-breasted bird bright against the background of the falling snow. "Look at that!" Delaney gasped, pointing at the bird. "He's so gorgeous."

"Like you," Josh said, and Delaney stopped walking for a minute before he stammered, "I mean… red like you… like your coat and hat."

She could tell by the color creeping into his cheeks that he was definitely embarrassed, but she couldn't help but laugh. "Thanks," she said, with an over-exaggerated tone. "It's been a long time since anyone said I was gorgeous."

He stopped and looked at her, and she gave him a fake wink, doing her best to imitate an old cartoon, and he began to chuckle. Clearly not knowing what to say, he shook his head and turned back around, walking away, though Delaney heard him mutter, "I find that very hard to believe."

"So is there any technique to this?" Delaney asked as they approached the fallen pine.

"Oh, I guess so," Josh replied. "Basically, you want to bend down, pick it up, and then move it to the trailer," he replied.

Delaney laughed at him as he went through the motions that

matched his instructions. "I see. Interesting. Can you go over that again?"

Chuckling, Josh moved to the end of the tree. "Why don't you try it with me?" he asked. "First, you bend down." Delaney dropped into a stance a little bit like a football player ready for the snap, making him crack up again. "Good. Then, you pick it up." She scooped the top portion of the tree into her arms and looked back at him awaiting instructions. He was too busy laughing to get much out at first, but finally, he managed, "And then you move it to the trailer."

"Are you going to help with that part?" she asked, as she began to move in the direction of the tractor, only the top portion of the tree moving, "Because it's a lot heavier than I thought."

"What? You can't get it on your own?" He stood back up now, his arms crossed against his gray coat.

Delaney made a mockery of trying to move the tree, pushing forward in the snow but not gaining any traction. "Nope, just not happening."

"Maybe you should think about lifting weights, working on your upper body strength."

She stopped moving and turned to look at him now. He was laughing, clearly giving her a hard time, but she narrowed her eyes. "All righty there, mister. We'll see who can move the tree."

"I was just teasing," Josh insisted, but before he could even step over to help, Delaney started to drag the tree in the direction of the trailer. "Seriously, let me get the trunk."

"I've got it," she replied, the tree coming along, though slowly. "I can manage." She adjusted her grip so that she had more of the tree in her arms, and even though the trunk was mostly dragging through the snow, she was making pretty good time. Within a minute or two, she had the tree back to the trailer. Setting the top of it against the back of the trailer, she let go and took a deep breath. "What do you think about that?" she asked, her eyes wide and her head tilted to the side.

"I think... you need to actually load the tree into the trailer if we're going to take it back to the customer," he said, slowly coming to a stop beside her.

Delaney's eyes widened in mock offense. "Give me a minute, and I will," she said, crossing her arms in imitation of him.

Josh continued to laugh at her antics. "You know what, you've exerted yourself quite a bit for now. Why don't you just go wait over there, and I'll do the rest."

"What am I? Some sort of a delicate flower?" Delaney asked. Shoving him aside playfully, she said, "All right. I've got this." The tree ended up being a lot lighter than she anticipated now that it was standing upright, and she was able to push it into the trailer without his help, even though he attempted to give her a hand. Once the entire tree was in the trailer, she turned to look at him and said, "There! See, I told you I could do it." She took a seat on the end of the trailer, breathing a little heavier than she was willing to let him see.

"Nice job," he replied, still smiling, though he'd finally stopped laughing. "Who'd have known my evil plot to con unsuspecting bakery owners into moving Christmas trees for me would actually work."

Delaney began to shake her head slowly from side to side as if she actually believed him. "I should have known there was something suspicious about you. I bet your name isn't even Josh Taylor, is it?"

"Nope," he teased. "In fact, I don't even work here. This is all part of a big Christmas tree black market racket. By midnight tonight, these trees will be exported to South America, and this unsuspecting farmer will never even know I was here."

Delaney couldn't hold back her laughter anymore, and by the time she finally caught her breath, the entire trailer was shaking. After a long moment, Josh sat down next to her on the trailer. "Are you okay there?"

"I think so," she replied. "I'm sorry. I guess I just don't get out much."

"No?" he asked, a lopsided grin on his face. "And here I thought I was just that amusing."

"You are," she assured him. "But I spend most of my days listening to little old ladies talk about their grandkids and which friend has pneumonia or to mothers reminding their children not to talk with food in their mouths."

"Well, then, I guess this is sophisticated conversation, then," Josh replied.

She had managed to contain herself by now, and looking into his hazel eyes, she suddenly couldn't remember what was so funny anymore. "Honestly," she said, swallowing a lump in her throat, "I think I was just so nervous about driving over here, wondering if you'd even remember who I was, I guess I'm just a little... slap happy. Sorry."

Josh's eyebrows arched and his grin morphed into a humble smile. "You really did come all the way over here just to see me?"

Delaney absently ran her hand through the strands of long brown hair that fell past her shoulders. "Yeah," she admitted with a shrug. "I hope you don't think that's too weird, but I really enjoyed our conversation at the bakery, short as it was, and I thought maybe you did, too. So... why not? It beats hanging out at the bakery all day listening to my teenage employees fit the word 'like' into every sentence, like, every other word."

"Well, that's pretty... cool," Josh said, looking down at the ground. Delaney wasn't sure how to take his remark at first. Did he think she was a stalker? That she was nuts? That she was a lunatic who didn't even know how to properly load a Christmas tree? Eventually, he returned his attention to her and said, "I really enjoyed talking to you, too. In fact, I would've stopped back by if I'd been headed that direction."

He ended his sentence with a bit of a lilt, and Delaney wondered if there was more he'd planned to say, but since he didn't add more, she smiled, and decided to accept his statement at word value. "Good," she said, "I mean, I know I can be a little silly sometimes, but that's just who I am."

"No, it's great," he replied, cutting her off. "You're great." He stood then, as if he didn't trust himself to say anything more. "Shall we get these other two trees back before the people who cut them down can't remember what they were doing here?"

"Yes, let's do," Delaney agreed, jumping to her feet. This time, as they approached the smallest of the three trees, she decided not to be so silly, though it was hard once they began to chat about the best way to work together to get the tree back to the trailer. By the time they had the third tree, the largest by far, loaded up and Delaney was sitting next to it, dangling her feet over the edge of the trailer and waiting for Josh to fire up the engine, her sides hurt from laughing so much. Somehow, she had gotten the impression that she could let her hair down with Josh, that she could be silly for no reason at all, and so far, it seemed that her intuition was correct. Regardless of whether or not he was actually having as much fun as she was, she knew this was a day she'd remember for years to come.

CHAPTER 10

Josh couldn't believe his eyes when he'd turned to find Delaney smiling up at him just an hour or so ago. At first, he though he'd grown delusional; he'd spent so much time thinking about her over the last week or so—had he finally begun to imagine that other women were her? Of course, he realized rather quickly that he was not hallucinating, and it was the real Delaney standing before him. He was still shocked, however, as she explained what had brought her to Taylor Tree Farm, and while he was ecstatic to have the opportunity to spend some time with her, he was definitely caught off guard. More than once in the short amount of time they'd spent together, he'd already found himself sounding utterly ridiculous. Luckily, she didn't seem to mind, and he'd already determined that she had the best sense of humor of all the women he'd ever met before.

As he steered the tractor back in the direction of the village, he tried to go as slowly as possible to make sure he didn't jostle her around too much. When he'd initially asked her to go with him, he had assumed she'd decline—not that he wanted her to, but the trailer wasn't exactly the comfiest place to sit while riding up and down rolling hills. She'd grabbed on with gusto, though, and watching her tackle that Christmas tree had been the funniest thing he'd seen in a long time. There was definitely more to the pretty little baker than initially met the eye.

Normally, it wouldn't have even crossed his mind to consider dating someone who lived so far from his home in Washington, DC. After all, he knew long distance relationships seldom worked out, and there was no reason to overcomplicate things when it wasn't necessary. If he really wanted to date, there were plenty of available girls in DC. He'd had his fair share of first dates over the years, even a couple of second ones. But lately, he had sort of given it up altogether. Most of the girls he met were shallow and never laughed at his jokes. Delaney was definitely different than those girls. Not only was she a hard worker who had taken the initiative to start her own business, she wasn't afraid to literally get her hands dirty, which was amazing. And anyone who thought his attempts at humor were even mildly amusing was okay in his book.

He pulled up next to the shaking station, which was thankfully off, and noticed Travis headed toward the tractor. He climbed down as his brother came to a halt in front of him. Though his hands were shoved inside of his coat, and he didn't seem to be in any hurry, his expression showed he was a bit put out, and Josh wondered what might be going on.

"Everything okay?" Josh asked, glancing over his shoulder to see if Delaney was having any trouble getting off of the trailer.

Travis opened his mouth as if he were going to let his brother in on whatever was troubling him, but he stopped abruptly as Delaney approached. "It's... nothing," he replied, his voice trailing off. "I'll tell you later." He was looking at Delaney expectantly as she came to a stop next to Josh, a smile lighting up her beautiful face.

"This is Delaney," Josh said, gesturing at her. "Delaney, this is my brother, Travis."

"It's nice to meet you," the older brother said, offering his hand, which she took.

"You, too," she said, still smiling. "I hope I wasn't interrupting anything."

"Not at all," Travis replied, shaking his head. "Are you the one who owns the bakery in Charles Town?"

Delaney looked from Travis to Josh, a puzzled expression on her face. She returned her gaze to Travis. "That's me," she nodded.

"I may have mentioned how good your cocoa is," Josh attempted to explain, hoping she didn't think he'd said anything specific to his brother about her personally.

"And our mom is having fits over the sorry excuse for hot chocolate she's been serving in the shop, so she's also mentioned that we should get you over here to 'fix it.'" He made air quotes to emphasize the final words.

Though she looked a little uncomfortable, as if she wasn't sure what to make of so much attention being placed on her cocoa, Delaney said, "Oh, well, then, I will definitely see what I can do."

"I'm sure Mom would love to meet you," Travis nodded, and then, as if he wasn't sure whether or not the comment might get him in trouble with Josh, he added, "I mean… because of the cocoa."

"Right," Delaney said, though now her expression looked skeptical. She was leaning away from Travis, and Josh wondered if she even realized she was doing it. She appeared to need a bit of rescuing.

"Thanks, Travis. We'll head in and talk to Mom. Do you mind helping Payton with those three trees?" Josh said, stepping past his brother and clapping him on the shoulder.

"Not at all," Travis said. "In fact, we're done in the field for today, so I'll be happy to run the tractor if you… have other things to take care of."

While Josh was more than aware what his brother was so un-tactfully trying to imply—that he might be interested in spending more time with Delaney—he both appreciated the offer and wanted to shake him for being so blunt. Rather than attempt a long explanation, he simply said, "Okay, thanks," and led Delaney toward the shop, hopeful that his brother hadn't made her want to run for the hills.

As they walked along, he could see Delaney looking around and realized she might be looking for her friend. "No sign of Melody?" he asked.

"I don't see her," Delaney replied, giving up and returning her attention to him. "I guess she could've headed out to find her tree. Or maybe they decided to go home."

"You say you drove?" Josh asked, making sure she had a way home.

"Yes," she nodded. "I borrowed my dad's old truck, just to make sure my tree fits okay, and I don't get any sap on my Charger."

"You drive a Charger?" Josh asked, stepping around a little boy who was attempting to persuade his mother to let him have one more turn at feeding the reindeer.

"I do," she said. "It's my pride and joy, though I don't get to spend as much time driving it as I'd like since my commute is only about ten minutes, and I never have much time to go anywhere besides work."

Josh nodded. "I hear you. I mean… about the not going anywhere part. Unless you count tree lots, and that's not as much fun as, say, a tropical vacation. And my work commute is actually pretty long, so maybe I don't understand what you're saying at all." She giggled at him, and he couldn't decide if he should stop talking or try to further explain. Eventually, he decided to just go with it. "I mean, I think a lot of people spend time in their cars but not going where they wish they were going."

"And where do you wish you were going?" Delaney asked. "Visiting a tropical location?"

"Sure," he shrugged. "Or taking a leisurely drive to visit someplace I've never been, I guess. Probably not hauling trees."

"You don't like hauling trees?" She glanced up at him and then returned her attention to where she was going to watch out for other people and potential slick spots in the snow.

"I do," he said. "I guess. I don't know." There really was no way to succinctly explain that he liked helping his parents out, but he wasn't sure that hauling trees was the life for him.

She looked at him again, her eyebrows arched, but she said nothing more. A moment later, they were standing outside the shop, and Josh realized what he was about to do. Taking a deep breath, he put his hand on the door pull, and waited. Delaney stopped in her tracks and looked up at him. "Delaney, you are about to meet my mother," he warned.

A curious smile crept across her face. "Okay?"

"I just want you to know that I don't normally introduce women to my mother so soon—as in before I've even had a chance to ask them on a date yet—so… please be forewarned. She's wonderful, but she is my mother, after all, and you just never can tell what might come out of her mouth."

Delaney laughed, and it didn't sound like nervous laughter either. It sounded like she was genuinely chuckling at his discomfort, which set him at ease a bit because at least she didn't seem scared to meet his mother. Of course, that might be because she wasn't interested in him at all, and after the way he'd just made that statement—"had a chance to ask them on a date yet"—could it be that this was all a bit ridiculous to her?

"I'm sure it will be fine," Delaney assured him. "After all, remember, talking to women your mother's age is sort of my specialty."

She was looking at him with large doe eyes, and he realized he was being silly. Of course she could handle his mother. They would definitely have baking in common, that was certain. Letting go of the breath he'd been holding, he pulled the door open and waited for Delaney to step inside, following after her.

Lydia greeted Delaney first, shouting a Merry Christmas over her shoulder as she finished arranging a few items on a shelf on the other side of the store. When she realized Josh was also there, she turned to approach them. "Oh, hi, Son. I didn't realize you'd made it in. Is the tractor holding up in the snow?"

"Yeah, it's not that deep yet," Josh nodded once Lydia had come to a stop in front of them. There were a few other customers in the shop, but they were preoccupied looking at the nutcrackers against the far wall. "Mom, this is Delaney. She owns the bakery in Charles Town."

Lydia's face lit up as if she were meeting a celebrity. "Delaney? It's nice to meet you!" Lydia gushed, taking Delaney's hand in hers. "I have heard such wonderful things about your cocoa."

"Thank you," Delaney replied. "It's nice to meet you, too, Mrs. Taylor."

"Oh, please, call me Lydia," the older woman insisted. "Why don't you two come in and warm up a little bit. I'd offer you some of our cocoa, but I'm sure it just wouldn't do."

Delaney followed her across the shop floor, taking her red gloves off as she did so and shoving them into her pocket. "I'm sure it's not that bad," she said politely.

Turning to look at her for a second, Lydia shook her head slowly from one side to the other. "It seems like it's all people can talk about. They love everything else, but they don't really dwell on that. It's all about the awful cocoa."

"Mom, only a few people have even mentioned it," Josh reminded her as he leaned against the counter where the cash register sat.

"Not too long ago, a cute couple came in with an adorable little boy, and the woman mentioned that she couldn't even drink it she was so hooked on yours," Lydia continued, looking Delaney in the eyes.

"Oh, that was probably my friend Melody," Delaney explained. "I'm sure she didn't mean to offend you."

"She didn't," Lydia replied, though clearly the comment had upset her. "I just thought to myself, 'I've got to meet this Delaney. She's world famous!'" Lydia chuckled, and glancing over at Delaney, Josh could see the color rising in her cheeks. "Here, you can take a sip," his mother continued with a shrug, and she went about pouring a bit of the dark liquid into a Styrofoam cup.

Delaney smiled as she took it, though he saw a bit of hesitation as her bottom lip quivered before making contact with the soft container. She swallowed and then paused for a moment before she withdrew the cup and forced the smile back to her mouth. "It's... not awful," she managed. "I mean... it tastes like the store bought kind, that you mix up. With water."

"That's what it is," Lydia assured her with a shrug. "What can I do?"

"Well," Delaney began, glancing at Josh who wasn't sure whether to rescue her or let Delaney finally give his mother an answer so she could stop dwelling on the cocoa issue. "How much do you usually sell in a weekend? I could bring you some of mine. You mix it with milk, not water, and it takes a few special tools to get it to mix just right, but I can explain how."

Josh watched as his mother's face lit up. "Would you mind, dear? I'm more than happy to pay for it, or give you whatever profits we make. I'd be so honored to have your cocoa as part of our Christmas village. I don't sell much cocoa now, but I'm sure if people knew it was yours, we'd sell a whole lot more. Oh, we could even use cups with your bakery name on them. What's it called?"

"Delaney's Delights," Josh answered before she could reply, and when she beamed up at him as if she were proud he could remember the name of her establishment, he could only shrug and hope his face wasn't turning too red. He'd only been dwelling on that name for the past two weeks.

"We could do something like that if you want," Delaney replied. "Whatever works for you. I wouldn't expect a whole lot of people to drive from Shepherdstown to Charles Town just to visit the bakery when I'm pretty sure there's more than one here."

"There is, but from what I hear, they're nothing compared to what you've got going on in Charles Town," Lydia replied, looking up at Josh and then back at her.

Rather than let his mother break into a description of how frequently he may have mentioned the bakery over the last several days, Josh attempted to move things on. "All right, now that we've got that settled, I think I'll take Delaney for a tour of the farm on the four wheelers. Travis said he had things under control with the trees."

"That sounds fun," Lydia agreed. "Aren't you starving, though? It's past lunchtime."

While Josh's stomach had been growling earlier, it had suddenly stopped when Delaney had showed up. "I guess so," he shrugged.

"Well, you could take her over to the house and fix some sandwiches from the leftover ham from last night, but I'm afraid you won't be able to use the microwave to heat it up," Lydia said, shaking her head and looking intently at the checkout counter.

Josh felt his stomach knot up. He knew that tone. "What's the matter with the microwave?" he asked.

With a sigh, Lydia began an explanation, her voice hushed so that the customers couldn't overhear, Josh supposed. "Your father was attempting to reheat his coffee when the boys went back for lunch a while ago, and he put it in for forty-five minutes instead of forty-five seconds. Of course, it didn't go that long before Travis realized there was a problem, but by then, the microwave had just about had it, and there's burned coffee all over the place."

"Oh, no," Josh mumbled, shaking his head. He was afraid something like this might happen someday soon. They were all very lucky that Travis was there to prevent a fire. "Is Dad okay?"

"He's fine," Lydia shrugged. "Travis said he went on like it was no big deal. He hasn't even come down here to tell me about it. But... well, I worry."

Josh nodded, and knowing his mother wouldn't say more in front of Delaney, he decided they could talk about it later. He glanced over at Delaney, and she had a concerned look on her usually cheerful face. She was chewing on her bottom lip, and while Josh was surprised his mother had mentioned it in front of her, he could see that she was absorbing the information as if she genuinely cared about his father as well, a man she'd never met. "I'll go check on him in a little while," Josh offered.

"Thank you," Lydia replied, exhaling. Then, shaking her head as if to clear it, she looked at Delaney and smiled broadly. "It was just lovely meeting you, Delaney. I'm so excited to get to try your cocoa for myself."

Smiling back at her, Delaney replied, "It was so nice to meet you, too. I'll talk to Josh, and we'll figure out the best way to get the cocoa over before next weekend. Does that sound good?"

"That sounds just wonderful," Lydia assured her, and before his mother could forcibly hug the young woman she'd only just met, Josh took her gently by the arm and began to lead her out of the shop. "Bye!" Lydia called and they both echoed her with a wave as they made their way back out into the falling snow.

Once they were back outside, Josh wasn't sure if he should apologize for his mother or try to put their conversation in context. Honestly, she had behaved herself quite well, except for the cocoa discussion, and Josh hoped Delaney didn't feel obligated to supply Taylor Tree Farm with cocoa, though the idea that she would be working as a sort-of supplier for them was kind of nice because it meant he might have more of a chance to see her. As he led her away from the shop, he stopped and turned to face her, touching her gently on the arm as he did so, "Thanks a lot for volunteering to help my mom with the cocoa," he began, not really sure what to say.

Delaney looked up at him, a smile on her pretty face. "Sure. Your mom is so nice. She seems like she really cares a lot about this place. And Christmas."

Josh couldn't help but chuckle. She'd hit the nail on the head. "My mom is a Christmas fanatic, and I think this is probably her favorite place on Earth."

"No tropical paradise for her?" Delaney teased, clearly referencing their earlier conversation.

"I don't know if my mother has ever even been to a beach," Josh admitted, thinking about when that might have happened. "I guess she would like it, but... I don't know."

"Everyone should go to the beach some time in their life," Delaney shrugged. "There's a reason the expression is 'life's a beach' instead of 'life's a mountain top.'"

"True," Josh replied, though the mountaintops he was standing amidst seemed pretty decent right about now. "Would you like to head back to my parents' house and grab some lunch before we go out on the tour? I know I'm taking up a lot more of your day than you might have planned, but my mom makes the best ham."

Delaney's smile broadened. "That sounds great," she said, nodding. "I didn't really eat any breakfast this morning."

"Awesome," he said. "I mean... that you want to have lunch, not that you didn't eat breakfast."

Giggling, Delaney swatted him on the arm playfully. "I knew what you meant." She looked around. "Do we walk to your parents' house? We could take my truck."

While Josh was thinking of taking his dad's old work truck that they often used to drive back and forth between the village and the house, it was possible someone else might need it, and there was no reason to leave Delaney's truck in the parking lot. "We can take your truck, if you'd like."

"Okay," Delaney replied. "I will have to actually pick out a Christmas tree before we go, though. Nana will not be very happy if I spend my whole day at a Christmas tree farm and don't bring her back the perfect tree."

As he led her off toward the parking lot, Josh said, "Don't worry. We'll find you the perfect tree." Perfect tree, perfect day, perfect girl. This mountainside was looking better and better all the time. Who needed a beach?

CHAPTER 11

The drive from the village to Josh's parents' house had been relatively quick, and Delaney hadn't said much. She was too busy concentrating on where she was going since most of the way actually crossed the acreage, and she couldn't see the ground well because of the snow. Originally, she had thought to let Josh drive, but he'd insisted that it wasn't far and that she wouldn't have any problems navigating what had become a pretty well-worn path even if she couldn't see it. When she'd pulled up outside a cozy log cabin and switched the engine off, she'd given a small sigh of relief before jumping down out of the truck and following Josh inside.

Meeting Josh's mom had been nice; Lydia seemed very sweet, and she wasn't pushy, nor did she seem to make any assumptions. While meeting one parent was enough for one day, Delaney did sort of hope that Josh's dad would be around, or that she'd have a chance to meet him later. While she'd tried to stay out of their private conversation, his forgetfulness had caught her attention, and she wanted to mention Nana, though it hadn't been the right time. Josh's father seemed like a nice man, and Delaney hoped she'd get to make his acquaintance sooner or later.

Josh led her inside what turned out to be an empty house, despite the various vehicles outside. The front room was decorated beautifully with a large Christmas tree, boughs of various evergreens draped in garlands and formed into wreaths, with large red bows and golden ornaments. However, as soon as they entered the kitchen, the overwhelming smell of burnt coffee hit her nostrils, almost making her gag and ruining a bit of the ambiance.

"Leave it to Travis not to clean that up at all," Josh muttered, approaching the microwave. "Sorry about that, Delaney."

"It's okay," she said, though she was sure her tone probably revealed her stomach was having other thoughts. "Can I help you clean it up?"

Josh stood back at arm's length and opened the microwave door. The smell was even worse now, and he began to cough. "You know what," he said, closing the door quickly, "I think I'll just set it outside. It might be time to get a new one."

Despite the green tinge to his face, Delaney couldn't help but giggle. "Do you want to take it out the back? I'll get the door."

"Sounds good," Josh said as he pulled the plug from the wall and shimmied the appliance out of its cubby above a built-in cupboard. Delaney went ahead of him and pulled open the back door before stepping in front to fling open the screen door. Despite having left her coat in the living room at the entry, she was happy to be outside in the fresh air again, even if the breeze did bite just a bit. Once Josh had the microwave on the edge of the porch, as far away from the door and windows as possible, she closed the door, taking another deep breath of mountain air.

"Thanks," Josh muttered, stretching his back. The microwave was a larger model and clearly it had been heavy. He shook his head as if he was still contemplating the whole situation.

"No problem," Delaney replied, wanting to mention she understood his concerns, but afraid to invade his privacy. Just then, she realized they were not alone. A large bloodhound with a substantial belly slowly made his way up the steps and approached her, his sad eyes begging to be petted. "Aww! Who's this?" she asked as she offered her hand for his approval before she began to stroke his head.

Josh's countenance changed immediately. He stepped over with a smile on his face and dropped to a knee, patting the dog on the back. "This is Critter," he replied. "How are you today, boy?" he asked. The dog dropped down and rolled over, a clear indication that he needed a belly rub immediately. Josh complied, and the whacking of the dog's tail against the porch showed his happiness.

"He's so cute," Delaney said as she stood and watched Critter enjoy the scratching.

"He's a good dog," Josh said, and she wasn't sure if he was talking to her or to Critter. "Older than dirt, but a sweet boy."

Delaney laughed. "He reminds me of our old dog, Skeet, although he was a Lab, so totally different. But Skeet loved to have his belly rubbed." Thinking of Skeet, who'd passed a few years ago, made her sad.

"You don't have a dog now?" Josh asked, standing.

"No," Delaney replied, realizing her bottom lip was protruding. "My parents have a couple of Goldens, but Nana is more of a cat person. She has barn cats that she insists on taking care of all by herself, though sometimes I notice she forgets to feed them so I do it for her. I miss having a dog, though."

"I'm definitely a dog person," Josh nodded, giving Critter one last pat and then standing. "Cats are too finicky."

"I agree," Delaney nodded, though she really enjoyed playing with the kittens she'd find in the barn when she was younger.

"Let's go in before your freeze." Josh held open the screen door, and Delaney waved goodbye to Critter who was beginning to make his way back into the yard, not even realizing she'd been shivering until she was back inside the Taylors' warm kitchen.

The smell had dissipated a bit with the removal of the microwave, but it was still there. "I'm really sorry about the odor," Josh said as he crossed back to the part of the kitchen they'd vacated earlier. "I wonder if my mother has something we can spray."

The idea of anything mingling with the burnt coffee made Delaney's stomach begin to flip flop again. Pine scented burned coffee? Mango breeze, perhaps? "It's fine," Delaney assured him. "I think it'll go away in a bit."

He opened the cabinet under the sink and brought out a can of pure Lysol, which Delaney thought might be better than nothing, and at least it was the clean-scented kind. He sprayed it over where the microwave had stood and the put it back under the sink. "I'd light a candle, but I don't think my mom keeps those around much anymore."

Something about the way he intonated the statement made Delaney think there was more he wasn't saying. "Why is that?" she asked, realizing it probably wasn't her business.

Josh crossed to the sink and began to wash his hands. At first, Delaney thought maybe he wouldn't answer. Realizing she had just petted the dog herself, she decided a good hand washing was probably in order and crossed to join him. He scooted out of the way and dried his hands on a towel as Delaney pumped some soap onto her hands out of a bottle she assumed was his mother's since it was "Sugar Cookie" scented. As he handed her the towel, Josh replied, "I think Mom's afraid Dad might light one and forget."

He was standing right next to her now, and without the weight of their bulky coats, she could see his muscular frame. His jaw was set, possibly to hold back the emotions from what he'd just said, and his strong hand gripped the corner of the granite countertop next to the sink. Delaney could still detect a waft of pine and mint, even over her own sugar-scented hands, and setting the towel aside, she gave him a sympathetic look. "Nana has a lot of trouble remembering things, too," she said quietly. "I worry a lot about her. In fact, I insisted she go over to a friend's house today while I was gone. She's alone enough as it is, and I'm afraid something will happen."

Josh sighed and ran a hand through his unruly dark hair. "It's just... my dad isn't even that old, you know?" he asked. "I mean... I'm not saying because your grandmother is older that makes it any easier. I just... I'm not sure what to do."

"I didn't take it that way," she assured him. "I know what you're saying. Has your mom talked to a doctor?"

"Not for a while," Josh admitted. "My dad is very stubborn and never wants to go."

Delaney couldn't help but giggle. Her dad was the same way, and to some extent so was Nana. "Maybe that would help. I'm going to take Nana first thing next month. I want to see if there are any supplements or medications she could be taking to help. I've also been doing some research, and there are some games and apps that are supposed to help."

Josh's face brightened a bit. "Right. I've looked into those myself. I'm not sure if any of them would help Dad because I can't imagine I could get him to use them. But...." He hesitated, and Delaney raised her eyebrows, wondering what it was he was contemplating telling her. Eventually, he shrugged and said, "I'm toying with the idea of designing an app myself."

"You can do that?" she asked, surprised. "What is your day job?" She realized she had never even asked.

He chuckled. "Currently, I work in IT, but my degree is in programing, so yes, I think I can do it. I'm just not sure exactly what I want it to do. The games and puzzles they say will help with brain development are great. I also want there to be resources for family members and some sort of a reminder system that will help with scheduling and maybe even alert to danger somehow."

"That would be awesome," Delaney proclaimed, turning to face him. "Nana has so much trouble remembering to do things. I've talked to her about setting alarms, but she's afraid of the sound they make."

"It would definitely have to be something gentle," Josh replied thoughtfully. "I don't know.... I'm still in the early stages of working it out. I want to make sure that it's helpful and not just some catchy, worthless technology that either serves as a crutch or takes the focus off of the real problem. Ultimately, we need to find a cure for... Alzheimer's."

His hesitation at even saying the word tugged at her heartstrings. Delaney could relate. To her, old age and a lack of short term memory were totally different than the disease he'd just named, and she'd always chosen to think Nana suffered from the former. But what if she was wrong? Would Delaney be able to accept that label either? "Well, I'd love to help you with it, if there's anything I can do. I think it's extremely important to continue to do research and find a cure as well, but in the meantime, if there's something that could make people's lives better, I'd be all for it."

His face brightened, and Delaney thought he looked genuinely reassured by her statement. "Thanks, Delaney. That's really nice of you to say. The biggest problem I have right now is there just doesn't seem to be enough time to work on it. Even though this is the only vacation I ever get to take, I don't have a lot of time to relax."

She hadn't thought about this being his only vacation. "Well, that stinks," she said, not sure what else to say.

He nodded and approached the refrigerator. "Ham sandwiches sound good to you?" he asked, pulling the door open.

"Sounds great," she replied. "What can I do to help?"

"Why don't you have a seat, and let me take care of it?" he asked, gesturing toward a barstool at the nearby island. He pulled out a covered plate, which Delaney assumed was the ham, along with some cheese and butter.

"Well, I guess I won't argue with that," she said. Even though Nana cooked dinner almost every night, Delaney couldn't remember the last time a man cooked anything for her. Certainly, Bradley wouldn't have entered a kitchen even if it was on fire and she was trapped inside. She had a seat on the the barstool and watched as he got out a frying pan and began to heat slices of ham in melted butter. "So I guess you're pretty busy working when you're in DC?" she asked, an attempt to continue their previous conversation.

"Yes," Josh called over his shoulder. "I tend to work more than anyone probably should." After a moment, he added, "You can probably relate."

"How do you know that already?" she asked, amazed at his perception.

"Well, you've recently given up at least one Saturday, it's pretty clear your business means a lot to you, and I assume anyone who runs a successful small business probably doesn't get to take too much time off," he replied, ending his statement by turning to flash her a smile that melted her heart almost to the degree of the butter in the pan.

"I do work a lot," she admitted. "I love my bakery, but there are times when I wish I could just take a week off. That hasn't happened since... forever."

He stepped to a bread box and pulled out a package of white bread. "I can imagine. So no beach for you either then?"

Delaney let out a sigh. "Nope. Sounds nice, though."

"Hey," he said, turning to face her, "I didn't mean to get you all depressed."

Letting out a giggle, she said, "I'm not. I mean, I love my job. I'm so lucky I get to go to work everyday and do something I love. But... there are some downsides, too. I wish I had someone who could run it for a while if I ever did decide to take a vacation."

He assembled the sandwiches and plated them, adding a hefty side of potato chips and a dill pickle spear before bringing Delaney her plate and setting his down beside it. "Do you drink soda, or are you strictly a cocoa kind of girl?"

She couldn't help but laugh as his hazel eyes stared at her in all sincerity. "Water would be just fine, thank you," she replied. The sandwich smelled heavenly, erasing all hints of the burned coffee, and as he set down a glass of ice water in front of each plate, she folded her hands and said a quick prayer and then dug in. It was just as delicious as it smelled. "Wow," Delaney said between chews. Swallowing, she managed, "This is so good."

"Thanks," he said, "although I can't take much of the credit. Mom did most of the work."

"She is definitely a fabulous cook," Delaney replied. "Maybe she should think of opening a restaurant or something."

"I think she would've liked that back in the day," Josh mused before popping a chip into his mouth. Once he finished chewing, he said, "Now, I think Mom just wants to spend time with the grandkids and make whatever she wants in the kitchen."

"I can understand that," Delaney nodded. "She's definitely talented though."

"I'll be sure to let her know you said so," he said with a smile. "It'll mean a lot to her. She likes you."

Delaney's eyes widened, happy for the news. "You think?"

"For sure. Which means... I'll get all sorts of questions the rest of the evening after you leave, but that's okay."

Delaney felt a blush invading her cheeks. She didn't know what to say, so she changed the subject. "You mentioned grandkids. How many nieces and nephews do you have?"

"Payton is the oldest. You met him. He's my sister Mackenzie's son. Then my brother Travis, who you also met, has two little girls named Chloe and Bridgette. While Mom loves all three of them, as well as her great-nieces and nephews and various cousins who spend a lot of time here, especially around the holidays, she adores those little girls."

"Oh, I bet they're precious," Delaney gushed. "How old are they?"

"Bridgette will be six in January, and Chloe just turned three," he replied, brushing his hands off and reaching for a nearby napkin out of a wooden holder. He handed one to her as well. "They are *all* little girl."

Delaney couldn't help but smile. She'd always hoped someday she'd marry and be the mommy of a little girl or two. "How sweet. And you're the only one who lives in the city?"

Josh let out a deep sigh, and Delaney wondered if she'd hit a nerve. "Yes," he finally said. "Although, my father has been asking me to take over the farm."

He was quiet, and Delaney wasn't sure what to say. Clearly, this was a sensitive issue for him. While it was tempting to launch into an argument for why that sounded like a great idea to her—after all, Shepherdstown was a lot closer to Charles Town than Washington, DC—she knew it wasn't any of her business, at least not at this point in time. "I guess that's something not to take lightly," she finally managed.

He forced a smile, his lips drawing into a tight line. "Definitely not," was all he said. They sat in silence for a long moment, and Delaney took a slow sip of her water, trying to think of something else to say. Nothing would come to her, so she waited, wondering how deeply he was lost in his thoughts.

It took a moment, but eventually, Josh said, "So, have you ridden a four-wheeler before?"

Delaney nodded. "Yes, my parents own a farm, so we started riding at a pretty young age. Back then, I don't think it ever even crossed my mind to put on a helmet or watch out for potholes. It's a wonder I'm still alive."

Josh laughed. "I can relate. We have helmets," he assured her. "Well, if you're ready to go, I'd love to take you out to the far acreage, let you see the view from the top of the hill, and maybe even introduce you to my dad if you don't mind me checking in on him."

"Sounds great," Delaney smiled, wiping her hands off on the napkin one more time. She followed him to the trash can and scraped off her plate before they both put them in the dishwasher, and Delaney noted that he sure was a good son, cleaning up after himself. He even rinsed the pan and put that in the top rack as well. While she was slightly nervous to meet the elder Mr. Taylor, she was excited, too. Things may have been moving a bit more quickly than normal, but she really liked Josh. The more time she spent with him, the more she wondered if this might have possibilities, particularly if he planned on sticking around Shepherdstown.

A few minutes later, she found herself bundled up in her coat, gloves, and hat, with a helmet atop her head straddling an ATV. It had been about a year since she'd ridden one, but she was sure it was like a bicycle, and it would all come back to her as soon as she started the engine, and once Josh signaled that he was ready to go, she cranked it up and followed him out across the snow-covered fields.

She realized he wasn't going that fast, probably considering she had never ridden here before and it was snowy, but even at the lower speed, the wind was whipping through her hair, and the snow crystals began to sting her face. It was coming down a little more now, and riding along amidst the dancing flakes gave her the sensation she was flying. Everywhere she looked, there was an untouched blanket of white spread along the hillside, up into the surrounding mountains, the boughs of Christmas trees reaching out to the heavenly blue skies. Delaney felt more free than she could remember ever feeling, and for a moment, she thought about lifting her arms, standing up, and letting the wind take her. What would it feel like if the breeze actually took her up into the sky, and she was free to fly like the cardinals that flittered between the trees to her right?

They began to climb up the hillside, and Delaney was careful to stay right behind Josh, certain there must be a path here she couldn't see. The higher they climbed, the steeper the terrain became, and she was cautious so as not to flip the ATV over. They rode through some heavier brush, and in a few places she was afraid a branch might snag her coat. Eventually, they came to a clearing on the top of a hill —or was it a mountain?—and there below she could see almost the entire Christmas tree farm laid out before her, like a miniature scene inside a snow globe. As she removed her helmet and climbed from the ATV, she gasped. It was one of the most beautiful sights she'd ever seen.

"It's something, isn't it?" Josh asked, stepping right next to her.

"Oh, wow. It's just gorgeous…." she agreed.

He began to point out the various fields where certain trees were grown, the village, which she'd spotted right away, his parents' house, and a few other locations that were clearly important to him. She listened intently, but mostly she just marveled at the beautiful, picturesque scene beneath her.

"It really is unlike anything I've ever seen before," she finally said, which was saying a lot considering she'd lived in West Virginia her whole life and farmscapes were a natural backdrop for most of her existence.

Leaning in close to her ear, he said quietly, "All of this could be mine, if I want it."

She could feel the warmth of his breath on her neck which sent a tingly sensation down her spine. The smell of pine and mint she knew to be his aftershave was even stronger than the woodsy smell of the trees behind them, and she wondered how it was that she felt so close to this man already, having just met him a couple of weeks ago. It took her a moment to form a coherent sentence. "You're not sure what you want to do, or you don't want to disappoint your parents?"

He sighed and took a step backward, which broke the spell she'd been under just a bit. "Both, I guess," he replied with a shrug. "I do love it out here. I love spending time with my family, and I want to be here for my parents when they need me. I just worry that I will miss my life in the city."

"You must have a lot of friends there," she offered, turning to face him.

"No, not really," he replied, chuckling, which Delaney thought was a little odd. "I mean, I guess I do. I just don't have a lot of time to socialize away from work. Here, I don't have a lot of time either, but I already know everyone. Family, friends, all the people I grew up with still live here for the most part."

"Are you afraid you'll miss working with computers?" she asked, taking a step toward him, her boot crunching in the snow.

"I think so," he admitted, "although my dad thinks I might have time to do some of that on a smaller scale in town. I honestly don't know exactly what it is that's keeping me from making a decision."

Delaney had never been in a similar situation; she'd known from the time she was in high school she would temporarily go off to culinary school and then come back to open her own bakery. That's exactly what she had done. It must be hard to dream of spreading your wings and flying away, only to find out there was a tether. "Do you have to decide soon?" she asked.

"No, I don't," he admitted, and his countenance changed just a bit, as if she'd reminded him to breathe. "When I stand up here, though, and look down there at all of those trees, my parents' house, the village, it reminds me that eventually I will have to make up my mind."

She nodded and offered a small smile. "Well, the good news is, today is not decision day."

His hazel eyes fell on her face, and he looked at her much the same way he had that first day in the bakery, as if he were attempting to memorize her face. "True. I don't have to decide anything right now."

"So... why don't we have some fun instead?" she asked, and before he had a chance to react, she bent to the ground and scooped up a handful of snow, forming it into a ball right before she launched it at his chest.

At first Josh looked shocked, his mouth agape and his eyes wide, but just as Delaney began to think perhaps she had inadvertently upset him, he shouted, "You will pay for that!" with a chuckle and bent down to begin forming his own snowy projectiles.

Laughing, Delaney looked around to see where she could take cover, an idea she might have come up with before she started the snowball fight if her judgment hadn't been clouded by the nice smelling man about to launch an all-out offensive. She quickly ducked behind a tree as he gathered together enough clumps of snow to pelt her for several minutes. Just as she was about to lob another imperfectly formed snowball in his direction, Josh tossed several in a row over at her, somehow managing to bend them around the tree, and before she knew it, she was fully engaged in a snowball war.

Within minutes, Delaney found herself chuckling harder than she could remember laughing in ages. While she had taken a few hits to the head and one to the arm, he wasn't throwing them hard enough to hurt her, and despite the fact that he was standing out in the open, she had a hard time hitting him, mostly because she was laughing so hard her aim was off. Eventually, she shouted, "Truce! Truce! I call a truce!" But rather than honor her cry of uncle, he charged ahead, eventually infiltrating her tree barricade. She took off running, not even knowing where she was headed, careful to avoid the drop off, but a few moments later he caught up to her, and she fell to the ground in a fit of hysterical giggling.

"Are you all right?" Josh asked, no longer able to stand upright himself, he was laughing so hard.

Unable to catch her breath, Delaney stuck up one gloved finger, a symbol that she needed a moment. "I'm... okay...," she managed.

"Good," he said, coming to rest in the snow next to her. "I didn't think I was throwing them that hard, but I couldn't really tell if you were laughing or crying. I was hoping it was laughing."

She finally managed to contain herself just a bit. "I don't think I've laughed that hard since Dana Hampton peed her pants in the seventh grade musical."

Josh looked at her, eyes wide. "Poor Dana Hampton."

"Oh, no, she totally deserved it. She was never nice to anyone," Delaney replied, leaning up on both elbows. "It's been ages since I had a snowball fight."

"Me, too," Josh said, "although I'm not sure why. I should get the little girls next time we're out."

Delaney had stopped laughing now. She brushed a strand of hair off of her face. "They would love it." Then, another thought occurred to her. "Have you ever made snow angels with them? Oh, those were my favorite."

Before he could even answer, she lay back onto the snow and began to brush her arms up and down, though he was in the way and took her cue to scoot over some. She moved her legs back and forth as well, attempting to make an angel in the snow. "Well, it's kind of rocky here, and the grounds not really very even, but you should definitely get Chloe and Bridgette to try it."

Josh scooted over from her and lay back into the snow. "You're right," he said as he began to mimic her motions. "It's been a long time since I've done this, too. I'm sure they'd get a kick out of it, even if they ended up stepping on it and messing it up."

"That's the trick," Delaney reminded him, "getting up without leaving a handprint or footprint." She decided to try standing, and carefully stretched her hands outside of the perimeter of what should be the wings. As she pulled herself to her feet, she began to lose her balance. Luckily, Josh was already standing next to her, and he caught her, pulling her up carefully, his hands around her forearms.

Delaney turned and realized his face was a mere inch away from hers. His hazel eyes locked onto her face, his lips so close to hers. He took a deep breath, and she froze, realizing she wasn't breathing at all. "Thank you," she managed to say quietly.

It took him a long moment to quietly reply, "No problem," and Delaney cleared her throat, slowly taking a step backward. He let go of her, once he was certain she had her balance, and she straightened her hair, biting her lower lip, and shifting her gaze back out to the valley below them.

"We should, uh... probably go see what Dad is up to," Josh muttered, taking a step back himself.

"Right," Delaney agreed. While she would have loved to discover what it was like to have Josh's lips on hers, it was way too soon for that. This wasn't even a date—was it? He began to head back over to his four-wheeler, and she followed, making sure her hat was on straight. Even though the magic spell had been broken, she'd still had the best time she could remember playing in the snow with Josh. She hoped this was the first of many such memories to come.

CHAPTER 12

Josh was fairly certain he knew where he could find his father. Despite the fact that Travis had said they were done, he suspected his dad would still be out in the western acreage checking on the saplings and making sure none of them would be affected by the snow. That's what his father did—check the trees. Josh didn't know for sure if that was the life he wanted for himself, but the idea of staying in Shepherdstown was becoming more and more appealing.

He'd been so close to kissing Delaney he could almost feel it. There she was, those bright eyes staring at him in wonder, her full lips parted just before his. She had that twinkle in her eye, and he really wanted to feel her lips on his. However, he'd only met her a few weeks ago, and he hadn't even asked her on a date yet. There was no reason to get carried away. If he was really meant to find a way to have a relationship with her, whether or not he went back to DC, then they would sort it out. Rushing things now would only lead to problems and potential heartache.

They found his father exactly where Josh expected him to be, amongst the smaller trees on the outskirts of their property. He looked up and waved as they came into view, though his forehead crinkled a bit when he saw Delaney, obviously not sure who she might be. Josh pulled his ATV to a stop a good fifty feet away from where his father was pruning a mid-sized spruce, and Delaney came to a stop behind him.

He waited for her to hop down from the four-wheeler and hang her helmet on the handlebars. He couldn't get over looking at her, she was so beautiful, and when she turned to him and smiled, he felt his heart skip a beat. "You ready to meet my old man?" he asked.

Delaney giggled. "I don't think he's that old, but sure," she replied, clearly understanding when he was joking around. That was something that just happened to come naturally between them; Delaney always seemed to know when he was kidding, and she always found a reason to laugh at his silliness. He considered offering her his arm, but thinking that might cause questions to arise in his father's mind, he walked alongside her as his dad finished his pruning and looked up expectantly.

"Hello there, Son," Kent called as they approached. The snow had let up, and now the only flakes flying by were coming off of the taller trees as the wind whipped by. "And who is this young lady?"

"Dad, this is Delaney. She's the baker from Charles Town I was telling you about. She stopped by to pick out a tree." Turning to Delaney, he said, "This is my dad, Kent."

"It's nice to meet you, Mr. Taylor," Delaney said, offering her hand.

Taking her gloved hand in his, Kent replied, "Lovely, to meet you, too, but I'm sure you heard—I'm Kent." He smiled and gave a little chuckle, which made Delaney's face light up. "What have you two been up to? He giving you the tour?"

"Something like that," Josh replied, staring at Delaney to see what she might say.

"He took me up there," she explained pointing to the hilltop they'd just come from, "and gave me a beautiful view of your land. It's just breathtaking."

Kent's face beamed with pride. "Why, thank you," he said. "I'm very proud of what we've built here. Couldn't have done it all myself though. Nope, got lots of help from Josh and some of the other kids. It's a lovely place, no doubt about it."

Josh smiled, happy to see his dad so proud of the farm, even though he didn't give himself nearly enough credit. "What are you working on, Dad? Shaping these guys for next year?"

"Sure am," Kent replied, eyeing the tree he'd just been working on. Turning to Delaney, he said, "You can't just expect a tree to grow out of the ground and be a perfect Christmas tree. No, getting them to be their best takes a lot of work."

"I can imagine," Delaney nodded, and Josh wondered if she was just being polite or if she really had an understanding for all of the work that went into what his father did.

"Did you get one picked out yet?" he asked, looking at her expectantly.

"Not yet," Delaney admitted. "What time does the lot close? I didn't even think about that."

Kent chuckled. "Don't worry about it, girly. You got all the time you need. We're happy you're here."

His father was smiling at her as if he'd just met his new daughter-in-law, and Josh couldn't help but wonder at how entrancing Delaney really was. First his mother, and now his father, both of them seemed to see the same qualities in her that Josh was seeing himself. She really was an amazing young woman.

"Thank you," Delaney said, a bit of color rushing into her cheeks.

"I think we ought to head back to the house," Josh suggested, seeing that Delaney might be growing a bit uncomfortable now with his father's full attention. She likely didn't want to interrupt his work either.

"It was so nice to meet you," Delaney said, offering her hand back to his father.

Rather than shaking her hand, Kent wrapped his arms loosely around her shoulders. "It was very nice to meet you, too, Delaney. Don't be a stranger now," he added as he released her. She was smiling, and she nodded as she stepped backward, looking surprised but not uncomfortable.

"Don't stay out here all evening, Dad," Josh called as he turned to go back to the ATVs.

"You know I won't miss your mom's cooking," Kent called back, and Josh couldn't help but chuckle. That was certainly true.

A few minutes later, they were standing outside of the log cabin near Delaney's truck, ATVs back in the outbuilding where they were kept. The snow had essentially stopped at this point, but the sun was beginning to fade behind the mountains, giving the white ground a pink luster. It was still chilly out, and he was sure Delaney was ready to get back into the truck. Hopefully, the heater was in better shape than some of the other features, like the paint job.

"You want to head back to the village and pick out a tree?" he asked, lingering at the driver's side door.

"That sounds good," Delaney replied, her hands shoved deep down into the pockets of her coat. "Are you going to come with me?"

"Of course," Josh replied. "I've got to make sure you pick out a good one."

Delaney giggled. "I think I know how to pick out a Christmas tree," she replied as he pulled open the truck door for her and she began to climb inside. He watched her settle in and then closed the door for her before going around to the passenger's side and joining her. The engine was cranked, and mildly warm air began to fill the cab. It wasn't nearly as hot as he had hoped, but it was getting there, and it did take a bit of the edge off of the frigidity.

"I'm sure you can pick out a decent tree," Josh said, shrugging, "but I'll help you make sure you get the best one possible."

She giggled again, and it was a sound Josh thought he would never tire of. She backed the truck out of the parking spot and waited for him to point her in the right direction down the makeshift lane that led to the shop. "I guess you probably know more about Christmas trees than I ever even dreamed there was to know."

"That's a good way of putting it," Josh laughed as they went over a bump in the field. "If you head that way, you'll see the village in just a second."

She was quiet for a moment, and he supposed she was concentrating. Once the village came into view, he saw her shoulders relax a bit. "Your father sure is sweet."

Without hesitation, Josh replied, "Oh, yeah. He's great. I wish he didn't work so hard though."

"Does he spend a lot of time out there pruning the trees?"

"Probably more than he should," Josh admitted. "That's one thing that he really doesn't like any help with, either. Says the rest of us do it wrong." He chuckled, and she turned to him and smiled. "I wonder if that's something he'll keep up even after he retires. I guess it's not too stressful, and it's not like he'd have to chop those trees down and haul them in."

"That sounds like a lot of work," Delaney offered. They were almost to the lane that led to the parking lot, and from here, Josh could see that there weren't many customers left. As it got darker, most people would head home, even though his mother had done a lovely job of stringing Christmas lights, which were twinkling around the buildings now.

"It is a lot of work," Josh agreed. "That's why he's looking for a long-term solution for getting out of the business."

"And why he wants you to take over?" she asked as she made the transition from the field into the parking lot. She found a spot near the entrance to the village and pulled in, turning to look at him in anticipation of an answer.

"Exactly," Josh nodded. The decision weighed heavily upon him again, and he let out a long sigh. Her brown eyes were staring at him in genuine concern, and he couldn't help but be drawn to her. It was as if he'd known her for years, not a mere matter of days. "He said I don't have to decide right away, but I know it will make things easier on him once he has my answer."

"And if you say no, what will he do then?" she asked, biting her bottom lip as if it were her own difficult decision.

Shrugging, Josh said, "He's talked about finding a cousin or another family member to take over, but I don't think he trusts any of them. Honestly, I think he'd end up having to sell most of the farm. Hopefully, he'd be able to keep the house and the land around it. It's all paid off, but they don't have a lot saved up. Most of the time, we are lucky if we turn a small profit each season after paying seasonal workers. And then there was the cost of building the village and upkeep on the equipment, all of those things. So, at the end of the holidays, if they still have enough to budget for the rest of the year, things are going good."

Delaney let out a sigh and nodded. "I can sort of relate to that. The bakery definitely has some months that are busier than others. Has he thought about diversifying? Growing pumpkins or apples—something else that might be popular a different time of year?"

Nodding, Josh confirmed, "He has. But he spends so much time taking care of the trees even in the off-season, he's always been afraid he wouldn't have time for both."

Blowing out a breath, Delaney said, "Well, I know it can't be an easy choice for you. You should pray about it. That's what I always do when I have a tough decision, and it always helps."

He couldn't help but smile. It was nice to know she was a woman of faith. "I've definitely been praying about it," he assured her. "I've asked God to lead me in the right direction and prevent me from making my decision for selfish reasons."

"Good," Delaney smiled. "Do you think you'll make up your mind this season or will you try to put it off?"

"I think I'll try to let Dad know soon. If I decide to take over the farm, I'll still go back to my old job for a while—at least a few months. I've got to make sure I'm in a financial position so that if something goes awry with the farm, I'll be able to make it for a year or two until I can either sell it or fix it."

"I can understand that," she said, a small smile, seemingly forced, playing at the corners of her mouth. She reached out and put her hand on his arm, just above his wrist. "I'll pray for you, too," she said. "If you don't mind."

Josh smiled at her. "Thank you, Delaney. I would really appreciate that."

She held his gaze for a few moments, the smile broadening, and he looked into her brown eyes, wondering how it was possible to feel so connected to someone so quickly. Eventually, he cleared his throat, and even though he liked the feel of her warm hand on his arm and he could've continued to stare into her eyes all evening, he realized it was getting late and she probably needed to get back to her nana soon. "Are you ready to go find a tree?"

"Yes," she said, and a look of genuine excitement lit up her face. "Let's go."

Josh climbed from the truck and met her in front of the pickup. This time, he offered his arm, and she slipped hers through. "About how tall were you thinking?" he asked as he led her toward the giant snowman sign he'd helped his dad make a few years ago.

"Well," Delaney said, looking up at the sky and creasing her eyes as if she were deep in thought, "Nana's living room ceiling is about nine feet tall, I think. So probably something around six or seven feet. She likes them really full, she said, which is sort of surprising since the fake tree she's been putting up for as long as I can remember isn't full at all."

"Fake tree?" he asked, looking at her with a scrutinizing glare. "Your Nana's a Fakey?"

Delaney giggled, as if she'd never heard the term before but could appreciate it. "She claims my grandfather preferred them because of the mess. I don't know. She's decided to go real this year, and that's what's important, right?"

"I concur," Josh agreed. They were inside of the village now, and he could see Payton over near the shaking station helping a little old lady with her tree. The tractor was gone, which means Travis was either out picking up another load—which was doubtful considering the number of patrons nearby—or he'd put it away for the afternoon, which was much more likely. "Why don't we grab a saw and head out a bit? I think I know of a couple of trees that might work."

"You know them personally?" she asked, giggling. "Like, do they have names?"

He stopped and stared at her for a moment before proceeding. "Maybe. What's wrong with naming a tree? They're living creatures, too."

Her giggle turned into a hearty laugh. "I guess that's true."

"You should name your trees. And talk to them."

"As long as they aren't talking back," she replied.

"Well, of course not. I mean… not usually."

She broke into a full-fledged laugh, the kind that required an arm across her midsection, and he was happy to see he was able to entertain her so well. He let go of her arm to retrieve a saw from the collection they kept on hand for visitors who wanted their own lumberjack experience. "If you're quite all right, I think we can head out now."

"Give me a minute," Delaney replied, wiping tears from her eyes. "I can't breathe."

"Listen, Bill is calling for me, so I've got to go."

That renewed her laughter, and he took her free hand and began to walk toward the tree lot, dragging her along behind him. "Bill? Is that the name of the tree you think might work for Nana?"

"Sure. Then there's Ed. Or Roger. But definitely not Mona. She is a spitfire, that Mona."

"Does she moan-a-lot?" Delaney asked, catching up to him so he was no longer pulling her along.

He couldn't help but laugh at her awful joke. "I see my sense of humor is starting to rub off on you."

"Oh, I've got plenty of dad jokes," Delaney explained. "My dad is the king of bad dad jokes, so I learned from the best."

"Is that so?" Josh asked as they began to weave through the trees. He honestly did have one in mind he thought she would really love if no one had cut it down earlier in the day. Since the chances that anyone trudged out this far in the snow were unlikely, he was hoping it was still there. "Well, I might not be a dad yet, but I've got plenty of bad uncle jokes. Just you wait and see."

"I believe it," she replied, still giggling. "You do know where we are going right?"

"Nope, not at all," he said, playfully. He turned to wink at her and felt his heart warm at her smile. Even though they both had on gloves, holding her hand felt natural, and using the ruse of getting her started in the right direction had been a nice way to see if she would be okay with it. She wasn't pulling her hand away in protest, so he felt like she didn't mind either.

About ten minutes into their walk, he saw the tree he had been thinking about off in the distance. It was a Douglas fir, a little over six feet tall with full branches and a lovely green coloring that had really stood out to him. He waited until they had almost reached it to say, "Okay—what do you think about that one?" gesturing in the direction he wanted her to look.

Delaney's face lit up. "That one over there?" she asked, and when he nodded, she let go of his hand and hurried to step in front of it. She took a deep breath and said, "Oooh," as she slowly walked around it. "It's really nice."

"I thought so. I've had my eye on it for years. It hardly needed any pruning at all."

"I love it," she said, beaming. "I think it's just about the right height, too. I bet Nana will appreciate how full it is. Do you think it will leave a lot of needles?"

"Nah," he said, still smiling at her giddiness. "Douglas firs don't really lose their needles as much as some of the other trees."

"It really is nice, Josh," Delaney smiled. She was looking around as if she were trying to find a tag. "How much is it?"

The tag was on the side of the tree next to him, and he quickly pulled it off and shoved it in his pocket. "I guess if there's no tag, it's free," he said with a shrug.

She looked at him skeptically. "I don't expect you to give me a free Christmas tree. I know this is your family's business."

"Are you kidding? You've alleviated my mother's cocoa nightmares, you put up with the awful burnt coffee stench in the house, and you helped clear the snow off of the hillside. On top of that, you've put up with my corny jokes. I can't possibly charge you for this Christmas tree."

Though she was still smiling, she stepped up next to him, and crossing her arms against the front of her bright red coat, she slowly said, "I insist on paying for the Christmas tree."

Josh opened his mouth as if he were about to respond to her but then he leaned in toward the tree instead. "What's that, Bill? Oh, yes, I agree. Okay, I'll let her know." Turning back to Delaney, he said, "Bill here says I should let you know that he's going home with you one way or another, and your money is no good here. So...."

Delaney giggled and her serious tone morphed into a more light-hearted one. "Well, you tell Bill here that I want to contribute to the Taylor Tree Farm so that there are many more years of Christmas magic to come."

"I can't tell him that," Josh said, shaking his head. "Besides, he heard you. It's not like he can only hear me just because I'm the only one that can hear him. Although, I bet by Christmas Eve, you'll be able to hear him, too." Setting the saw he was holding down on the ground as she continued to giggle at him, Josh placed his hands on her arms just above her elbows. "Listen, Delaney, I know what you're saying—you didn't come out here expecting for me to give you a tree. But we always give family friends free Christmas trees. It's part of my dad's culture of giving back, and I have had such an amazing time with you today, there's no way I could take you into the shop and ring up this tree. That would be ridiculous. So please, consider it a Christmas present if you must, but take the tree. Bill really wants to go home with you, and I want to know that, when you're home with your Nana, basking in the light of a thousand twinkling stars, gazing at this tree, maybe you'll also remember this wonderful, magical day that we shared together. What do you say? Will you accept my gift and take home the tree?"

Delaney was quiet for a long moment, and Josh thought he saw tears forming in the corners of her beautiful brown eyes. He wasn't exactly sure what he might have said to elicit such a response, but just when he was about to ask if she was all right, she said, "Thank you, Josh. I would love to take this tree home to Nana, and you can be sure I'll remember this day for many, many years to come."

Josh felt warmth spreading up his body from where his hands still rested on her arms. She was smiling up at him, and this close, he could smell the scent of peppermint and cookies he'd always noticed when Delaney was around. She was so beautiful with her hair billowing out around her in the light breeze, her cheeks flushed from the chilly air. Now would have been the perfect time to lean in and press his lips to her luscious mouth. But he truly believed Delaney was a lady unlike any he'd ever met before, and she definitely deserved to be treasured. Taking his time getting to know her and giving her the respect she merited was very important to him, so even though he thought he saw her tilt her head up slightly, as if she were also pondering what it might be like to share a kiss, he took a deep breath and a step backward.

Smiling at her, Josh moved his hands off of her arms and said, "All right then, let's get this tree in your truck so you can get it home where it belongs."

He dropped to the ground, and even though she asked if there was anything she could do to help, he declined, and it only took a few minutes for him to have the tree cut down. Normally, he'd take it in with the tractor, but since it wasn't that big, he was fairly certain it wouldn't be a problem to haul it back to the village.

"Can I help?" she asked as he began to tug on the trunk.

Looking at the tree and then at Delaney, Josh replied, "You can carry the saw, if you'd like."

She took the tool by the handle and he began to drag the tree behind him as they walked back to the village. The snow was beginning to crust over a bit as it grew colder, which mad the surface a little easier to glide the tree over, and it really wasn't a problem at all to get it to move.

"Are the rules the same for saws as they are for scissors?" Delaney asked as they headed back in.

"Oh, yes, for sure," Josh nodded. "You never run with a saw."

She giggled. "Did you learn that the hard way."

He let out an over-exaggerated sigh. "Unfortunately, I learn most things the hard way." She laughed, which was his intent, but he was glad he didn't have to tell her he wasn't really joking. It seemed like there were a lot of things in life he'd had to mess up once before he got them right. This time, however, if he decided he was going to date Delaney, he wanted to do it right the first time. The more time he spent with her, the more he realized she wasn't the type of girl one dated a time or two and then decided to never call again. She was the type of girl you brought home to your parents. After all, he'd already done that, and they both seemed to love her. That spoke volumes about her personality and character, two things that were critical to Josh.

Once they reached the village, virtually everyone else was gone, though Josh could see his mother's outline through the window in the shop where a soft glow illuminated from the Christmas lights she liked to use inside as well as out. He hauled the tree over to the shaker station. He assumed Travis was around somewhere, though Payton probably left already since it was getting late and his mother preferred for him to be home before dark. He took the saw from Delaney and returned it to its rightful position. Then, Josh set the tree into the shaking machine, and turning to Delaney he said, "You might want to cover your ears." She complied, and he flipped a button, starting up the machine which began to vibrate the tree back and forth dislodging any loose needles, bugs, and basically anything else that might fall on the customer's flooring and make a big mess. It didn't eliminate all shedding, but it was definitely better than nothing at all.

After a few minutes, the tree seemed to stop losing needles, and he turned the machine off.

"Boy, that things sure is loud!" Delaney said, removing her hands from her ears.

"I know. Sometimes I hear it in my sleep," he mused. "I'll tie the tree up so that you can get it inside more easily." Grabbing some of the rope they always kept on hand for customers, he wrapped it around the tree several times so that the branches were secure.

"Thank you," Delaney said, once he had it all packaged up. "That should make it easier to get it through the front door."

Josh took the tree down and began to hoist it toward her truck. Delaney followed along, her feet crunching through the snow. "Do you have someone that can help you get it set up?" he asked.

"My dad can come over if he needs to," she explained. "He only lives a few minutes away. But I think I should be able to manage. So long as Bill cooperates."

He chuckled at her reference to his earlier joke. "And you have a stand?"

"Yep. I got it down from the attic earlier this week."

They reached her truck, and Josh could see the tree would fit in the bed with no problems. He put it inside, and then just to be sure it didn't become a projectile once she reached highway speed, he secured it to the truck to keep it from flying out. Once that was all done, he climbed back down. She was waiting next to the truck, her hands folded in front of her, her lips drawn together tightly, her eyes on the ground.

"Everything okay?" he asked, offering her a small smile.

She looked up at him and blinked before returning his smile. "Yes. Everything is… perfect," she replied. "I just want to thank you for being so nice when I showed up announced like this."

He scoffed. "Are you kidding? I'm so glad that you did. I had an amazing day, Delaney."

Her smile broadened. "Me, too."

He held her gaze for a long moment, not knowing exactly what he should say next. Finally, he managed, "Well, uhm, can I have your phone number? I mean, you might have tree related questions…."

"Bill might need to call and chat."

"Right," he laughed, "and we'll need to figure out what to do with the cocoa—assuming you're still okay with my mother's request. That is, I hope you don't feel obligated to help."

"Oh, no, that's no problem at all," Delaney replied, waving him off with one hand as she fished her phone out of her coat pocket with the other one. "Your mother is so sweet."

"She is, but once she gets her mind wrapped around something…." He let the comment trail off. No reason to get into his mother's obsessions at this juncture. He took off his glove, unlocked his phone, opened the contacts, and handed it to Delaney, taking her phone from her outstretched hand. He entered his information then handed it back to her. It took her a second longer, then she completed the exchange.

He smiled at her and then slipped his phone back into his pocket, not exactly sure what to say. "Well, thanks again," he said, trying to keep the awkwardness at a minimum.

"Thank you," she said, returning the smile.

"I'll call you soon," he promised.

"Sounds good." She took a step toward the truck, and he opened the door for her, stepping out of the way. She smiled at him and put one foot in.

He realized it was a long way up and there was no running board. "Here, let me help you," he offered giving her a hand. She easily lifted herself into the driver's seat with one hand on his arm and other gripping the steering wheel. "Have a safe drive back, Delaney."

"I will," she assured him. "Bye, Josh." She took her hand off of his arm, and he felt as if all the warmth had left his body.

"Bye, Delaney." With one last smile, he stepped back and pushed the door closed. She cranked the engine and the transmission clunked into reverse as he backed out of the way toward the front of the truck. With one more wave, she turned and headed out of the lot. Josh stood in the snow and watched her go until he could no longer see the gleam of the truck's rear lights. Today had not been anything like what he'd expected when he awoke that morning. Today had quite possibly been the best day he'd ever had in his whole life.

CHAPTER 13

Delaney had managed to get the tree inside that night when she'd arrived home, but Nana had decided to wait until after church Sunday to put the decorations on, so Delaney had decided to do something she rarely had time for. Rather than turning on the TV or getting out her laptop, she curled up next to the fireplace with a good book and listened to the familiar clink of her grandmother's knitting needles. The romance novel reminded her just how much she loved to read, and she was glad she'd taken a few hours to do that, especially since the book was by one of her good friends, Olivia Kensington, and she'd been meaning to read it for weeks. Now, the next time she came into the bakery, Delaney wouldn't have to tell the same little white lie that she'd started the book but hadn't had time to finish it yet. Even though she'd gone to bed with a hundred pages or so to go, at least she'd actually read most of it.

She'd been surprised that Nana hadn't asked more questions about her day. Once Delaney mentioned Reid and Michael, a lot of the questions had centered around them, and Delaney was able to keep the focus on what Melody had been up to. They'd exchanged a few texts the day before, and it sounded to Delaney like there was a romance blossoming, though Melody insisted that wasn't the case. Still, they had plans to see each other again, and that seemed like a good sign to Delaney.

It wasn't until she had begun to put the lights on the tree that Nana, cozy in her recliner across the room, made an observation with the hint of a question. "This tree sure is pretty, darling. It must have cost quite a bit. Do you need me to give you some money, sweetheart?"

The lights were anything but tangled, thanks to her smart storage plan from the year before, but Delaney secretly wished they were in a knot so she could pretend she was so focused on getting it out that she couldn't answer. Since that wasn't the case, she said, "Oh, no, Nana. It's fine. Don't worry about it."

"Nonsense, child," was the reply. "You could at least let me pay half. It's my house, after all."

"It really wasn't much," Delaney answered, winding the strand of clear lights around the top of the tree first and working her way down.

"Good, then you won't have a problem taking half of not much."

Delaney let out a sigh and turned to face her grandmother who had her head tilted at the "no nonsense" angle. "Nana, I actually ended up getting the tree for free—sort of like a prize."

"What's that? Since when do lots give away trees as prizes?"

"Well, not a prize exactly. I helped them with a few things, and they insisted on giving me the tree for free." She hated being anything but forthright with her answer to Nana, but she didn't want to tell her about Josh, not yet anyway.

Nana's lips were drawn together in a tight line before she asked, "What did you help them with?"

Delaney shrugged. "Mrs. Taylor had some cocoa questions. I'm going to help her with the cocoa they sell at the little shop. I also went on a tour of the farm and met some of the workers. It was nice."

"So that's why you were out so long," Nana replied.

"Yes, it was a nice time. And when I was done, they insisted that I take the tree. I tried to get them to take my money, but they wouldn't hear of it."

"Hmmm," Nana said, her mouth still drawn taught. "Seems... fishy."

Delaney turned and looked at her before she returned her attention to the tree and put the last of the lights around the bottom. "Nana, they're just really nice people, and they wanted me to have it. That's all."

"And this wouldn't have anything to do with that tree farmer who came into the bakery, would it?"

Swallowing hard, Delaney went about getting the garland out of the box, pretending like she wasn't exactly sure what Nana was talking about. "Uh... well, I saw him there, I guess."

"Um hmmm," Nana said again. "And how was Josh?"

She was only slightly surprised that Nana remembered his name. Even though her everyday memory was beginning to slip, she never forgot a name or face. "He was good," Delaney replied. "Busy. But good, I think."

"Well, this morning in Sunday school, Brother Mitchell talked about Christmas being a time for magic. He reminded us that the Lord gives gifts in many ways, but one of those ways is in the form of rekindled relationships and new friends. Maybe this Josh feller of yours is meant to be a new friend."

Delaney knew her grandmother well enough to know precisely what she was getting at. With a sigh, she dropped the garland and found a spot on the couch. "Okay, Nana. I did see Josh, and we spent a lot of time together. He's a very nice man, and I really enjoy his company." Nana's face beamed. "But," Delaney continued, "he lives and works in Washington, DC, most of the year. He's only at the farm now because he's helping his folks out around the holidays."

"So?" Nana asked, giving one of her famous shrugs.

"So," Delaney replied, "I'm not sure I'm ready for another long distance relationship. You know how things worked out with Bradley."

"Bradley?" Nana repeated. "That Bradley was never good enough for you, Delaney. Why, never once in the whole time that the two of you went out did he ever come to the house to pick you up. He never even brought you flowers. The day that Bradley said goodbye was the best day of your life."

Delaney shook her head. Her former relationship was so much more complicated than her grandma could possibly realize. "I'm not sure that flowers and door opening are the most important things in a relationship."

"Sure they are," Nana insisted. "They are the hallmarks that show whether or not a man is a gentleman or just a common good-for-nothing, take-it-or-leave-it, dime-a-dozen hooligan."

Delaney couldn't help but giggle at her grandmother's list. "I know what you mean, Nana. But don't you think it will be hard if Josh decides to stay in DC?"

"It might be hard," Nana agreed, "but most things in life that are worth having are a little hard, especially in the beginning. But if it's meant to be, you'll figure it out. Does he like you the same way you like him?"

She felt her cheeks warm and knew she was likely as red as the Christmas bulbs waiting to be hung on the outstretched boughs of the tree. "I think so," she said quietly.

Nana's face broke into a wide grin. "Of course he does. Pretty, sweet girl like you. If it's meant to be, it'll happen. You pray on it, honey."

Delaney nodded, pursing her lips together to keep her emotions in check. Despite her grandmother's apparent nosiness, she always felt better when she had a heart-to-heart discussion with the wise woman. "I will, Nana," she promised.

"Good girl. Now, let's see about that garland. Can you make it drape down and wrap around the outer portions of the branches? I really like it when it's all fluffy and soft."

Giggling at her oddly worded request, Delany said, "I think I can do that," and stood to address the tree. "Bill" certainly looked pretty already with his twinkling lights, and as much as Delaney wanted to tell him that, she decided she'd wait until Nana had gone to bed. There was no sense trying to explain to her grandmother why she was talking to the Christmas tree.

Josh had managed to evade his mother's game of twenty questions by telling her that he'd had a nice time with Delaney and he'd call her later that week. Then, he pretended he didn't feel well and needed to rest. He didn't like being dishonest with his mother, but by the time he'd returned to the house, his stomach definitely didn't feel normal. Of course, it was likely nerves brought on by being in the presence of a beautiful woman most of the day, but it allowed him to retire to the basement where he'd been living the last few weeks without having to answer any questions he honestly didn't know the answer to. She'd also brought him some soup later, which was much appreciated, though he'd paid with a renewed line of questioning regarding Miss Young.

Sunday afternoon, he was out in the field again, bringing in trees customers had selected for their homes. Many of them were still wearing church clothes, and some of the little girls looked like ice princesses twirling around in the snow in their long dresses and coats. Chloe and Bridgette had even stopped by, and he was glad his mother had something else to focus on for a bit. Her questioning had let up, but he knew she wouldn't stop asking until he'd either told her that he and Delaney were not planning on seeing each other again—or they were married.

Once he was certain the trees were all brought in and there wasn't an immediate need for him to stick around, he'd grabbed one of the four-wheelers and taken off for the high ground, eventually coming to a stop where he could still see the tracks he and Delaney had left in the snow the day before. He realized, though he had visited this precise point hundreds, if not thousands, of times, he would never look at it the same way again. Now, that overgrown pine would forever be the place where Delaney had tried to evade his snowballs. That ridge would be where he and Delaney had attempted to make snow angels, where he'd helped her up and first contemplated kissing her. This had always been a special place for Josh, but from now on, no matter where life took him, this place would always be where he first realized he was falling in love with Delaney.

Standing with his boots planted in an inch of snow looking out at the fields of Christmas trees below, many of them still blanketed in white, he knew the way he was feeling didn't make logical sense. How could he be falling in love with her already when they'd only just met? He hadn't even known her last name until she plugged it into his phone. But, there was no doubt in his mind that was what was happening. Unlike all of the other girls he'd dated in the past, with Delaney, he could see a future; he could picture spending his days with her—waking up in the morning next to her, kissing her goodnight every evening. He could envision coming home from work at the end of the day to the smell of her baking, hearing the sound of their children's laughter ringing in the air. That was exactly the future he wanted for himself: a loving wife and children, a house that felt like a home, someone to share his dreams with. Regardless of how many days it had been since they met or how long they'd spent together, he knew already that Delaney could be that woman, the one he'd been dreaming of.

Of course, when he pictured himself coming through the door at the end of the day, he had no idea where that door was or what job he was returning from. Would Delaney be interested in dating him if he decided not to move to the farm? Could they handle a long distance relationship? Eventually, she'd have to move to Washington if he decided that's where he needed to be. Would she be willing to sell the bakery? He could help her find another location, but he knew it wouldn't be the same. What about her family? There were so many things to think about, and he knew eventually they would all need to be considered. For now, however, as he stood staring out at the peaceful valley below him, he took Delaney's advice and said a little prayer that God would guide him in the right direction, that if he was meant to stay in Shepherdstown, he would know that's where he was meant to be, and if he was supposed to be be in Washington, DC, that choice would also become clear.

As he turned to climb back aboard the four-wheeler and head back to the village, he let go a long sigh. He had pretended to listen to trees yesterday when they were joking about her Christmas tree being named Bill, but Josh knew sometimes it seemed equally as difficult to hear God as it was to hear imaginary talking trees. Hopefully, when the answer was sent, Josh would be listening with his whole heart.

CHAPTER 14

Delaney arrived at the bakery earlier than usual Monday morning. She hadn't been getting a lot of sleep since she'd spent the day with Josh, and while it was just the day before yesterday, it seemed like ages ago since she'd talked to him. She'd hoped he'd call or text, but Sunday went by without her phone ringing at all, and though she'd considered giving him a call herself, she decided not to. It was best to let the guy call first, or at least that's what both Nana and her mother would say.

She was pleased to see all the dishes washed and put away in the kitchen, the tables cleaned, and the chairs stacked neatly. Sometimes when the teenagers closed the shop on a Saturday afternoon, she'd come in to a bit of a disaster Monday morning. It was nice to see that these kids were responsible enough to make sure everything was ready to go bright and early Monday morning, especially since she'd seen through the app she used to monitor sales just how busy they had been on Saturday.

Once she'd finished walking through the bakery, she checked the cocoa reserves and saw that they would definitely be needing more today. She also needed to make sure she had enough ingredients on-hand to take with her to Shepherdstown for the shop in the village. Most of the ingredients she used were common kitchen reserves that were used in lots of her recipes, but the one secret ingredient she needed for her cocoa was hidden in a place where no one else knew where or what it was. Behind the giant sugar bags in the back closet, there was a little cutout in the floor her father had designed just for this purpose. As she moved the bags out of the way and popped the wood plank, she immediately realized something was different. The tin that she kept her secret ingredient in was situated differently than it always was. She was consistently very careful to make sure she put it back exactly the same way so that she would know if it had been moved. Something wasn't right.

Delaney pulled the container out of its hiding spot and took the lid off. There didn't appear to be any missing; she was always very careful to observe how much was left so that if something fishy happened, she could tell. There was quite a bit of the secret ingredient left in the container, and it didn't look as if anyone had actually opened it, although it might be hard to tell if someone had judging by the contents alone. Was it possible somebody had seen where she hid it, opened it, and sampled it trying to determine exactly what it was?

Shaking her head, Delaney returned the wood to the floor and replaced the sugar. As soon as she was done making the cocoa, she'd put the container back, but for now, there was no reason to let Cameron or anyone else who might wander in know about her secret hiding spot. Clearly, someone else did know, or else, how could the container have moved? Surely she didn't put it back in the wrong position without noticing?

Deciding there wasn't much she could do about it—and since the recipe was only kept in her own head anyway—Delaney went about making a big batch of cocoa for the shop, hoping it would last a couple of days. She'd need to order some more of just about everything to make sure she had enough to get her through the week and help Lydia as well. While most of the ingredients were ordered through the shop like everything else, the secret one would require a special trip to a specialty grocery store in an adjoining town, a journey she only made by herself. She'd plan on doing that another evening this week.

She had just slid the container back into its hiding place and replaced the wood flooring and bags of sugar when she heard steps outside the back door, followed by Cameron's key in the lock. She'd decided he needed his own key, just in case she didn't make it in on time one morning, and he was responsible enough to trust with it.

"Good morning," he called, as bright and cheery as ever. He took his coat and backpack off and hung them up in their usual place.

"Hi," Delaney said, smiling. "How are you today?"

"Great," Cameron said. He was almost always this chipper in the morning, which made Delaney happy since most teenagers she knew were not. "We were so busy Saturday, it was insane!"

"I know," Delaney replied as she went about prepping to bake a batch of muffins. "I saw on the sales report."

"Francine and Bonnie ended up staying until close just to help us out." He tied his apron on and went about his usual morning duties.

"Really?" Delaney asked, a bit surprised to hear that. "You, Joanna, and Courtney couldn't handle it by yourselves?"

"Well, Courtney ended up leaving early. She said she wasn't feeling very good," Cameron explained.

Delaney hadn't noticed that on the spreadsheet she kept for time cards, but she'd have to check again. "That's too bad," she muttered, wondering if Courtney was really ill or just wanted to go.

"Yeah, she was acting kinda weird all day," he said, shaking his head and getting a cloth out of the drawer to go wash down everything up front again.

Delaney thought back to when she'd stopped by Saturday morning. Courtney had seemed a bit odd, and Joanna and Cameron were also acting a bit... teenager-y. Whatever was up with Courtney, she hoped she would get over it by Saturday so that she could still attend the formal she'd been talking about. Thinking of the dance made her remember how Cameron had been looking at Joanna, and a small smile pulled at the corners of her mouth. He was in the shop now, and she could hear him getting the chairs down so he could wipe everything off and prepare for customers.

Walking into the shop area a few feet, she said, "Cameron, are you going to the Winter Formal?"

He turned and looked at her, and a bit of a shadow passed across his eyes. "I'd like to," he said. "I mean... I'm not much of a dancer, but... well... there's this girl."

Delaney's face lit up. "Anyone I know?"

Even in the dim glow coming from the strands of twinkling Christmas lights that illuminated the room in lieu of the bright fluorescents they'd switch on at opening, she could see he was blushing a bit. "Yeah, you know her."

Delaney couldn't help but smile. "Oh, you like Joanna, don't you?" she gushed, clasping her hands together in front of her. "She's such a sweet girl. Quiet—but so smart. And she really is pretty."

"I know," Cameron said, brushing his long bangs back over his forehead. "But... I asked her if she was going, and she said no. She said she hates dances."

Feeling her joy being pulled away from her, Delaney protested. "Asking someone if they are going to go and asking them to go with you are two different things," she reminded him.

Cameron turned back to the table he'd been wiping down and swiped at it a few more times. "I guess. I just... I mean, what if she says no?"

"She won't." Delaney was quite sure of herself.

He seemed to consider her words. "How do you know?"

"Because I saw the way she was looking at you, too," Delaney replied. "Ask her."

Cameron turned back to face her now. "What about the 'no dating' policy the bakery has? You know, where employees can't date each other?"

Delaney had to fight back a guffaw. "What's that now?" she asked.

"Courtney said that you have a rule that employees can't date each other."

Her eyes wide, Delaney tried to process what he'd just said. Why would Courtney say such a thing? "Uh, Cam, you're the first guy I've ever employed. I've never said anything about any of my employees dating since most of them are married women, and then there are the two teenage girls. I didn't think that would be an issue."

His face puckered up. "Well, then, why would she say that? I mean, I hadn't even said anything to her about wanting to ask Joanna. She just volunteered the information."

"I honestly have no idea," Delaney said, shaking her head and crossing her arms. "She has a boyfriend anyway. It's not like…." She stopped herself. Was Courtney actually jealous of Joanna? That would be a first. It didn't matter. "That's definitely not a policy. If you want to ask Joanna to the dance, you should."

He absorbed the information for a second before nodding and turning his attention to the next table. Though she wasn't sure what that reaction meant—or didn't mean—Delaney decided she'd been enough of a matchmaker for one day, and she went back to the kitchen to get the muffins in the oven.

A few minutes later, Cameron came into the kitchen. "Everything's wiped down and straightened up. I'll turn the lights on and flip the sign in a minute."

Delaney glanced up at the clock and saw that they had about two more minutes to spare before opening time. "Awesome," she said. She was working on a pan of croissants that would go in the oven next.

Cameron leaned on the counter next to where she was working. "Delaney, can I ask you something?"

His face was just about as serious as Delaney could ever remember seeing it. She stopped working on the croissants and looked at him expectantly. "Absolutely."

He let out a loud sigh. "I was hoping Joanna would be at the dance so that I could ask her to dance, but I don't want to ask her to go to the dance with me."

Her eyebrows arched, Delaney asked, "Why is that?"

With another deep sigh, Cameron said, "Because I don't have a car. I'll have to ride my bike to the dance, and I guess I could ask her to meet me there, or something, but I feel like the guy should pick the girl up at her house, you know? And I can't do that."

Delaney felt her heart melt just a bit. "And you can't borrow your parents' car?"

"No," he replied quickly. "My dad has the night off, so he can watch the kids, but my mom has to work, and she'll need the car to drive to the super-center."

Without another thought, Delaney said, "You can borrow my car."

Cameron's eyes widened. "What? Your car? Oh, no, Delaney, I wasn't trying to get you to lend me your car. I just wanted to see if you thought she'd still want to go if she had to meet me there."

Delaney knew Joanna didn't have a car of her own either, that she usually rode in her mom's minivan to work because she didn't have her license, and while she might be willing to meet him there, Cameron was right. It would be more meaningful if he was able to pick her up, especially if he was driving a nice red sports car. "Cameron, I totally trust you to borrow my car. As far as I know, I don't have plans Saturday night, but if that changes, my dad has an old work truck I can borrow that I've driven lots of times, and he just lives down the road. Please, feel free to take my car."

His face lit up, and though he was slowly shaking his head back and forth like he was saying no, his words said otherwise. "I can't believe this. Wow, thank you so much, Delaney."

Before she knew it, he had his arms wrapped around her, and while she let out a small giggle at his enthusiasm, she hugged him back. "You're so welcome. Now, make sure you ask that girl first thing this morning so she can plan her dress."

"I will," Cameron nodded, letting her go. "We have first period together."

Delaney patted him on the back as he stepped around her, headed to the front, his face still beaming. While she was confident Joanna wanted to go, she honestly wasn't sure if she'd be brave enough to say yes. She was hopeful that she would be willing to take a leap of faith and tell Cameron she'd go with him. She was also hopeful that

Courtney wouldn't find out, at least not for a few days. After all, Courtney was acting peculiar, and she had a bit of mean girl in her. If Courtney did something to ruin this for Joanna, Delaney would be greatly disappointed.

Before long, the bakery was hopping. Cameron had left for school, and Edie was doing her best to man the front while Delaney kept the baked goods coming. She'd decided to try a new recipe that morning, a Christmas cookie she'd found online, and while it turned out delicious and was very popular, it had also slowed her down a bit. There were more customers than usual, and she'd spent more time up front than she'd wanted to.

Right before lunch, the door chimed and Delaney looked up to see her friend Olivia's smiling face. Her blonde hair was a bit wind blown despite the beret she had on her head, and her porcelain skin had a bit of a rosy glow to it, likely from the sharp breeze. "Hey, Olivia!" Delaney called. "How are you?"

"Good," she nodded. "I'm sorry I haven't been in recently. I've been so busy."

"Writing the next best seller, no doubt," Delaney smiled. "What can I get you?"

"Just a large cocoa," Olivia replied, then added, "to go."

"You can't stay a while?" Delaney asked, her shoulders slumping in disappointment. She turned to the cocoa machine and began to make her order.

"No, I've got a fast approaching deadline, and I'm not sure how I'm going to get this book finished before the end of January."

Delaney slid the cocoa across the counter to her friend. "Is it the next book in the Virginia Sweethearts series?" she asked. "I am almost done with the last one, and it is so good, Olivia."

Olivia smiled, humbly. "Thank you. I'm glad to hear it. Yes, it's the sequel. And I have to have it finished by January twentieth to meet my deadline." She let out an exasperated sigh. "With the holidays and family visiting… I just can't get as much done as I'm used to."

Delaney nodded. She could definitely understand busy. "Well, I for one hope you finish it soon. I can't wait to see what happens next. I think Elliott is one of my favorite fictional characters of all time."

Olivia giggled. "Everyone loves Elliott. I think I'm just going to rent a cabin up in the mountains, the same place dad used to take us when we were younger, and just lock myself inside for a few weeks and get it done."

"You'll wait until after Christmas though, right?" Delaney asked.

"Yes," Olivia sighed. "I have to. But luckily my folks are going to Cabo for New Years, so the day after Christmas, I'll just be looking for some peace and quiet!"

Giggling, Delaney said, "Well, good luck." Then, deciding her friend looked like she could use a pick-me-up, she took out one of the new cookies she'd just baked and slid it into a paper envelope. "Here, you need this."

Olivia looked at the cookie, then back at her friend. "Oh, Delaney, you don't have to do that."

"I insist," Delaney said. "They're a new recipe, and they are delicious. Now, get out of here. You've got to finish this series so I can find out if Margot and Elliott get together!"

"What do I owe you?" Olivia asked, digging in her back pocket.

"Girl, please," Delaney said, shaking her head. "For the hours of entertainment you've supplied me and the rest of the world, I owe you."

Olivia's smile broadened. "I didn't come in here to take advantage of a small business owner, you know?"

"I know," Delaney replied. "It was nice to see you, though. After you finish the book, we've got to do something fun together."

"Definitely," Olivia replied. "Melody, too." She took out a five-dollar bill and slid it into the tip jar.

Delaney remembered all the fun times they'd had together in high school. The three of them had been almost inseparable. Now, she didn't think Olivia and Melody had done much more than say hello since Melody had been in town. She'd like to help change that. "Absolutely," Delaney nodded. She said goodbye and watched Olivia return to the blustery weather outside.

The rest of the day was just as busy, and before she knew it, it was time for her to head home. She hated to leave Edie when it was so busy, so she decided to stick around and wait until Courtney and Joanna arrived. Even though it would make almost an eleven-hour day for her, they were running low on chocolate chip muffins, one of their most popular items, so she decided to pop another tray into the oven while she waited on the girls. Joanna almost always got there a few minutes before her shift began whereas Courtney would likely be a few minutes late.

When Joanna arrived, Delaney tried to read her expression to see if she looked any happier than usual. She didn't; in fact, as the young girl went about hanging up her backpack and putting on her apron, Delaney thought she actually looked a bit upset. "Is everything okay?" she asked.

"Fine," Joanna mumbled, tightening her ponytail.

"You don't look fine," Delaney observed.

Joanna said nothing, only adjusted her glasses and shrugged her shoulders as she headed toward the front.

Delaney was just about to go ask her if she wanted to talk when Edie came into the kitchen. "Delaney? Josh is here. He's asking for you." Edie was beaming, and Delaney could hardly believe her ears. While she was pleasantly surprised, she'd been working all day and could only imagine what her hair and makeup must look like now. Edie brushed a few loose strands of brunette hair behind Delaney's ear as the baker wiped her hands on a towel. "You look beautiful," Edie assured her.

"Right," Delaney mumbled, setting the towel aside. "Thanks."

Once she saw him, standing against the counter, smiling in anticipation, she was no longer concerned with what she might look like, and she felt her face begin to glow. Joanna was ringing him up, and he slipped her some cash as Delaney approached. "Hi," she said, running her hands along the sides of her jeans. "I didn't expect to see you here today."

He laughed. "I know. I would've called, but I was just headed back from Winchester and thought I'd stop in and see if you were here. I didn't know what time you got off."

Delaney glanced at the time. "About two hours ago."

"Right," he said, chuckling. "I know how that goes."

She wasn't sure what to say, she was so happy and surprised to see him. He did look a bit tired, as someone might who had been delivering Christmas trees all day. But his hazel eyes were twinkling, and his smile lit up her heart. "It's great to see you."

"You, too," he replied. "I actually can't stay too long. I've got one more load to drop off on the way back home. But, while I was in Winchester, I saw a sign for a community production of *A Christmas Carol*, and I thought that might be fun. Do you want to go? It's Friday night."

Delaney was shocked. She certainly hadn't expected him to ask her out on his quick stop just to say hello, especially not in front of Joanna and Edie, who were clearly listening in, but before the question was even out of his mouth, she was nodding. "Yes, I'd love to." He could've asked her to a bathroom cleaning convention and she would've said yes.

"Friday?" Edie echoed. "That's the night of the Christmas parade."

Delaney realized she was right, and even though attending the Charles Town Christmas Parade was an event she'd never missed in her entire life, at that moment, she couldn't have cared less. "That's okay," she shrugged. "I've seen it. Lots of times."

Josh chuckled nervously. "If you'd rather go to the parade, we could do that instead," he offered.

"No, I'd love to go see a play. I can't remember the last time I went to anything like that," Delaney insisted. She'd loved theater when she was in high school, but that seemed like a million years ago, and while Winchester's hometown production wasn't likely to be stellar, it would definitely be an event to remember.

"Well, if you're sure, I'll give you a call later this week and you can give me directions to your house."

"Perfect," Delaney smiled. "And we can talk about the cocoa then, too," she added.

"Yes, we need to do that as well," Josh nodded, and Delaney wondered if that meant his mother had been driving him crazy about cocoa for the last few days. Raising his to-go cup, he said, "It was nice to see you, Delaney."

"You, too," she smiled. "Talk to you soon." She watched him cross to the door, and just as he had done last time, he paused with one hand on the exit and looked back at her. Delaney felt her knees weaken, and she knew her cheeks were ablaze. She didn't care; that man had to be the most handsome one she'd ever seen, and he was sweet, caring, compassionate, smart—perfect. For her anyway.

Once he was gone, Edie said, "Well, willing to miss the Christmas parade for that fellow, hmmm? I do believe you're smitten, Delaney."

There was no use denying it. "I guess you could say that," Delaney replied. She was definitely glad now that she'd decided to stay until the girls got there.

Thinking about Joanna and Courtney caused her to look up at the clock. It was well-past the time Courtney was supposed to be there, and she had yet to show up. Looking to Joanna, Delaney asked, "Do you know where Courtney is?"

Joanna shrugged. "I don't know. I talked to her this morning, but when I smiled at her at lunch, she acted like she didn't know me."

Joanna looked so sad at reliving the experience, Delaney's heart hurt. Courtney could be so rude. "Okay," she said, giving Joanna a sympathetic smile. Maybe that's why she seemed so glum, even though if Cameron had asked her to the dance, Delaney would've expected her to be over Courtney and focused on Cam. "I'll go call her."

As Delaney went to the back to call Courtney in private, the back-door swung open loudly, and a flustered Courtney came in. "Sorry I'm late," she said." Her hair was untamed and she had streaks down her face, as if she'd been crying.

"Is everything okay?" Delaney asked.

"Yeah, everything is fine," Courtney replied as she went to get her apron and threw it on. "It's just been an awful day."

Delaney didn't like the sound of that. Maybe Courtney hadn't been trying to be rude to Joanna. Maybe she just had something else going on. "Anything you want to talk about?"

Courtney looked at her as if she might say something, but then she shook her head. "I'm fine," she said.

Delaney wasn't sure if she trusted that or not, but she decided not to press the issue. She certainly wouldn't feel comfortable talking if Delany tried to force her to. "All right," she said. "Well, call me if you need anything. I'm going to head out."

"Okay," Courtney mumbled, and without saying goodbye, she stepped past Delaney and went to the front. Edie said hello, and Courtney mumbled hi, but she didn't speak to Joanna at all, and when Joanna turned to look at her as if she might greet her, Courtney turned away.

Edie made her way to the back, glancing over her shoulder at the two teenage girls. "I do believe the peace has finally been breached," she said. Edie had been warning her for months that those two just didn't "gee and haw" and that eventually Courtney would do or say something so nasty to Joanna that she wouldn't be able to work with her anymore. While Delaney thought that might be possible based on their personalities, she'd been hopeful that they were both mature enough to keep their differences outside of work. The tension today, however, made Delaney uneasy, and she considered staying until the bakery closed to make sure the girls got along.

As if she was reading her mind, Edie said, "Delaney, you have to go home and get some rest. You can't work a twelve hour shift today."

"Sure I can," Delaney replied. There'd been lots of times when the bakery had first opened that she'd worked much longer than that.

"Not today, not as busy as we've been. Go home and get some rest. I'll be here for another half hour or so, and I'll subtly make sure they know it's imperative that they get along until closing. Okay?"

Delaney wanted to trust Edie, wanted to trust the girls as well, but this was her business they were talking about. What if the girls started arguing in front of the customers—or worse? Surely, nothing like that would happen. Eventually, Delaney gave in. "Okay," she muttered.

Joanna and Courtney would only be alone for an hour. Surely, they would be okay for an hour, wouldn't they?

With one more glance around, Delaney slipped her coat on and grabbed her purse. Looking up at the front, she saw Joanna working the cash register while Courtney refilled drinks and gathered dirty dishes. *Everything would be just fine—right?* It had to be.

CHAPTER 15

The next morning, Delaney walked through the back door of the bakery half expecting to see the entire shop trashed. However, everything was in its place and it was clear that the girls had taken the time to wipe everything down before they left the afternoon before. All the money in the register was counted and bundled correctly, the trays were prepped, and Delaney was able to jump into her morning routine just as usual. With a sigh of relief, she started her baking, hoping whatever was happening between the two teenage girls was over.

She hadn't even gotten the first tray of muffins in the oven when the back door opened. It was a bit too early even for Cameron, and she was surprised to see Courtney standing there, looking dressed and ready for school, with a worried expression on her face.

"Courtney?" Delaney questioned, shocked. Courtney had never come in early before, ever. Even when she was supposed to. Delaney set the tray of baked goods aside and turned to face her. "What's going on?"

"I'm sorry to bother you so early," Courtney said, crossing over to her. "But something has been bothering me, and I needed to talk to you about it, even though I'm not sure how."

Delaney felt her stomach tighten. Was Courtney in some sort of trouble? "What's going on?"

Letting out a loud sigh, Courtney reached into her pocket and took out her phone. "Now that I have a job, I thought it would be nice to buy my family Christmas presents for once. So, I've been doing a lot of looking online, trying to decide what to buy. Well, last night, while I was looking for something homemade to buy my mom—you know how she likes crafts and all that stuff—I found something that I thought you should see." Courtney pulled up a website on her phone and handed it to Delaney.

Her forehead crinkled, Delaney looked at the website. It was one of those sell-your-own-crafts sort of sites, something like Etsy, but not one Delaney was familiar with. It was a picture of a little girl drinking hot cocoa out of a bright red mug. While Delaney didn't recognize the child and supposed it could've been a stock image, the description certainly caught her attention. The listing was for "award winning hot cocoa, just like your nana used to make." Customers could order the dry powder for delivery to their home, and it came with directions for how to mix it yourself.

Confused, Delaney handed the phone back to Courtney. "Okay. I'm not sure what it is you're trying to say."

"I looked at the shop address," Courtney explained, swiping at the screen with her finger. "Look."

Delaney looked at it again. It was an address in Charles Town. She was even more confused now. "Are you saying you think someone's trying to sell my cocoa?"

Courtney sighed heavily. "Delaney, that's Joanna's address. She's attempting to sell your cocoa online and pass it off as her own."

Delaney's eyes widened in disbelief. She really didn't see how that was possible. She began to shake her head.

"I caught her in the closet the other day snooping around," Courtney continued. "I asked her what she was doing, and she said nothing. Ever since then, she's hardly spoken to me. Now, she's hanging out with Cameron a lot. I don't know him very well, since he's new and all, but maybe they're working together. I don't know...."

I just felt like you should know so you can make her stop. I mean, I didn't want to say anything because I'd hate to see either one of them lose their job, but it's not right for them to try and sell your cocoa as their own."

Delaney really wasn't sure what to say. That explained the canister being moved, but how would Joanna even know where she kept it? And did she know enough about baking to guess what the secret ingredient was? Could she replicate her cocoa recipe? Her head was swimming, and she leaned back against the counter, not even sure what to say.

"I want to go before Cameron comes in," Courtney said, backing toward the door. "I don't know if he's involved or not. But... please don't let them know I told you, okay? Can you just say you found it yourself?"

Delaney nodded. "Sure."

"Thank you," Courtney said, offering a weak smile. "I'll be on time today. I promise."

"Okay," Delaney replied. "Have a nice day," she added, forcing a smile

"You, too." Courtney stepped out into the cold, and Delaney tried to return to her muffins, wondering how it was possible that the two kids she trusted the most might be trying to take advantage of her.

It wasn't too long before the door opened again, and Cameron came through. She could tell almost immediately that something was wrong. His disposition was not at all cheerful like it usually was. "Good morning," he muttered as he went to hang up his backpack and grab his apron.

"Hey, Cameron," Delaney said, turning to face him. "What's the matter?" She wondered if Joanna had said no when he'd asked her to the dance or if he was about to tell her he'd helped steal the cocoa recipe.

He sighed, and brushing his hair out of his eyes said, "I'm not sure if I should talk about it at work."

Delaney forced a smile. "You can talk about anything you'd like to to me."

He managed a small smirk. "Well, I took your advice and asked Joanna to the dance. She seemed surprised. She said yes."

Delaney couldn't help but smile at that.

"But then... later, she looked really sad. I asked her what was going on, and she said she'd heard some really bad rumors about herself, like things I don't even want to repeat. It turns out, they were started by someone she trusted, someone she considered a friend. She wouldn't tell me who. Anyway, she was just so gloomy the rest of the day. I wanted to come by yesterday afternoon to check on her, but I couldn't get away. I'm just worried about her."

She couldn't help but feel concerned for Joanna. Delaney had never been the victim of those kinds of vicious rumors, but she'd heard plenty of them when she was in high school. "Does Joanna know who started them?"

"She thinks so, but she wouldn't say. She said she didn't want me to worry about it. But I heard a few of them myself, Delaney, and they weren't nice at all."

Realizing she didn't want to hear them for herself and that he likely wouldn't repeat them even if she asked, Delaney wondered, "What did you say when you heard them?"

"I told the kids repeating them to shut up, that they weren't true. I told them I know Joanna, that we're going to the formal together, and I know for a fact none of it's true. It's just someone who's jealous of her out to dirty her name." He was shaking his head, looking down at the ground. "Delaney, I've met a lot of girls in a couple of different states, but I've never met anyone like Joanna. She's so... nice. And smart. And she's really pretty, too, even though she doesn't like people to notice her. The fact that someone would treat her like this really... sucks."

Delaney didn't care for that word, but she agreed. It wasn't nice at all. "I'm so sorry, Cameron. Hopefully, whoever is spreading these lies will let up now, especially if people like you continue to stand up for Joanna. Just try to help her focus on the dance, keep her mind off of it. It'll blow over eventually." She hoped that what she was saying was true.

CHRISTMAS COCOA

Cameron nodded. "Thanks, Delaney. You really are a good listener. And thanks for telling me to ask her out, too. I'm so glad I did."

"Me, too," Delaney smiled. He went about his usual routine, and she returned to her muffins. She'd known Joanna for years. They even went to the same church. She'd never known her to do anything underhanded or sneaky. Likewise, Cameron was a nice young man who always went above and beyond to make sure he was doing the best job possible. He was working hard to help his family. She just couldn't believe either of them would try and steal her cocoa recipe. There had to be another explanation.

Delaney fished out her phone and pulled up the website Courtney had shown her earlier. She had to do some searching to find the listing, but eventually she did. The mailing address for the company might be Joanna's, but that wasn't the address she was interested in. She might not know too much about technology, but she knew someone who did. She took a screenshot of the listing and returned her focus to the muffins. Once Cameron was off to school, she might have a chance to send what she knew to Josh. She was willing to bet he could figure out where the listing had come from. If anyone was able to track an IP address, she knew Josh could.

JOSH HAD JUST FINISHED UNLOADING his second shipment of Christmas trees for the day when his phone rang. He was pleasantly surprised to see it was Delaney. Climbing back into the cab but not starting the truck, he answered, "Hello?"

"Hey, Josh. Sorry to bother you," she said. The sound of her voice sent tingles down his spine.

"You're not bothering me at all. What's up?" he asked. Her voice sounded a little different than normal. He hoped she wasn't calling to cancel their date. He'd already picked up the tickets earlier that morning.

Delaney sighed into his ear. "I was wondering if you knew how to track an IP address. Like really track it, not just pinpoint a town. I need to know who listed a certain homemade cocoa for sale on one of those sell-from-home sites."

Josh now realized what the concern in her voice was about. "Sure, I can do that," he replied, "although there might be other ways to figure out who listed it. Someone's trying to sell your cocoa?"

"Yes," she replied. "One of the girls who works here says it's the other one, and maybe Cameron. I don't know, Josh, I'm just not buying it. I don't think Joanna would do something like that. She's such a good kid. And Cam? No way."

While he didn't know Cameron personally, he'd been in the shop when Delaney had hired him, and he agreed, he seemed like a good kid. "Can you send me a screenshot of the listing, and I'll take a look?"

"Yes, I have it all ready to go. I just wanted to talk to you about it first. Thank you so much, Josh. I really appreciate your help."

"Of course," he replied. "Any time." Then, he added, "I'm sure you're very busy, but I'm so glad you called. It's nice to hear your voice."

"It's really nice to hear yours, too," she replied, her tone completely different than it had been when he'd first answered. She seemed more relaxed and calm.

"I picked up the tickets while I was in Winchester this morning," he continued. "It's sure to be a great show—starring Lindel Hurst."

"Ooh, who's Lindel Hurst?" Delaney asked.

"I don't know," he admitted, "but I'm sure he's Winchester's finest."

She giggled. "You were in Winchester this morning, and you didn't stop by on your way to say hello to me?"

"Well, it's a lot faster if I take the interstate," he explained. "And besides, my folks are very demanding. They get very angry if I don't stay on schedule." None of that second part was true, of course. He'd considered stopping by to see her both on his way this morning and on his way back, but the interstate did save him quite a bit of time, and while he was always excited to see her, he wanted to wait until Friday to see her again. He needed to attempt to focus on his work—not that he didn't spend the entirety of his long drives dreaming of her brown eyes.

"Whatever," she said in a teasing tone. "I guess I'll let you get back to work and go help Edie out myself. She's swamped over there."

"I'll call you back once I've had a chance to figure this out," he promised.

"All righty," she said. "Thanks again, Josh."

"Talk to you soon." He waited for her to say goodbye and then hung up the phone, still cradling it in his hand, thinking of how nice it had been to hold her hand in his. A few seconds later, a text came through with a picture of the listing in question and a message thanking him for being a "lifesaver."

Josh peered at the picture for a moment and noticed the mailing address was in Charles Town. That didn't necessarily mean the IP address came from the same residence though. He'd need a computer to figure it out, but he assumed there were more clues in the posting, and once he had a chance to sit down and work on it, he was certain he could get Delaney an answer. The idea that someone was trying to pass off her cocoa as there own was troubling, and he knew she had enough on her plate right now without having to worry about hot chocolate thieves.

Putting his phone away, he started the truck and put on his seatbelt, letting his mind wander to what Friday night might be like. He had no idea who Lindel Hurst was either, but if this date ended up being half as good as he imagined it would be, Mr. Hurst would definitely be receiving a five-star review from him.

CHAPTER 16

Delaney hadn't waited around the bakery to see how Joanna and Courtney interacted when they came in. By the time her usual departure time of 2:00 rolled around, she was ready to go. Edie said she'd stay and make sure the girls got settled in and call her if there were any problems, but she hadn't called, and Delaney took that as a good sign, even though she was certain Edie wouldn't have called her anyway unless there had been an actual fight on the shop floor of the bakery.

She'd come home to the wondrous aroma of Nana's beef stew and sat on the couch with her while she strung popcorn chains for the tree, which already looked beautiful now that it was fully decorated. But if Nana wanted popcorn chains, then that's what they would have! Delaney had declined helping since she was more likely to poke her finger with the needle than actually work it through a piece of popcorn anyway.

Nana was excited that Delaney had gotten to watch both episodes of *Judge Judy* and the evening news with her. They were calling for more snow, which made Delaney decide to go chop some firewood before it got too dark. She put on her coat and went out back, turning on the back porch light as she went.

Her dad was nice enough to bring wood down every few weeks, but it wasn't chopped and corded correctly most of the time, and Delaney didn't mind piecing it out so that it would fit in Nana's fireplace. She had a gas heater, too, but the wood stove was cheaper, and that's what they relied on most of the time. As Delaney picked up the axe and positioned one of the larger pieces of wood so she could break it into smaller pieces, she reflected on the day. With each swing of the axe, she felt more and more frustration leave her body. Whoever it was that was trying to steal her recipe, she knew Josh would figure it out. And whatever was supposed to happen with Josh, they would figure that out, too.

The sun had gone completely down below the mountain tops by the time she was satisfied that they'd have more than enough wood to replenish whatever they used of their reserves over the weekend, and Delaney put the axe away and headed back toward the house. She was a little sorer, a little more tired, and a lot more satisfied with life.

A little later, she was sitting in her room going over some numbers on her computer when the phone rang. Glancing down, she was happy to see that it was Josh. With a smile on her face, she answered, "Hello?"

"Hello, can I speak to the world's finest hot cocoa maker, please?" he said in the type of voice a tell-a-marketer might use.

"This is she," Delaney giggled. "How may I help you?"

"I'd like to order five thousand gallons of delicious hot cocoa, please, and I need it by 5:00 AM tomorrow morning."

"Luckily for you, we have a tanker truck out back that holds just that much," she replied, playing along with his little game.

"Wonderful! Let me give you my fake address, and you can go ahead and drive that on over."

She started laughing, glad to be reminded of his sense of humor. "I'd rather have a real address, thank you very much."

"You would?" Josh asked. "Good. Because I have one for you."

"You do?" she asked, catching her breath. She thought he might be fast, but she didn't realize he'd be that fast.

"Yes," Josh replied. "I used the IP address to trace an actual address, but I just used that for confirmation. It really wasn't that difficult to get a real address."

Delaney was puzzled. "It wasn't?"

"No, the shop the cocoa was listed in is new, but it was made from an existing account on the website, so I looked at the mailing address on that account, and it's different. That original shop has been in existence for about five years, so I'm sure that's the legitimate address. The shop sells various homemade craft items, and it's owned and operated by a Shannon Tobak who lives on West Fifth Street in Charles Town. Do you need the exact address?"

Delaney knew he was still talking, but she'd stopped listening when she heard the name Shannon Tobak. She gasped, unable to believe her ears. "Did you say Shannon Tobak?" she repeated, once she was able to formulate a sentence.

"Yes," Josh confirmed, his tone indicating his concern. "Everything all right, Delaney?"

It took her a moment to answer. "Yes, it's just... that's Courtney's mom."

"Okay," he said slowly, the word coming out more as a question than a statement.

Delaney realized he probably had no idea why that was such a shock to her. "Josh, Courtney is the girl who told me that Joanna stole the cocoa recipe. It wasn't Joanna at all. It was Courtney. Why would she do that?"

"Oh," Josh replied, clearly thinking before he replied. "I don't know. Is there some reason why Courtney would want to see Joanna get in trouble?"

Delaney had no answer for that. The girls had worked together for a year with no problems. "Maybe something happened at school?"

Josh was quiet for a moment before he asked, "Could it be Cameron?"

"No," Delaney answered quickly before she even thought about a response. "I mean... I don't think so. Courtney has a boyfriend. Kyle or Skyler or something. I can't imagine she'd be upset at Joanna because Cameron asked her to the Winter Formal."

"When did Courtney tell you about this cocoa posting?"

"The day after Cam asked Joanna, but whoever messed with my cocoa tin did it before that because I noticed it the morning I told Cam to ask Joanna out."

"Is it possible Courtney knew Cameron liked Joanna and started formulating this plan in advance?"

Delaney's head was beginning to hurt and her heart sank. How could Courtney do something so underhanded. "I don't know," she admitted. "Maybe. I guess I need to have a chat with Courtney tomorrow."

"Maybe she'll confess. She's just a kid. She might not have really thought about what she was doing."

"I guess so," Delaney said, shaking her head slowly from side to side in disbelief. "She's worked for me for almost a year. I just can't believe she'd be so sneaky."

"It might be possible that someone else is trying to frame her, but I find it highly unlikely. Especially since the IP address indicated a spot very close to her residence, and it is her mom's account."

"Right," Delaney sighed. "Well, thank you so much for helping me out with this. I can't tell you how much I appreciate it."

"No problem," Josh replied, his tone changing from concern to a more sincerely content tone. "I'm glad you thought to call me."

"Are you kidding?" she asked. "I thought of calling you immediately." She realized what she was saying a moment to late, but then, surely he knew by now she was spending most of her time thinking about him—didn't he? Before he could say anything else about her admission, she asked, "How's your dad? Did you find a doctor?"

"My mom's going to take him to a specialist right after the holidays," he said, with a sigh. "He doesn't want to go, of course, but she said she wouldn't bake her pecan pie if he didn't agree, and well, that did it."

Delaney giggled. "Your mom must bake one amazing pecan pie then."

"It's the best in the world," he replied. "I mean, unless you also bake a pecan pie, then it might be the second best."

She burst out laughing again as he began to back track. "I do bake a good pecan pie, but Josh, don't worry about having to choose between your mom's baking and mine. I'm not jealous of other people's skills—except for maybe when it comes to cocoa. That's the one thing I will defend to the ends of the earth."

"Is that because it's a family recipe?" he asked.

"Yes, it's Nana's recipe, and it's based off of her grandmother's recipe, so it's generations old. There's a lot of Young family pride in that cocoa recipe." She was thoughtful for a moment before she added, "I guess that's why it hurts so much to see anyone try to take advantage of it."

"Kids don't always appreciate history and tradition like we do," he reminded her. "Sometimes you've got to live a little before you can really understand what life is all about."

Reflecting on his statement, she realized he was right. "How'd you get to be so wise?" she asked.

He chuckled. "Life will do that to you sometimes, I guess."

She decided it wasn't necessary to ask him any more about trials and tribulations at that moment. "I'm really looking forward to seeing you Friday."

"Me, too. The show starts at eight, so I guess I should pick you up before seven to make sure we get there on time."

"Okay," she replied. "I'll text you my address. Even though it's out in the country, Google works."

"Sounds good. I thought we could grab a bite to eat afterward, unless you need to get back home sooner. Or is that too late to eat? Should we eat before?" He sounded nervous as he shifted from one question to the next.

Delaney tried not to giggle at his indecisiveness. Perhaps he really didn't date that much. "It will be a little late for dinner, but that's okay. I can bring us a snack for the drive if you don't mind crumbs in your truck."

"I was actually going to drive my car for a change. It's been in the garage for a while. But, no, I don't mind a few crumbs."

"I think Nana will let me stay out until at least midnight, although if I'm not in by then she might ground me," Delaney teased.

"I might turn into a pumpkin at midnight, and then you might be tempted to turn me into a pie," he replied, a playful lilt to his voice.

"Well, then I guess we better be back here before then."

He laughed, and Delaney enjoyed the sound of it, realizing she might not speak to him again for a few days. "I think I can manage that. Have a good night, Delaney."

"You, too, Josh," she said, hanging on to his name as he said goodbye and she repeated it back to him before hanging up. She stared at her phone for a second, wondering how she got so lucky. She'd thought her relationship with Bradley was the real thing, but only a few minutes after meeting Josh she knew he was such a better man than Bradley.

Sighing, she leaned back against the headboard. Surely, Josh wasn't just taking her out because he needed a break from the tree farm with the plan to never see her again after this, was he? He was really interested in her, right? She knew he was concerned about living so far away, and it didn't sound like he was ready to commit to taking over the tree farm. But Delaney thought what they had was at the very least the promise of a lasting relationship. She was hopeful that he would be willing to take a leap of faith with her. If not, she didn't know what she would do. It hadn't been that long on the calendar since he'd first walked into the bakery, but she was already fully invested in being with him for the long haul.

Eventually, she returned her attention to the spreadsheet before her, which reminded her she'd have to have a very difficult conversation with Courtney the next day. She prayed that God would give her the right words to say to help Courtney to come clean and realize why what she did was wrong. She hated confrontation, but Delaney knew she had an opportunity to help this young lady learn a very valuable lesson if she handled it correctly. That, too, was a lot of pressure, and after a few minutes, she put her laptop aside and started to pray, asking for guidance. By the time she was done, she thought she knew how she would handle it, and she went about getting ready for bed with a lot less weight on her shoulders.

WEDNESDAY MORNING, Cameron had seemed a little more like himself, but he still said Joanna was having issues, and Delaney's heart ached for the young girl. She didn't say anything to Cameron about the cocoa, though. She knew he likely had no idea what Courtney had done. He mentioned that Joanna was still upset that someone was spreading rumors about her, but Cameron still didn't know who it was. Unfortunately, Delaney was pretty sure she did.

She decided not to tip Courtney off that she knew what she was up to or else she might not come in to work at all that day, so she waited for the girls to come in for their shift, going over what she thought she might say for most of the hours she was baking that day. Eventually, school was out, and Joanna came in through the back door. She managed a smile when Delaney greeted her, but Delaney could easily see everything wasn't okay, and she felt terrible that Joanna was having to go through this.

Ten minutes later, and five minutes after her shift was supposed to start, Courtney bounded in. "Sorry I'm late," she said when she noticed Delaney standing near the counter looking at her expectantly. "Ugh, Holly wanted a ride, but then she got busy flirting with Rich, and I couldn't get her to go. And then Kyler needed to go back for his cell phone...." She rolled her eyes and let out a long sigh, like her boyfriend forgetting his cell phone was the end of the world.

Without acknowledging everything else she'd just said, Delaney replied, "We need to talk." She'd already let Edie know she'd be occupied for a while once Courtney arrived, though she hadn't hashed everything out with her other employee, so she knew they'd get a bit of privacy. Nevertheless, Delaney gestured to the closet, thinking it would be best if they could go in there and shut the door.

Courtney's eyes grew wide. "Okay," she said slowly. She took off her coat and hung it up but she didn't bother to put on an apron. She followed Delaney into the supply closet and waited next to boxes of ingredients, her arms crossed in front of her.

Delaney closed the door and turned to face her. She looked at her intently for a second, remembering how her mother used to break her with just such a look. Maybe that would work on Courtney as well. Clearing her throat, she asked, "Is there something you want to tell me?"

Digging the toe of her left Kick into the tile, Courtney said, "I'm not sure I know what you're talking about."

With a calm tone, Delaney said, "I think you do."

"Um, is this about Joanna?" Courtney asked. "Because I didn't really say any of those things about her. I mean… I heard them, and I didn't, like, disagree, but I didn't really start any of the rumors."

Her eyes widened, and Courtney's expression told her that the young girl realized Delaney hadn't known for sure she was involved in the rumors until just now. Courtney attempted to backtrack, "Oh, that's not what…."

"The cocoa, Courtney. I wanted to talk about the cocoa. But… you were involved in the rumors, too?" Delaney asked, her heart feeling even more heavy than it had before. "I thought Joanna was your friend."

"She was, I guess," Courtney shrugged. "I mean, we don't really talk that much at school. She's not really like the other girls I hang out with. I try to be nice to her, but she's just so… weird."

Delaney swallowed hard. "It really hurts to hear you say that. Joanna is very nice. Sure, she's smart, and sometimes that can make a person stand out, but to hear you say you helped spread rumors about her…. Courtney, I thought you were better than that."

"You don't understand, Delaney," Courtney shot back, her voice raising. "I try to be nice to her, but she doesn't even care. And then… when Cam started talking to her at school, and all the other girls were like, 'Why is that cute guy from your work so interested in Joanna?' it made me mad. Like, why does he care so much about her?"

"So you're jealous that Joanna's gotten so much of Cameron's attention? But you have a boyfriend."

"I know," Courtney said, flipping her hair over her shoulder. "But Kyler's a dumb jock. And Cameron's, like, a real guy. I mean, he's like an adult. He's cool. Everyone likes him. I guess... I just didn't like that he was so interested in Joanna and not me."

"So you decided to spread some rumors about her and try to get her fired?" Delaney asked, trying very hard to maintain her cool even though she was starting to grow more than a little upset.

Courtney was carefully studying the floor again. "I didn't mean to get her fired," she said quietly. "I just wanted her to get in trouble. I thought if Cameron knew she was stealing your recipes, maybe he wouldn't like her so much."

"But you tried to tie him to it, too," Delaney reminded her.

With a big sigh, Courtney said, "I thought if he got in trouble, maybe I could make him feel better."

Delaney shook her head slowly from side to side as Courtney looked up at her, tears in her eyes. "Wow, Courtney. I'm so... disappointed in you right now. You've worked here for almost a year, and we've never had any major issues. Sure, you've been late a few times. But you've been trustworthy and easy to get along with. This whole thing just makes me really sad."

Tears were streaming down Courtney's cheeks now. "I'm sorry, Delaney. I never meant to disappoint you. I didn't really steal your recipe. I just wanted you to think someone had. No one ever ordered it, and if they had I wouldn't have been able to ship it anyway, because I don't know it. And... I know I've been just awful to Joanna."

"Yes, you have," Delaney agreed. "Listen, if you're truly sorry for what you did, then you need to apologize to her, not me. And you need to make sure those rumors stop, too. I'll go cover for her, and she can come back here, and you can tell her how you feel, okay?"

"Yes, I'll apologize," Courtney agreed, brushing the tears away on the back of her hands. "Am I fired?" she asked, a solemn expression on her pretty face.

"No, you're not fired," Delaney said, shaking her head. "I believe in second chances. But you've got to promise that nothing like this will ever happen again."

"Thank you," Courtney said, flinging her arms around Delaney. "My mom said if I got fired I'd be grounded for a month, and that would mean I'd have to miss the Winter Formal." She realized it might not be appropriate for her to hug her boss at that moment and promptly let go. "I promise you'll never have another issue with me again. I'll never even be late again."

"Okay," Delaney agreed, doubting the latter part of that statement was true. She reached for the doorknob but then stopped. "By the way, how did you know where I keep the tin with my secret ingredient?" she asked.

"Oh, I discovered it a couple of months ago when I was getting a bag of sugar," Courtney replied. She stepped on top of the board that Delaney popped out of place to access her hiding place and there was a little squeak. "My grandma has a secret hiding place in her kitchen where she keeps her stash, too, and it makes the same sound when you step on it."

Delaney shook her head. She had no idea that board squeaked. She wondered if everyone knew her secret ingredient was down there, and no one ever mentioned it. She'd need to find a new hiding place. "What's your grandma's secret stash?" she asked out of curiosity.

"I don't know," Courtney admitted. "I can't tell what it is either. But I will tell you she bakes the most delicious pecan pie on earth."

Delaney had to fight back a fit of laughter, thinking about the conversation she'd had with Josh the night before. Perhaps a pecan pie bake off was in order. "I'll go get Joanna," she said. "Thank you for being honest with me, Courtney. It means a lot to me that you were willing to apologize and accept responsibility for your actions."

"Thank you for giving me another chance, and I promise I'll delete that website as soon as I get home."

"I believe you," Delaney said, smiling before she went out. She hoped that Courtney would actually hear "I believe *in* you." Sometimes all it took was a little faith from someone who didn't have to give it to teach a lesson that would last a lifetime.

Delaney went up front and told Joanna that Courtney needed to speak to her. The blonde looked a little nervous, but Delaney gave her a reassuring smile, and she headed to the back. A few minutes later, the teens emerged smiling, with their arms around each other. Delaney took off her apron, and turning to Edie she said, "My work here is done." Edie laughed, and Delaney went to the back to hang up her apron, grab her purse, and sneak out the back door like the hero from a western movie riding off into the sunset. Of course, unlike The Lone Ranger, she'd have to ride back in the next day, but at least for now she had saved the damsel in distress and brought the villain to justice… or something like that.

CHAPTER 17

Delaney was wearing a long red velvet dress and thick black tights with black boots. She planned to wear her long black dress coat as well. She wanted to look nice, but she also wanted to be warm. It was a bit windy outside and there was a chance of snow. Nana had insisted she borrow her mistletoe earrings, which her grandfather had given his wife as a gift a few years before he passed away, and even though Delany thought it was a little cheesy, she'd agreed to wear them. Her hair was pulled back in a half updo with little curls framing her face, so she didn't think the earrings were too terribly noticeable, though she had a feeling Josh would love that she had borrowed something sentimental from her nana should the topic come up.

She was ready to go well before he was due to arrive. The excitement building inside her had been too much for her to handle, so she went ahead and got ready, and now she sat on the sofa near Nana's recliner trying to watch *The Santa Clause*, though she really hadn't heard a word Tim Allen had said in the last twenty minutes. The twinkling lights on the Christmas tree were a constant reminder of the wonderful day she'd spent with Josh, just as he said the tree would be, and she spent most of her time staring into the warm glow wondering what fate had in store for her tonight.

Finally, a little before 7:00, Delaney heard the familiar crunch of gravel outside and knew that Josh had arrived. Planting both feet firmly on the floor, she leaned forward and took a couple of deep breaths, trying to calm her racing pulse.

"Is he here?" Nana asked, her hearing no longer as good as it used to be.

"I believe so," Delaney replied, straightening her dress.

Nana's face lit up. "Oh, goody. I finally get to meet him."

She gave him a moment to get out of the car and approach the porch. Two quick knocks on the door, and Delaney slowly pulled herself to standing. As she walked by, Nana reached out and squeezed her hand.

Delaney glanced through the glass at the top of the door to make sure it was him and was delighted to see his familiar face smiling back at her. She pulled the door open with one last deep breath. "Hi, Josh," she said, smiling, hoping he couldn't see how nervous she was.

"Hi," he replied. He was wearing a nice brown coat with matching dark slacks and a green shirt with a red tie. His hair was about as tamed as she'd ever seen it, and she couldn't help but think he was the most handsome man she'd ever seen. "This is for you," he said, holding out a wreath. "My mom made it."

The wreath was freshly cut and smelled wonderful. Golden jingle bells and red ornaments adorned the sides with a big red bow at the bottom. "Oh, it's so pretty," Delaney said, holding it at arm's length so she could admire it. "Look, Nana," she said, stepping toward her grandmother.

"Isn't that nice," Nana said, smiling but not getting up from her comfy recliner.

As Delaney walked over to her so she could get a better view, she remembered her manners. "Oh, Josh, you can come in. I'm sorry," she said.

He stepped through the door and pushed it closed behind him.

"No problem. You must be Nana," he said, and Delaney realized he probably didn't have any idea what her real name was.

"Nana, this is Josh. Josh, this is Nana. Her real name is Nora Jean but everyone calls her Nana."

"That's right," Nana said, taking his outstretched hand. "Awful nice to meet you, young man."

"It's wonderful to meet you, too," he said patting her hand gently with his free one. "Delaney has told me how much she enjoys living with you. And I sure am impressed with your cocoa recipe."

Nana snickered. "She gives me too much credit. I know she's made that recipe all her own. But she's a good girl, and I'm lucky to have her here to take care of me."

"You take care of me, too, Nana," Delaney reminded her.

"You kids be careful tonight. Don't drive too fast," Nana warned as Josh released her hand.

"I'll take good care of her," Josh assured the grandmother.

Delaney set the wreath against the table near Nana's chair, thinking she'd hang it up when she got home. She leaned over to kiss Nana's cheek. "Night, Nana. See you in the morning." She knew Nana would be in bed long before she got home. She liked to go to bed early so she could get up with the roosters.

"Night, dear. It was so nice to meet you, Joshua," Nana added.

"Nice meeting you, too," he replied, and Delaney thought it was sweet that he didn't insist she call him Josh or attempt to correct her.

"Are you ready?" she asked.

"Yes," Josh replied, gesturing toward the door.

"The cocoa's right there in that big tin, if you want to grab it," Delaney said, gesturing toward the tin she'd purposely set by the door earlier in the evening so she wouldn't forget it. He reached down and picked it up as she held the door for him. "The directions for how to mix it are on the side. I taped the lid closed, so hopefully it won't spill all over your car." She slipped her coat on and grabbed her handbag where she'd stashed a couple of cookies and little bottles of water for the snack she'd promised.

"Spilling it would be bad," Josh agreed as he carried the container out toward his car. Delaney looked out to see a black Mustang in the drive. It was nice and shiny and looked like it might go really fast. Just her type of car.

"Do you want me to get the door and you can put it in the back?" she asked.

"If you'll get the driver's side, that would be great," Josh replied as Delaney hurried over and did just that. He set the tin down in the back while Delaney waited, and once he had it situated, he followed her around to the passenger side so he could get the door for her.

"Thank you," Delaney said with a smile as she slid into the seat. He was already so much more of a gentleman than Bradley had ever been.

The ride to Winchester would take about forty minutes, and Delaney was certain they would spend the whole time chatting. Josh was so easy to talk to; she didn't even have to try with him. It was nice to be able to converse with someone interesting and not constantly have to struggle to come up with something to say. With Josh, it was natural.

The first topic he'd asked about was the situation with the girls at work, and she'd filled him in on what had transpired as they munched their cookies. Since the conversation she'd had with Courtney and Joanna, the girls had been getting along much better, and she was almost as excited about tomorrow's Winter Formal as the kids.

"I think it's so nice of you to loan Cameron your car," Josh said. "He seems like a really good kid."

"He is," she assured him. "I wish I could pay him more so he could get his own wheels soon. But he's trying to help out his folks, and I'm not sure how long it might take for him to save up."

"A lot of trucking companies around Winchester are hiring. Maybe his dad should look over here," Josh suggested, and Delaney made a mental note to suggest it to him. "Are you sad you're missing the Christmas parade?"

"Not really," Delaney said, though she was sure it would be a good time. "Who would rather go stand outside in the cold to watch a parade than see the great Lindel Hurst on stage, live and in person?"

"You do have a point," he laughed. "I just hope his performance is as good as last year's. The local newspaper described it as, 'a treasure to behold.'"

"That will be hard to top," Delaney giggled. "No, the parade is a big deal, but the bigger deal is the Christmas Festival, which happens every year on Christmas Eve. If you really want to have a good time in small town Charles Town, that is the place to be."

"Oh, yeah?" he asked, glancing at her briefly before returning his attention to the road. It was dark by now, but there was a bit of traffic, and Delaney could easily see the winding highway in front of them. The mountains on either side still had a dusting of snow which was illuminated by the starlight.

"Every year, the Baptist church in town hosts the Festival, but everyone participates. Practically the whole town comes to the booths during the day to shop and eat way too much food. We always have a ton of customers that day. And then there's a performance in the evening with lots of different choirs and musicians. The children's choir is always adorable."

Josh ran a hand through his hair. "That does sound like a lot of fun. I might be being a bit presumptuous, but if you can stand me after tonight, maybe we could go together."

Delaney felt a rush of warmth to her face. They hadn't even been on this date for an hour and he was already asking her out again. "That sounds like a lot of fun," she said.

"Unless of course, you already have plans."

She laughed. "No, this time of year, I don't have a lot of time. Nana and I usually go together, and my parents meet us there."

"I would love it if Nana went with us. She is... a gem."

"She really is," Delaney agreed. Thinking of her grandmother warmed her heart, and she was so happy that Josh could see how precious she was in just the few minutes he'd spent with her. She was certain they would be fast friends in no time at all.

"Do you think things will slow down after the holidays?" he asked, slowing behind a big truck.

Delaney sighed. "I don't know. Part of me hopes so, but it's been nice not to have to worry about any of my expenses this month."

He nodded. "I can imagine. Running a family business is so difficult."

"Is your dad ready for a break?" she asked, straightening her hair.

"I think so," Josh replied. "He would never admit it, though."

She studied his profile for a moment before she said, "I bet they hate for the holidays to end because they know you'll be leaving soon."

Slowly, Josh nodded. "I try to come and visit them a couple of times each month, but it's not the same as being home."

Not sure she wanted to hear the answer, she took a deep breath and asked, "When will you go back to Washington?"

He checked his mirrors before answering, surely a sign he was stalling. Eventually, he said, "I'm supposed to be back at work January fifth. I usually go back the Saturday before."

Delaney didn't say anything. Thoughts of Josh being so far away made her sadder than they should since she hadn't even known him that long. She had no idea at this point if he'd want to see her after the holidays or not. She hoped so, but she also knew how difficult long distance relationships could be. The last one she'd attempted hadn't lasted, and even though she already felt her connection with Josh was very different than what she'd had with Bradley, being apart was never easy.

They began to enter the outskirts of Winchester, so she said nothing in response. A few minutes later, they were pulling into a parking lot outside of the local auditorium. It wasn't big, but it was larger than any performance center in Charles Town for certain. The snow was coming down softly, and Delaney made sure her coat was secured before she reached for the door handle.

She didn't get a chance to open it. Josh quickly moved around the front of the car and pulled the door open for her, offering her his hand. With a beaming smile, he said, "Are you ready to see some community theater?"

Giggling, Delaney slipped her hand in his. "As ready as I'll ever be." They walked hand in hand into the auditorium, and Delaney pushed thoughts of what might happen in January aside. She was here with Josh now, and that's all that mattered.

The auditorium was decorated with Christmas wreaths, garlands, and dozens of twinkling trees of various sizes. Delaney loved the red velvet bows and the gold ornaments that sparkled in the dim light. Josh presented his tickets, and they were ushered to their seats, which were toward the front in the center. The plush red matched the décor, and Delaney took her coat and draped it across her lap on top of her handbag, realizing she'd inadvertently worn a dress that also matched the seats.

Josh didn't seem to notice. "What do you think?" he asked, hanging his own coat over the back of his seat.

"It's nice," she replied. "Great seats."

"Well, you know, if you're going to see a production of this caliber, you've got to be willing to spend a little cash."

She giggled. "I really love *A Christmas Carol*," she said. "I read it when I was younger, and I think I've seen every version of the movie ever made."

"Even the Muppets version?"

"Oh, yes. That's one of my favorites," she replied, grinning. "I love the song Kermit sings with the little frog guy. What's his name?"

Josh thought for a second. "I believe his real name is Robin, but he's playing Tiny Tim."

"Well, yes, I knew he was playing Tiny Tim. Robin. That's right. Why do you know that?"

Letting out a sigh, Josh said, "I have nieces remember. They love that movie, too."

"It's so cool that they've watched it. It's older than we are."

"True. I like for them to watch the classics," he nodded. "Muppets, Charlie Brown, the original Grinch—not that Jim Carrey nightmare."

Delaney giggled again and didn't bother to mention she actually liked the remake. "I love that you spend so much time with them."

He tipped his head back and smiled. "I miss them a lot when I'm at home. They're growing up so quickly."

Nodding, Delaney said, "I can imagine it must be hard to leave them."

Josh slowly nodded but didn't say anything more. A few minutes later, the house lights dimmed, and Delaney turned her attention to the stage, hoping that this small town performance was entertaining. She knew these weren't professional actors, per se, but she admired anyone who was willing to get up on stage in front of this many strangers. She had her fingers crossed that Lindel Hurst and company would give the performance of their lives.

Delaney wasn't disappointed. Despite the sets being a bit amateurish and the actor playing Bob Cratchit forgetting a line that required a prompt from Scrooge, the performance was actually very good, and Lindel Hurst made the old geezer quite believable, particularly when he transformed into a benevolent, generous soul at the end. The cast earned a standing ovation, and the little boy playing Tiny Tim was so adorable, when he came out to bow everyone cheered even louder. By the end of the production, Delaney's cheeks hurt from smiling so much.

Before they made their way out of the hall, Josh leaned over and whispered into her ear, "See, I told you Lindel Hurst wouldn't let us down."

"He was wonderful!" Delaney proclaimed, absolutely meaning it. "I really think he was just about as good as Michael Cain."

"I don't know about that," Josh replied as they began to make their way out of the row of seats to the aisle. "But he was definitely better than Jim Carrey."

Delaney laughed so hard, the person in front of her glanced back to see if she was okay. "You really have something against Ace Ventura, don't you?" she asked.

"I guess I've just never been a fan," he admitted with a shrug.

"Well, I am a fan of Lindel Hurst's for sure," Delaney said, and though part of her was exaggerating for humor's sake, she really did think the actor had done a phenomenal job.

"Maybe he'll repeat his performance next year, and we can make this a tradition," Josh offered.

Delaney felt her cheeks turning red, and she was glad he was behind her and might not be able to see. Was he really that comfortable with her that he thought they might be together at this time next year? Without turning completely around, she said, "I hope so. If he doesn't get signed by some major production company between now and then."

They were out of the auditorium now, and Josh led her to the side so he could take her coat and hold it open for her to slip into. "That's a possibility," he admitted, smiling. "Would you like to go get a bite to eat? I saw a little Italian place that looked promising when I was picking up the tickets the other day."

"That sounds amazing," Delaney replied. Once her coat was on, he took her hand and smiling, led her out into the falling snow. Even though it was cold and windy, snowflakes dancing down from the heavens and collecting in her long brown tresses, Delaney felt just as warm as she did when she was home by the fireplace.

THE RESTAURANT WAS NEARBY, but it wasn't as crowded as Delaney thought it might be considering the crowd leaving the auditorium all at the same time. It was quaint inside, with pendulum lights hanging over each table. They sat in a booth with a window, a red and white checkered tablecloth and a faux candle setting the ambiance, and Delaney enjoyed watching the snow falling outside as she sat cozy in Josh's company.

She ordered the lasagna, her very favorite Italian dish, and was nibbling on her salad, trying to wait until her entrée arrived to dig into the fresh bread, but it smelled heavenly and she wasn't sure how long she could wait. Josh was not waiting for his spaghetti to sample the steaming breadsticks, and when he let out a groan of satisfaction, she gave up and reached for one herself. "This is melt-in-your-mouth good," she said between bites. "Why was I trying to wait?"

He laughed. "I have no idea. The bread is the best part."

She shook her head. "I know. But as a baker, I have to be extra careful about calories. Someone has to eat that thirteenth treat every time to make sure they're right, you know?"

"Ha, I don't think you have anything to worry about," he said, and

Delaney felt her face flush. He was quiet for a moment before he said, "How is it that you don't have a boyfriend?"

She felt her face turn even redder. She set what was left of her breadstick aside and let out a sigh. "I did. His name was Bradley, and he lived in Baltimore. It was just... too hard living so far away from each other. We lasted about a year, but six months ago, he said it was too much. And I haven't heard from him since."

Josh's expression was very sympathetic, as the corner of one side of his mouth creased and he began to slowly shake his head. "I'm sorry to hear that, Delaney."

"No, it's okay," she assured him. "I mean... he was right. It was hard. And he was a lawyer, which meant he was busy a lot of the time. I couldn't drive over every weekend because of the bakery. We were better off calling it quits before it got too serious."

"Still, it's never easy to end a serious relationship," Josh replied, offering her a smile.

Delaney shrugged. "No, it wasn't. But I'm definitely past it now." She pulled off another hunk of bread, but before she took a bite, she asked, "What about you? When was your last serious relationship?"

He ran a hand through his hair and seemed to think for a second. "Honestly? College. I mean... I've been so busy at work I haven't gone on more than a date or two with any woman in the last four or five years. There have been a couple of girls I thought I might want a relationship with, but they're never quite who I think they are."

Though she was surprised to hear that, Delaney quickly brought her raised eyebrows into check. "Dating is hard," she admitted. "I never make it a priority. It's just been easier to focus on work and assume I have years ahead of me to worry about it."

"I agree," he said with a chuckle. "But..." he looked up at her, "when the right person comes along, it doesn't seem so hard anymore."

Delaney felt the heat rising in her cheeks again as she stared into his hazel eyes, and if it hadn't been for the waitress bringing their food right then, she thought she might be caught in his spell forever. She turned her attention to the lasagna, but she couldn't help but smile between bites, her heart flittering in her chest. Every time she glanced up at him, he was smiling back at her. Josh definitely had a point; there was nothing difficult about this date at all. Of course, things might change when he went back to Washington. For now, she'd try to stay in the moment and fully enjoy the time they had to spend together, even if it might only be a few more weeks.

They chatted over dinner about anything and nothing, including more favorite movies, such as *White Christmas* and *It's a Wonderful Life*. They discussed favorite Christmas carols and who sang the best rendition of "Oh, Holy Night" on the Christmas radio station they were listening to. On the way back to the car, Josh held her hand and only let it go long enough to run around to the driver's side and climb in, reaching for it again as soon as his seatbelt was buckled.

The ride home was relatively quiet as they enjoyed Christmas carols on the radio and the gentle lull of the falling snow tinkling against the windshield. Delaney loved the feel of his strong hand in hers, and she could imagine many, many more such drives in their future. Hopefully, the distance they had to travel to see each other would just be between Shepherdstown and Charles Town and not on to Washington, but Delaney knew that if Josh was as committed to her already as she was to him, they would find a way to make it work.

Eventually, they reached the road that wound its way up to Nana's house, and Delaney let out a deep breath, sad to see the night end. The snow was falling faster now, and Josh put the car in park and gave her hand a squeeze before coming around to open her car door.

Delaney stepped out into the snow and hooked her arm through his as he led her to the front porch. The light was on, but she could see through the window that the fire was low and the house lights were all off, a sign Nana had gone to bed. Turning to Josh, she said, "Thank you so much for such a wonderful evening."

He smiled down at her, the tips of his shoes just in front of hers. "Thank you. I really had a great time."

"Me, too," she assured him, looking up into his hazel eyes.

"I hope we can go out again sometime really soon."

"Me, too," she repeated. She realized her eyes had fallen from his eyes to his lips, and she quickly raised her gaze, hoping he hadn't noticed.

He must have, though, because when she looked up, his eyes were locked on her mouth instead of her eyes. She broke into a giggle. "You know, I don't usually kiss on the first date," she said, a teasing tone to her voice.

His face contorted into a crooked grin. "Oh, yeah, right. I just...."

"Of course, if you wanted to count this as a second date.... I mean, technically, you did ask me to go on a tour of the farm with you, so...."

Before she could finish the statement, he leaned forward and caught her lips with his. His mouth was as warm and soft as she had imagined it would be, and Delaney inhaled the comforting scent of pine and mint. He pulled away almost as suddenly as he had kissed her, but he was smiling, and taking a step back toward the car, he said, "Goodnight, Delaney. I'll talk to you soon."

"Goodnight," Delaney replied, certain her face must match her dress. She watched him bound away and continued to stand on the front porch watching his car until he'd turned and disappeared down the lane out of sight.

She took a deep breath, inhaling the fresh December air, and took a few steps off of the porch so she was standing in the yard. She spread her arms, and slowly began to twirl, the dancing snowflakes accumulating on her black coat, on her handbag, and in her hair. Tipping her head back, she opened her mouth and caught some of those flakes on her tongue as she gazed up into the starlit skies. She knew up there, the God of the heavens was smiling down at her, and she finally felt He'd answered her prayers and sent her a love to last a lifetime.

CHAPTER 18

It was the last Saturday before Christmas, which meant the tree lot was busier than ever, and once Josh had the cocoa set up for his mom, he was busy all day bringing in trees and helping customers. He'd only had a few minutes to check on his mother, but she said the hot cocoa was a huge hit, and she felt so relieved knowing that the customers had absolutely nothing to complain about. Everyone was having a wonderful time.

While Josh drove the tractor, his mind returned continuously to his date with Delaney. He knew they'd have fun no matter where they went, but Delaney had watched the performance with a sense of wonder he usually only saw in small children, such as his nieces, and he loved how she grabbed life with gusto. Everything she did was full of joy, and he absolutely loved every moment he spent in her company. When he'd mentioned going out again and potentially making a tradition out of watching *A Christmas Carol*, he'd done so because he couldn't help himself; he wanted to be with her for every Christmas to come.

Hearing the specifics about her last relationship had made his heart heavy. He knew she was leery of starting another long distance relationship, and he couldn't blame her. They often didn't last. But he was certain he would find a way to make it work, even if he had to commute to Charles Town every weekend, maybe even in the middle of the week. Regardless of whether or not he decided to take over the farm, he'd still have to go back to work at the firm for at least another year. It wouldn't be that long, would it? Hopefully, he could spend the next few weeks solidifying their relationship so that by the time he had to go back, Delaney would be just as enthralled with him as he was with her—if that were possible. He did know for sure that when he'd kissed her, he'd felt electric tingles like he'd never felt before, and when he glanced down at her smiling face, she seemed to be feeling it, too.

The tree farm was about to close when he realized his cell phone was ringing. Thinking it might be his dad asking him to do one more run before he called it an evening, he pulled it out of his pocket and was surprised to see it was his boss from the firm. Wondering what he could possibly want, he pulled his glove off and answered. The conversation was brief, but by the time it was over, Josh felt sick to his stomach. He needed to see Delaney right away.

DELANEY KNEW the bakery would be busy that day, and when she looked up at the clock to see it was almost 5:00, she couldn't believe it. She was exhausted, but she'd seen more smiling happy faces than she could remember. A lot of the children stopped by after visiting Santa at the library, and their excitement was palpable. It was almost Christmas, and everyone was overjoyed.

She'd let Joanna and Cameron go home early to get ready for the dance, and Courtney had ended up asking off, getting Edie to cover her shift for her. When Cameron asked her for the keys to her car, Delaney had hugged him. She was pretty sure she was almost as excited as he was, though he was trying to play it cool. He promised to send her pictures the next morning, and Delaney couldn't wait to see Joanna in the new pink dress she'd bought.

"So if Cameron has your car, how are you getting home?" Edie asked, flipping the sign on the door to "closed" and turning the lock.

"My dad is picking me up," Delaney explained. "I'm actually kind of excited. I know it seems silly, but it's been a long time since my dad picked me up from work."

"Aww, how precious," Edie gushed. Just then, they heard a knock on the back door, and Delaney realized it had to be her dad. Edie said, "Go ahead. I'll finish up. The kitchen's done. I'll just need to wipe these tables and counters off."

"Are you sure?" Delaney asked, glancing around. "You already had to come in on your day off."

"It's fine," Edie assured her. "Go on."

"Thanks," Delaney replied, giving her friend a quick hug before she bounded off to get her coat and purse before her father froze to death. She pulled open the door to find him standing there like the freezing temperatures were no big deal at all. "Hi, Daddy," she said, pulling the door closed behind her. "Thanks for coming to get me."

"Hello, princess," he said as she slipped her arm in his. "Everything all locked up?"

Delaney appreciated him looking out for her, even though it wasn't necessary. "Edie is still here. She'll make sure to lock the door."

He was driving his old work truck, the one she'd be driving until she got her car back from Cameron, and she hopped up into the passenger seat, glad he'd left it running so it stayed warm. "What do you say you come home for dinner? Mom's making her chicken and dumplings."

There was no way Delaney would argue with that. "Sounds delicious. What about Nana?"

"I stopped by to see if she wanted to come over, but she said she had a few Christmas presents she needed to finish knitting, and she didn't want to bring them with her because they are for us."

Delaney smiled. Nana was no nonsense when it came to finishing her presents on time. "I see," she said. "She knows I'm going with you then?"

"I told her you might would," he replied, and Delaney giggled at the familiar phrase unique to her dad and his folks. He was quiet for a moment, but Delaney could tell by the way he looked at her out of the corner of his eye every once in a while there was something more he wanted to say. Finally, he said, "So... Nana says you had a date last night."

Delaney held back a grin. She'd been thinking about Josh all day, but she wasn't sure she was ready for her dad to see just how serious she was about him. "Yeah," she said, with a shrug. "He's a nice guy."

"From Shepherdstown?" David asked, his tone light, though Delaney could tell by his eyes he was more interested than he sounded.

"Yes, but he lives in Washington."

Her father shook his head slightly. "Oh," he said. "That's pretty far away."

"I know," she said, with a nod. "We're taking it slow," she assured him. She hoped that was true. Honestly, she wasn't sure if they were taking it slowly or not. Her mind told her that was a good idea, but her heart said otherwise. She was falling for Josh pretty quickly.

"Well, I know you're a good judge of character," he replied. "Just be careful."

"Dad," Delaney said, and it was suddenly a three syllable word. "I will be."

"I know. I know," he said, adjusting his hat. "You're my little girl, though. I don't care how old you are. That last guy, well, he's lucky I'm not a violent man."

Delaney held back a chuckle. She knew how overprotective her dad could be. She honestly didn't feel like there was anything for him to worry about, but she patted her dad on the shoulder as they pulled into the driveway, and she was so thankful she had two parents who absolutely loved her more than anything. Even though she was closer to thirty than she was twenty at this point, she really would always be their little girl.

Having had no time to stop to eat that day, Delaney greedily devoured two bowls of chicken and dumplings before she finally felt full and sat back in her chair, letting her bloated belly rest for a few minutes before she hopped up to help her mother with the dishes. A few minutes later, there was an unexpected knock on the door, and her father walked into the kitchen to let her know a young man was there to see her.

Delaney felt her heartbeat hasten. Who would be there to see her? If it was Josh, was everything okay? Glancing at her mom, she shrugged and dried her hands on a dish towel before she made her way into the living room.

Josh was standing by the door, still wearing his work coat. He was smiling, but he had a concerned look on his face, and Delaney was immediately worried that something had happened to one of his parents or another family member. "Josh? Is everything okay?" she asked as she approached him.

"Everything is fine," he assured her. "I just needed to talk to you. Nana said I could find you here. I hope I'm not imposing."

"No, we've just finished dinner," she said.

"Would you like some chicken and dumplings?" her mother asked, and Delaney turned to see her parents had followed her.

Josh declined politely, and Delaney said, "Josh, this is my mom, Maggie, and my dad, David."

"Nice to meet you both," Josh said, shaking their hands in turn.

"Let me get my coat and we can go for a walk," Delaney said, clearly seeing that whatever Josh had to say to her, it was important and needed to be said in private.

As she slipped her coat on, her mother warned, "Be careful, honey. It might be slick out."

Delaney didn't reply, and Josh held the door open for her as she stepped out onto the porch.

It was dark. The porch light was on, but other than that, only the moon and stars lit the path that led around toward the barn. Delaney started slowly walking that direction, not quite sure where to go, and Josh walked alongside her. "What's going on?" she asked, afraid to hear the answer. Surely, he wouldn't have driven all the way over here to tell her he didn't want to see her anymore when they'd had such a good time the night before.

Josh took a deep breath and let it out, an icy fog forming in front of his mouth. "I got a phone call from my boss today," he explained. "I wanted to tell you in person, and I wanted to tell you now." He was slowly shaking his head. "I'm sorry for barging in on you. I guess it could've waited, but, I felt like you need to know what's going on."

Delaney turned to look at him, her steps becoming even slower as she did so. "What is going on?" she asked.

There was another deep sigh. "The company wants to run an update to the software while everyone is away for the holidays. They've been talking about updating the system for some time, but they've been putting it off because everyone uses the program that needs to be updated in order to do their jobs. We're a headhunting company, specializing in lobbyist and political jobs. This is the best time of year to let everyone take a week off so that the programs can be updated without interrupting anyone's work."

Delaney was confused. "So… if everyone is getting the week off, why is that a problem?"

"Because that means I have to go in to update all of the software," he explained. "No one else will be there, except for me and my team."

She suddenly understood. "So everyone else gets the week off, but you have to work."

"Exactly," he replied.

"Even though you already asked off?" she said, the injustice hitting her right in the gut.

"Yes," he confirmed with a nod. "My boss apologized and said I could take a different week off once everything was up and running, but that likely won't be until late January, maybe February."

Delaney stopped walking and turned to face him. "That really stinks, Josh. What does that mean, then? When do you have to leave?"

He kicked at the snow on the ground with the toe of his boot. "The update has to start on Christmas Eve in order to be finished running by the time everyone comes back on January fifth."

Her eyes widened. "It takes that long?"

"Yes," he assured her. "It has to be run in phases, and there are a lot of computers that will need updating. Even though there are two other people on my team, it'll take us the entire time, probably working late, to get it done. I'll give the other guys the day off on Christmas Day because one has little kids and the other is practically a kid herself, but that will make it just that much harder to get it done on time."

Delaney couldn't believe her ears. Here she was, thinking this would be her best Christmas yet. She'd spend Christmas Eve with Josh at the festival and then see him again on Christmas Day. They'd likely see each other several more times before he had to go back, maybe even spend New Year's Eve together, and now it was gone, all gone. Shaking her head, she asked, "What did your parents say?"

"They didn't like it, of course," he admitted. "But they understand. They know how important it is that I do my job well."

She could understand that, she really could, but the idea of not spending the holidays with him brought tears to her eyes. Slowly, she asked, "And what… what if you decided not to go back? What if you decided to stay at the farm and take over like your dad asked?"

He let out a heavy sigh and tipped his head to the side before he said, "Delaney, even if I did decide to do that, I can't just tell my boss no and never come back. What kind of a person would that make me? It would be awfully irresponsible."

"So what?" she asked, hardly believing it was her own voice. "They could find someone else to do it. They'd figure it out. Is it really complicated or something?"

He shrugged. "I don't know. But Delaney, it's my job. Believe me, I really wish I were able to stay here with you, go to the Christmas Festival with you, like we talked about, but… I can't just walk away from my life in Washington."

Delaney wanted to argue with him, to tell him of course he could —that if he were falling for her the same way she was falling for him, there would be no question. But she didn't say any of those things. Instead, she said the responsible thing, the words that would protect her heart the most. "Okay, Josh," she said, quietly, realizing he must not quite be exactly who she thought he was after all. "Thank you for letting me know." She turned on her heels and began to walk back toward the house, wiping the tears from her cheeks as she did so.

Josh caught her arm. "Delaney, please, don't," he said, though she continued to walk, despite him tugging her backward a few times and then releasing her. "I would stay if I could."

"No, I understand," she said. "They need you. They are important, and they need you."

"You're important, too," he reminded her. This time, he pulled on her hard enough to make her stop, and she did turn to face him. "Delaney, please believe me when I tell you no one is more important to me than you are. I just… this is something I have to do."

She swallowed the lump in her throat. She wanted to believe him, but she'd been told she was important before. She'd been told she was significant. She'd even been told she was loved. None of it was true before, so why would it be now? "Josh, I understand the importance of keeping your word and following through with your responsibilities. You told your boss you'd be there, and now you are obligated to do so. I get it. I just hope… someday… instead of being told I'm important, someone will step up and show me that I am."

Delaney pulled away from him again and finished crossing to the porch. She knew he was behind her, but he didn't say anything else. When she reached the porch, he said, "Delaney… I'll call you later, okay? I know we can work this out."

Before she turned to face him, she thought about how wondrous the night before had been and how she'd spent all day dreaming of a life with this man. Was she overreacting? Should she give him a chance to prove how much he cared for her even though he had to go? At that moment, she wasn't sure, but she did know she was not in the state of mind to make a rational decision. Without turning to face him, she called over her shoulder, "Fine. Merry Christmas." Then, she bounded up the stairs and into her parents' house, slamming the door behind her.

THE NEXT DAY AT CHURCH, the pastor's message had been all about the gift of Christmas and how each of us has an opportunity to be a gift to someone else, not only this time of year but every single day of the year. The message was wonderful and well-delivered, the songs had been divinely sung, and Delaney usually would have left with a skip in her step, revived and ready to go out into the world and be the light of Christ. But she'd spent most of the service thinking about Josh, even though she tried to focus on the sermon, and by the time she left, her heart was aching more than it had been when she walked in. She just couldn't understand why God would let this happen to her again when she'd tried so hard to live a godly existence.

Delaney had gone to church her whole life and understood it wasn't a trade-off; God didn't do favors for His people because they did what He said. Yet, she felt like she'd spent the last six months praying for a good man to come her way and that God had finally answered that prayer, only now to have that man decide she wasn't as important as he'd led her to believe.

Nana had reminded her the night before, as Delaney cried on her shoulder, "Sometimes God puts a little trial and tribulation in our lives so we can see His gifts a little more clearly." She'd urged Delaney not to give up on Josh, to give him a chance to get things sorted out at home and then see if he was really the one for her. She knew her Nana's words were wise, and she'd be smart to take them to heart. But right now, she felt betrayed, and even though logically speaking, it made sense that Josh would want to return to his job and tie up loose ends there, she'd already planned her Christmas with him. The thought of anything less than all of him made her heart ache.

That afternoon, she sat in her bedroom with her laptop open, trying to concentrate on her weekly earnings, but she was struggling to stay focused. Her phone vibrated on the nightstand next to her, and she was thankful to have a distraction from her distraction. Though she didn't recognize the number, she answered it anyway and was surprised to hear Lydia's voice on the other end.

"Hi, Delaney. I hope you don't mind me calling. I just wanted to tell you thank you so much for the cocoa. It's been such a big hit! I'm hoping we have enough left to last us through the rest of the afternoon," she said, her tone as chipper as Delaney remembered it.

"That's good," Delaney replied. "I'm glad everyone likes it. Do you need me to bring you some more?" She was hopeful the answer would be no. She couldn't imagine driving over to Taylor Tree Farm under the current circumstances.

"Thanks for offering, but the village will be closing for the season in a few hours. Sometimes we open on Christmas Eve, but this year we are just about out of trees, so this will be the end of the year for us."

"Oh," Delaney said. "Well, congratulations on selling out."

"Yes, thank you," Lydia responded. "It's definitely been a good year. I was hoping that we could work together next year right from the very beginning. I know how much people love your cocoa, and I'd love to give them yet another incentive to visit Taylor Tree Farm."

The idea of working with Lydia next Christmas reminded Delaney of what Josh had said about making *A Christmas Carol* a tradition, and the hole in the pit of her stomach began to ache even more. Still, she managed to say, "That would be nice."

"Oh, good," Lydia gushed. "I was hoping you might stop by soon so that I can pay you for the cocoa."

"You don't need to pay me anything…"

"Of course I do," Lydia cut her off. "We'll gladly pay you whatever you would normally charge for that much cocoa."

Delaney wasn't even certain how she might calculate that since she didn't usually sell it in powder. "I… I'm not sure how much it would be," she admitted. "I'll have to look into it."

"Okay, dear. Whenever you know, just get me an invoice. We would love to have you over for dinner before Josh goes back to the city."

Swallowing the lump in her throat, Delaney wondered if he'd even spoken to his mom about their conversation the day before. Rather than get into all that now, she said, "I'll probably be pretty busy at the bakery this week."

"Oh, I hope you can come over. He'll be leaving Wednesday.

Maybe you could stop by Tuesday afternoon? Tuesdays are usually pretty slow, aren't they?"

Everything she said made perfect sense, and yet the idea of sitting around the dining room table with the Taylor family knowing Josh would be gone soon seemed like an impossibility. "Maybe," she finally said. "I'll... talk to Josh about it."

"Wonderful," Lydia replied. "Oh, Delaney, we are so thankful to have gotten the chance to get to know you. I know it won't be easy when Josh goes back to Washington, but he cares so much for you, as I'm sure you know. And you are just... delightful. Just like your bakery says!"

She chuckled at her joke, one Delaney had heard more than once, but she sounded so sincere, the comment actually brought a tear to her eye. "It was lovely to meet all of you as well," she said, and she really meant it. She'd almost imagined she could be part of the Taylor family someday... almost.

"Well, I better get off of here. Thanks again for the cocoa, dear," Lydia said. "It was nice chatting with you. Take care."

"Goodbye," Delaney said, trying to keep her voice cheerful, but once she'd hung up, she let the tears roll down her face again. She had no way of knowing if Lydia had let Josh know she was going to call, though she imagined she hadn't mentioned it to him. She assumed she really did know about the conversation they'd had the night before and she was just trying to patch things up, like any good mother might do. But Delaney knew in her heart she wouldn't be able to see Josh again before he left. She hoped eventually, once the holidays were over, maybe, she'd find the strength to give him another chance, but for now, she'd have to find a way to get through the holidays on her own.

JOSH SAT on the back porch with Critter at his feet, trying to memorize this scene so he could envision it once he returned to Washington. He had tried not to be too upset with his mother when she explained what she'd done. Of course, he'd mentioned to both of his parents that Delaney was more than a little upset that he would be leaving before Christmas, and yet Lydia had snuck her number from his phone and called her anyway. His mother thought there was a chance Delaney might be willing to come over for dinner before he left, but Lydia hadn't been there to see her face when he'd told her he had to go. There was no way Delaney would ever agree to dinner, and he'd be very lucky if she ever stepped foot in his house again.

With a deep sigh, Josh took a sip of his coffee. He figured he'd never be able to drink hot cocoa again; it would always remind him of Delaney. He knew what he had to do. He'd worked for the same company for years, and he couldn't just walk away now, not when they needed him for this update. Surely, Delaney would come around to understand that eventually, wouldn't she?

His father quietly made his way out the back door and into the seat next to him, making Critter get up and scoot over just a tad so that he was now resting on one toe of Josh's boot. Kent said nothing for the longest time, and Josh was hopeful that there would be no more discussion of taking over the farm, moving closer, or of Delaney. He had made up his mind, and everything else could wait until after the holidays. It was easier not to think about it at all.

After several minutes, his dad said, "Did I ever tell you about how I first got to try your mother's pecan pie?"

Josh felt like he must have heard a hundred different stories about his mom's pie over the years, but he wasn't sure he'd heard this one. "No, I don't think so."

"It was Thanksgiving, 1984, and I was supposed to be at my uncle's house taking care of the livestock. He ran a dairy farm, you'll recall."

Josh nodded, wondering where this story was headed.

"I had been dating your mom about a month, and I was as smitten with that woman as a fellow could be. Earlier that week, she'd called me up and invited me over for Thanksgiving dinner. Well, of course I said yes. How could I say anything but yes? But then, your uncle reminded me that I was supposed to work that day. 'The cows still have to eat, even on Thanksgiving Day,' he'd said. Of course, he was right. They did have to eat. And I swore to him I'd be there. I was a responsible young man, now, mind you. If I said I was going to do something, by golly, I was going to do it."

Glancing over at him, Josh could see in his eyes how sincere he was, and he fought back a chuckle. His dad had always been responsible. "And?" he asked.

"And... I didn't show up," he replied. "I went to your mother's parents' house instead. We had pecan pie for dessert, and I knew that day I'd marry that woman. Oh, it wasn't just because of the pie, of course. But it sure didn't hurt."

His eyes wide, Josh asked, "What about the livestock?"

"They lived," Kent assured him. "My uncle was hot for a while. He'd had to go out and do it himself, but he made it happen. Course it would've been easier for me to do it. Would've saved him some trouble. But I was always bending over backward to make sure I put in extra work to make that farm functional, and I never got a thank you or a pat on the back for any of it. It wasn't until that day that my uncle really realized just how hard of a worker I was."

Josh swallowed hard. "What are you saying, Dad?"

"I'm saying, being responsible is all fine and good, Son, but sometimes there are things that are more important. Sometimes being responsible will make you miss out on the pie. And sometimes taking a different route will show your worth, but chances are, none of the cows will die."

Before Josh could say anything else, Kent stood and patted him on the shoulder and made his way back into the house, leaving Josh alone to ponder cows, pie, love, and the universe beneath a field of twinkling stars.

CHAPTER 19

The week was a long one. Delaney had been excited to see Cameron and Joanna's pictures. They'd had a lovely time at the Winter Formal, and Courtney had, too, with her date, Kyler. Hundreds of customers stopped by throughout the holiday week to share a special treat with a family member or warm up from the cold with a mug of hot cocoa. Delaney had gone about her days trying not to think about Josh, wishing Christmas could just be over already.

Christmas Eve was Thursday night, so lots of people stopped by Wednesday on their way to and from picking up last minute Christmas gifts. That morning, Delaney was in the kitchen, trying not to think about Josh leaving when her phone began to vibrate. She glanced down to see his number but decided not to answer. She didn't need to talk to him again, not right now. After the holidays, she'd give him a call or send him a text. For the time being, she thought it was best to push thoughts of him aside until she could think clearly and make a rational decision about whether or not she still felt important enough to him to continue to date.

A little while later, she glanced at her phone to see he'd sent her a text. *"I'm heading back to Washington today. I hope we can talk soon. I miss you, Delaney."* She slipped her phone inside her pocket without bothering to answer.

Finally, a few hours later, she realized she was acting both selfish and immature. Even though she refused to speak to him, she could at least let him know she was thinking about him. She messaged him back, *"Have a safe trip,"* and left it at that. She understood his job was important, but it broke her heart to think it was more important than spending the holidays with the people that should mean the most to him--including her.

THURSDAY MORNING, Josh arrived at work bright and early. His other two team members, Janet and Carlos, would be in shortly, and his boss, Mr. Cooper, said he'd come in that morning just to make sure he didn't have any questions. The update was something they'd been talking about for a long time, and Josh was fairly certain he knew exactly what needed to be done, but he appreciated the fact that Mr. Cooper was willing to spend part of his vacation in the office to make sure he was comfortable with the install before he and his wife were off to Aspen for the holidays.

Being back in his cubicle felt stifling. It did every year when Josh came back from the farm, but this time, it was even worse. Josh had felt more alive than ever out in the mountain air with Delaney by his side. Making snow angels, tossing snowballs at each other, walking hand-in-hand in the falling snow. Now, with no windows and only a picture of his folks in front of a Christmas tree to remind him of what it was like at home, he felt isolated and depressed.

"Hey, Josh!" Carlos said as he came in. "Welcome back."

"Thank you," Josh replied, trying to force a smile. "How have things been?"

"Same old same old," Carlos replied. He was older than Josh, and his career in technology was one he'd started after a lengthy stint in the military. He was about as hard a worker as they came, and Josh was glad to have Carlos on his team.

As they were chatting, Janet came up behind Carlos. She was fresh out of college, but computers were her passion, and she was also very good at her job. "Nice to see you," she said, grinning and adjusting her glasses. "I'm surprised Cooper managed to talk you into coming back early."

Josh pushed aside his personal feelings. "Well, this update is really important," Josh reminded them, "and it will take quite a while to run."

"True," Janet nodded. "But we both told Cooper we could handle it without you."

"Yeah," Carlos agreed. "It's like he thinks we can't do anything on our own." Clearly realizing what he said might be taken the wrong way, he quickly said, "No offense. I mean, it's definitely easier when you're here. But we can do this."

"For sure," Janet agreed. "I mean, I can stay here and work or go to my parents' house and listen to my nieces and nephews complain about not getting enough presents, you know?"

Josh grew frustrated at what he was hearing. If they'd both told Mr. Cooper they could handle this without him, why was he here? Josh shook his head as if that would clear his thoughts. "I'll talk to Mr. Cooper when he gets here to see what his rationale was," he replied, "but for now, we should probably get started. I have some ideas that might speed it up a bit."

"Mr. Cooper left already," Carlos stated, glancing at Janet for confirmation, and she nodded. "He left early yesterday afternoon. Told us all to have a Merry Christmas."

Josh could hardly believe what they were telling him. "He told me he'd come in and meet with me before we got started. This morning."

"Must've changed his mind," Janet shrugged.

While Josh was beginning to feel downright angry at Mr. Cooper's audacity, he did his best to keep his emotions in check. "Okay," he said, exhaling deeply. "I guess we may as well go ahead and get on it then."

Once Josh had Carlos and Janet working on installing the update, he placed a call to Mr. Cooper. It went straight to voicemail, and Josh thought it might be too early for him to answer if he was already in

Aspen. He left a message asking his boss to call him back, hoping his voice sounded even and the rage he was beginning to feel was tempered.

It wasn't until after lunch that Mr. Cooper finally managed to return the call. By then, Josh's fixes for speeding up the installation were already proving their value, and he realized that Janet and Carlos would be able to install the program in its entirety, without him, in only a couple of days, even if they didn't work at all Christmas Day. He'd already sent them home to spend Christmas Eve with their families and was sitting behind his desk staring at the picture of his parents on his cubicle wall when his cell phone rang, and he took a deep breath before answering.

"Josh, my man," Mr. Cooper said, "How is it going? You and your busy bees getting that update installed?"

"Hello, Mr. Cooper," Josh replied, thinking his tone sounded fairly even. "The install is running. Everything is on schedule."

"Great." The word seemed to have several extra vowels in it the way Mr. Cooper said it. "I knew I could count on you."

"About that," Josh began, "as you know, Carlos and Janet are both very good at their jobs. I'm pretty sure they can handle this. In fact, I know they can and that they will be done by Tuesday or Wednesday of next week."

"Oh, I don't know about that. They're good, but when you're not around, they tend to get a little…lazy."

Josh was offended on behalf of his team. "They're actually quite good at their jobs whether I'm here or not, sir. In fact, they handled everything that came their way these last few weeks while I was gone without even needing to call or text me once."

"Right," Mr. Cooper said. "Well, we haven't had too much going on with the holidays and all."

"I know, sir. I'm just saying, if it's all the same to you, I'd like to go back home and finish the holidays with my family, now that I'm certain Carlos and Janet have everything under control here."

"Oooh, I'm sorry, Josh, but I'm afraid that won't be possible. I'm going to need you to go ahead and stay there and make sure it gets done. It's not just me, mind you. The higher ups are counting on this install doing exactly what we want it to. You understand."

Try as he might, Josh couldn't hold back anymore. It was quite clear to him now that he was being taken advantage of, and that Mr. Cooper had been treating him this way for several years. His father's words came flooding back to him. How many times had he gotten a thank you or a pat on the back? None. In all the years he'd worked there, he'd never once been told how much he was appreciated. "Mr. Cooper," Josh said, still fighting to keep his voice even despite his anger and disappointment, "I will be going back to my family to finish the vacation I asked off for eleven months ago. And when I return in January, it will be for two weeks so that you can find someone else to take my position full-time."

"What?" Mr. Cooper nearly shrieked. "Josh, you can't be serious."

"Oh, I'm quite serious," Josh assured him. "But don't worry. I assure you no cows will die. Now, if you'll excuse me, I have a date with a baker. Merry Christmas, Mr. Cooper."

He didn't wait for Mr. Cooper to reply. Instead, he hung up his phone and hastily typed up a letter of resignation, printed it out, signed it, and tossed it on Mr. Cooper's desk before he gathered up his items and left. He'd call Janet and Carlos later to make sure they knew he wouldn't be back before the install was done, but he was certain they would both be happy for him. Then, he set off for home, hoping he'd make it back in time to salvage what he had with Delaney.

DELANEY WASN'T GOING to attend the Christmas Festival at all. In fact, when her parents had stopped by to pick up Nana, she'd declined, despite their insistence that she come along. But she didn't feel like celebrating or seeing friends. All she wanted to do was stay in her PJs and watch old Christmas movies until she fell asleep curled up on the couch, the lights on the Christmas tree she'd picked out with Josh extinguished.

Somewhere about midway through *It's a Wonderful Life*, she

changed her mind. She wasn't sure if it was the promise that, "Every time a bell rings, an angel gets its wings," or the thought that the world couldn't go on without George Bailey, but she knew she had to get up off that couch and head to town.

Wiping the tears from her eyes, she hurried to her room to throw on the Christmas dress she'd been planning to wear for weeks. She rushed through her make-up and ran a brush through her hair before shoving her feet into a pair of ballet flats and grabbing her coat on her way out the door, shouting, "See you later, Bill."

It was snowing again, and the town was lit up with thousands of twinkling Christmas lights. She knew she'd have to hurry if she was going to get to the church before the end of the children's choir performance. She was lucky enough to find an empty parking spot behind the bakery, then she took off at a jog to try and reach the church on time, careful not to slip on the iced-over snow.

The sanctuary was packed, every eye on the chorus of cute cherubs as they sang "Silent Night." Delaney was shocked to see her friend Melody at the piano. The thought that she had finally found her song again brought a fresh wave of tears to Delaney's eyes, though she managed to hold them back. She stood in the entryway for a moment before finally spying a row with an empty spot or two at the back and sliding in next to an older couple who smiled at her in welcome.

As the children were finishing up, Delaney realized someone was standing next to her. She looked up in surprise as her brown eyes met familiar hazel ones. Covering her mouth with her hands, she stared in awe.

"Is this seat taken?" Josh asked, a hopeful smile pulling at the corners of his mouth.

Without a word, Delaney shook her head and then scooted over so that he could fit in beside her. Once the song was over, the congregation burst into applause, and the house lights went up a bit as the children began to make their way back to their parents.

Delaney finally found her voice. "What are you doing here?" she asked.

"I realized you meant more to me than anything else," he replied as if it was the easiest statement in the world. "How could I stay in Washington at a job where I'm not appreciated when everything I've ever wanted in the whole world is right here in Charles Town?"

Delaney felt her face light up. "Do you really mean that?" she asked.

"More than anything in the world," Josh assured her. "Delaney, I hope it doesn't sound too crazy to you to hear me say this when we've only know each other a few weeks, but I've never met anyone like you before."

Feeling her heart begin to flutter, Delaney nodded. "Me neither. I couldn't imagine Christmas without you, Josh."

He smiled and took both of her hands in his. "You'll never have to again, Delaney, I promise. From now on, your Christmas traditions are my Christmas traditions. I love you, Delaney Young."

"I love you, too, Josh Taylor," Delaney beamed.

Josh wrapped his arm around her, pulling her head against his shoulder as the lights went down, and Delaney realized that Melody was singing the most beautiful Christmas song she'd ever heard. She listened in silence at the breathtaking beauty of her sweet friend's angelic voice filling the room around them. Delaney's heart was so full of love, she thought it might overflow. God really did answer prayers, and tonight He'd sent more than one Christmas miracle to the little city of Charles Town.

When Melody was done, everyone clapped, and Delaney turned back to face Josh, realizing she'd have to explain the significance to him later. "When this is over," he whispered in her ear as the adult choir took the stage, "what do you say we go have a cup of Christmas cocoa?"

Delaney smiled, "And some of the world's best pecan pie?"

"We'll save that for tomorrow… if you'll spend Christmas Day at the Taylor Tree Farm."

Delaney wished she could kiss him right then and there but knew that would also have to wait. "There's no place in the world I'd rather be," she assured him. Delaney nestled her head against Josh's shoulder as the "Hallelujah Chorus" rang out, and she knew spending Christmas Eve with Josh would be a tradition that would last a lifetime.

The End
Find *Winter Woods*, book 3, here.

A NOTE FROM THE AUTHOR

Thank you so much for reading *Christmas Cocoa*. I hope that you enjoyed Delaney and Josh's story. Please consider leaving a review. Reviews help other readers to know whether or not this book is right for them. They also let me know what you like about the series. There are plenty more books to come, so I'd love to hear your thoughts.

The next book in the series follows Olivia, Delany's author friend, as she takes off to the woods in an attempt to finish her book. Will cowboy Memphis, who happens to be staying in a nearby cabin, prove to be too much of a distraction? Find out in *Winter Woods*.

If you'd like to skip ahead in Delaney's story, you'll want to read *From This Moment*, book one in the new Charles Town Brides series. You can find it here.

Please consider signing up for my newsletter! You can download several of my books for free when you sign up. Discover your next favorite book here:

https://books.bookfunnel.com/idjohnsonnewslettersignup
or sign up here:
https://www.subscribepage.com/f3d2p5

A NOTE FROM THE AUTHOR

To find links to the other books in the series, please check the "Also by ID Johnson" section. Thanks again!
ID Johnson

ALSO BY ID JOHNSON

Stand Alone Titles

All I Want for Christmas is Pooch

(sweet contemporary romance)

Christmas Memory

(sweet contemporary romance)

The Doll Maker's Daughter at Christmas

(clean romance/historical)

Pretty Little Monster

(young adult/suspense)

The Journey to Normal: Our Family's Life with Autism *(nonfiction)*

Duology

(psychological thriller/literary fiction/women's fiction)

Beneath the Inconstant Moon

The First Mrs. Edwards

The Motherhood

(dystopian romance)

Rain's Rebellion

Rain's Run

Rain's Return

Ashes and Rose Petals

(contemporary romance/retelling of Romeo and Juliet and Cinderella)

Girl in the Attic

Girl From the Tomb

Girl On the Beach

Nashville Country Dreams

(contemporary romance)

Meant to Marry Me

Lead Me Home

You Are the Reason

Forever Love series

(clean romance/historical)

Cordia's Will: A Civil War Story of Love and Loss

Cordia's Hope: A Story of Love on the Frontier

The Clandestine Saga series

(paranormal romance)

Transformation

Resurrection

Repercussion

Absolution

Illumination

Destruction

Annihilation

Obliteration

Termination

A Vampire Hunter's Tale (based on The Clandestine Saga)

(paranormal/alternate history)

Aaron

Jamie

Elliott

Christian

The Chronicles of Cassidy (based on The Clandestine Saga)

(young adult paranormal)

So You Think Your Sister's a Vampire Hunter?

Who Wants to Be a Vampire Hunter?

How Not to Be a Vampire Hunter

My Life As a Teenage Vampire Hunter

Vampire Hunting Isn't for Morons

Vampires Bite and Other Life Lessons

Gone Guardian

Death Does Not Become Her

Blood of the Vampire Hunter (based on The Clandestine Saga)

(paranormal romance)

Night Slayer

Shadow Stalker

Queen Catcher

Mother Hunter

Ghosts of Southampton series

(historical romance)

Prelude

Titanic

Residuum

Heartwarming Holidays Sweet Romance series

(Christian/clean romance)

Melody's Christmas

Christmas Cocoa

Winter Woods

Waiting On Love

Shamrock Hearts

A Blossoming Spring Romance

Firecracker!

Falling in Love

Thankful for You

Melody's Christmas Wedding

The New Year's Date

Charles Town Brides (based on Heartwarming Holidays Sweet Romance)

(Christian/clean romance)

From This Moment

Can't Help Falling in Love

It's Your Love

When You Say Nothing At All (coming soon!)

Reaper's Hollow

(paranormal/urban fantasy)

Ruin's Lot

Ruin's Promise

Ruin's Legacy

When Kings Collide

(steamy historical romance)

Princess of Silence

Collections

Ghosts of Southampton Books 0-2

Reaper's Hollow Books 1-3

The Clandestine Saga Books 1-3

The Chronicles of Cassidy Books 1-4

Celestial Springs Collection

Heartwarming Holidays Sweet Romance Books 1-3

Heartwarming Holidays Sweet Romance Books 4-7

Websites: https://books2read.com/ap/xX7ZD8/ID-Johnson

For updates, visit www.authoridjohnson.blogspot.com

Follow on Twitter @authoridjohnson

Find me on Facebook at www.facebook.com/IDJohnsonAuthor

Instagram: @authoridjohnson

Follow me on Bookbub: https://www.bookbub.com/authors/id-johnson

Made in the USA
Monee, IL
13 October 2023